Arsenic *with* Austen

Arsenic *with* Austen

A Crime with the Classics Mystery

KATHERINE BOLGER HYDE

Minotaur Books
A THOMAS DUNNE BOOK
New York

A THOMAS DUNNE BOOK FOR MINOTAUR BOOKS.
An imprint of St. Martin's Publishing Group.

www.thomasdunnebooks.com
www.minotaurbooks.com

Library of Congress Cataloging-in-Publication Data

Names: Hyde, Katherine Bolger, author.
Title: Arsenic with Austen / Katherine Bolger Hyde.
Description: First edition. | New York : Minotaur Books, 2016. | Series: Crime with the classics ; 1 | "A Thomas Dunne book."
Identifiers: LCCN 2016001444 | ISBN 978-1-250-06547-6 (hardcover) | ISBN 978-1-4668-7242-4 (e-book)
Subjects: LCSH: City and town life—Oregon—Fiction. | Inheritance and succession—Fiction. | Man-woman relationships—Fiction. | Murder—Investigation—Fiction. | GSAFD: Romantic suspense fiction. | Mystery fiction.
Classification: LCC PS3608.Y367 A89 2016 | DDC 813/.6—dc23
LC record available at http://lccn.loc.gov/2016001444

Our books may be purchased in bulk for promotional, educational, or business use. Please contact your local bookseller or the Macmillan Corporate and Premium Sales Department at 1-800-221-7945, extension 5442, or by e-mail at MacmillanSpecialMarkets@macmillan.com.

First Edition: July 2016

10 9 8 7 6 5 4 3 2 1

To my parents,
James and Charlotte,
who did not live to see this day
but are no doubt rejoicing in it

• Acknowledgments •

Upon publication of one's first novel, it is virtually impossible to thank every person who has materially contributed to the work of many years coming at last to fruition. I have had more friends, encouragers, teachers, mentors, colleagues, critique partners, beta readers, and budding fans than I can count or mention. But if you have stood in any of these relations to me, please know that I thank you from the bottom of my heart. I would not have made it this far without you.

Particular thanks must go, first, to my husband, John Hyde; my children, Lena and Nicholas Cooper and Elizabeth and John Hyde; and my sister, Anne Ramirez, all of whom have supported me in every way along this journey. Next, to the first friends in whom I confided my aspirations to write, Susan Shisler and Monk Ignatius; to my longtime critique partner, ego-bolsterer, mutual commiserator, and general great friend, Charise Olson; to my dear friend Molly King, who has spared me many hours of carpool driving and been a second mother to my son; to the Santa Cruz writers' lunch bunch, who have encouraged me in disappointment and cheered for me in success; to my parish, St. Lawrence Orthodox Christian Church in Felton, California, where artists of all stripes are not merely tolerated but encouraged; to beta readers Bev. Cooke and Carrie Padgett, who made invaluable suggestions for improving the manuscript; to my fabulous agent, Kimberley Cameron, who believed in Crime with the Classics from the moment she saw the concept; and to everyone at Thomas Dunne/Minotaur, especially my excellent editor, Marcia Markland, and her efficient assistant, Quressa Robinson.

My gratitude also goes to the Rockaway gang (you know who you are), a group of friends who meet annually at Colonyhouse in Rockaway Beach, Oregon, to write, encourage, critique, drink wine, and laugh uproariously far into the night. Not only did Rockaway Beach inspire the setting of this series, but my time there has been crucial to keeping me sane during the years of struggle and learning. As for the rest, well, what happens in Rockaway stays in Rockaway.

Last but greatest, I will say with the immortal J. S. Bach— *soli deo gloria.*

· one ·

"Change of scene might be of service—and perhaps a little relief from home may be as useful as any thing."
—Mrs. Gardiner to Elizabeth Bennet,
Pride and Prejudice

A gentle late-spring breeze ruffled the tender leaves of the maple and cherry trees on Reed College's front lawn, flirted with the skirts of the graduates' robes and tugged at the edges of their mortarboards, then swirled up three stories to tease Emily's upswept hair as she stood at her open office window. Of late this scene had become the favorite of her whole teaching year, because it meant the year was over.

She shrugged gratefully out of her heavy doctoral robes and smoothed the lace-trimmed ivory linen dress she wore underneath. When had teaching literature ceased to be a joy she looked forward to each morning and become instead a dreaded chore? When had her students and colleagues become a band of indifferent strangers instead of her own beloved community? *Sometime after you left me,* she said aloud to Philip, whose presence was one only she could perceive. *None of it means anything anymore.*

You only get out of it what you put into it, his voice repri-manded her. He never seemed to say anything new these days—only things she'd heard him say a thousand times before. Death must put a damper on one's creativity.

Maybe I need a sabbatical. Time to write that book, finally. She'd been planning it for years: the definitive work on Dosto-evsky's conflicted relationship with his Orthodox faith. But Reed's emphasis on teaching over publication had allowed her to keep putting it off.

Philip, for once, was silent. What would he say? *You can't run away from your problems; you have to face them.* Or: *It's about time you stopped talking about that book and actually wrote it.* Or, most maddeningly: *You must do as you think best, my dear.*

Too late to ask for a sabbatical for next fall, anyway. She could defer the decision awhile. As she seemed to be deferring all action these days.

She straightened the few remaining papers on her desk, filing some, placing others in her briefcase. Among them was a pile of mail she'd picked up from her campus box on the way up. Lit and Lang Department memos, a sweet handwritten note of thanks from a thesis advisee, next year's academic calendar—and one stiff white envelope that had come through the regular mail.

The return address was in Tillamook: MacDougal & Simpson, Attorneys at Law. *What on Earth . . . ?*

She stared at the envelope in her hand until Philip's voice nudged her. *Only one way to find out, my dear.*

Apparently, the letter opener had left for vacation ahead of her; it was nowhere to be found. She ripped the flap open and extracted a folded letter.

Dear Mrs. Cavanaugh:

As the legal representatives of your great-aunt Beatrice Runcible, it is our melancholy duty to inform you that Mrs. Runcible passed away on May 22 of this year. Her funeral will be held at two P.M. on May 27, 2013, at St. Bede's Episcopal Church in Stony Beach, Oregon, with interment to follow.

As a legatee under Mrs. Runcible's will and coexecutor of her estate, we beg you will visit our office at your earliest convenience, preferably before the funeral. Please telephone 503-555-1407 to confirm a time.

Your obedient servant,

James P. MacDougal, Attorney at Law

Emily stared at the letter, unable to realize Aunt Beatrice was dead.

She'd been in—what, her early fifties?—a thousand years ago, when Emily's father used to dump his children on Beatrice's doorstep each summer while he toured the Northwest in search of his next teaching job. So she must be well into her eighties now. Must have been, when she died.

Emily was surprised by the strength of the pang that drove her into her chair. Aunt Beatrice, dead. That vibrant, seemingly ageless woman whose will and energy galvanized the entire village of Stony Beach, most of which she owned. How could she be dead?

And how could Emily have neglected her all these years? She'd written from time to time, but they hadn't seen each other since—great heavens, could it be since Emily and Philip's wedding?

It must be. Aunt Beatrice hadn't wanted to leave Stony Beach for anything less than a wedding or a christening. There had never been any christenings. And Emily had never been able to bring herself to return to Stony Beach. Not since the summer she was sixteen. Not since Luke . . .

A tidal wave of emotion flooded her body, stinging her eyes and clenching her gut. A wave far stronger than her grief for Aunt Beatrice. She'd kept thoughts of Luke at bay for so long, she would have sworn she'd forgotten him.

But clearly she hadn't. And probably never would.

His face sprang before her, undimmed by any trick of memory, unchanged by the passage of years. His thick dark hair and sun-reddened cheeks, his teasing smile, the deep gray eyes that could shift in a heartbeat from laughter to longing. Eyes that could render her breathless in one glance.

"Luke . . ." she whispered, but his image faded on her breath. How could she go to Stony Beach and risk seeing him again?

But no. He wouldn't be there. He'd left at eighteen, vanished, untraceable. And Stony Beach wasn't a place people went back to when once they'd gotten away.

She'd go and pay her respects to Aunt Beatrice. She owed her that much. After all, it was Aunt Beatrice who'd opened the world of literature to Emily in the first place—the world she'd inhabited peacefully and, in the main, contentedly for the last thirty-five years.

Emily read the letter again, wincing at the dangling modifier (which would have horrified Aunt Beatrice) but this time taking in its meaning: *legatee and coexecutor*. Clearly it was her duty to go, whether she wanted to or not.

Legatee. Aunt Beatrice had been a wealthy woman all those years ago. Some of the property, Emily vaguely remembered, was tied up under Beatrice's late husband's will, but the house was not—nor the library it contained. If Aunt Beatrice had left Emily her books . . . ! That would be a legacy well worth claiming.

Funeral on May twenty-seventh. Emily glanced at the calendar on the wall. May twenty-seventh was tomorrow!

With shaking fingers she fumbled for the telephone, pressed 9 for an outside line and then the number of the lawyer's office. A youthful, high-pitched male voice answered, and Emily pictured a Dickensian clerk, a Guppy or a young Bob Cratchit, slaving away with a quill on a high stool. Only, of course, such a clerk wouldn't have had a telephone.

She introduced herself and heard the young man's tone shift into full attention mode. "Oh, Mrs. Cavanaugh! I'm so glad our letter reached you. We weren't entirely sure we had the right address."

"I just got it today. Pretty squeaky timing. Tomorrow is not only the funeral but my first day of vacation—I might not have gotten the letter till August if it hadn't come today."

"Yes, I'm sorry about that. But as I say, we couldn't be sure. . . . At any rate, you will be able to come? For the funeral?"

"I'll be there. I can meet with Mr. MacDougal on my way down, if that's convenient."

"Certainly. Would ten o'clock suit you?"

Tillamook was about ninety minutes from Portland. Not too early a start. "Fine."

Emily finished packing up and paused in her office doorway for a last look around. *Well, Philip, it looks as though I'm going to get a change whether I want one or not.*

A little change will do you good, my dear.

But something told Emily that whatever lay before her, "a little change" would hardly be an adequate description.

Tillamook lay in a green bowl between the coastal mountains and Tillamook Bay. A placid town, as quiet and unhurried as the dairy cattle that peppered the rolling slopes to each side of the road. You had to love cattle to live in Tillamook—their reek pervaded the air, their milk fueled the cheese industry that kept the town alive. Cheese, of course, was essential to life, but Emily preferred to obtain it from a grocery store well removed from its pungent source.

Luke used to tease her about her aversion to cows. *What's not to like about cows?* he'd say. *Gentlest creatures in the world.*

They're big and scary and they stink, she'd insist.

He'd laugh, slinging his long burly arm around her summer-freckled shoulders. *One of these days I'll take you to my uncle's and introduce you to Bessie. Nobody could be scared of Bessie.*

One of many promises he never kept.

She shook off thoughts of Luke like a cow flicking its tail at a fly. He was gone. This trip was not about him. It was about Aunt Beatrice. Aunt Beatrice, who was dead and whose lawyer wanted to speak with her.

She found the lawyer's office with no difficulty in Tillamook's regular, numbered grid of downtown streets. At ten o'clock precisely, she tried the door of MacDougal & Simpson, only to find it locked. She stepped back in annoyance but then saw a slight young man with a violent shock of red hair and a dense coating of freckles bustling up to the door.

"Mrs. Cavanaugh?" he asked. She nodded. "I'm so sorry—had

trouble starting my car." He nodded toward an ancient Honda parked next to her PT Cruiser. "Just give me a sec."

He got the door open and ushered her into an office that looked more like a professor's than a lawyer's. Two venerable wooden armchairs faced an enormous battered desk piled high with leaning stacks of papers, while books overflowed the bookcases on the back wall to form piles on the frayed carpet.

Emily glanced pointedly toward the door that she assumed led into an inner office. "Will Mr. MacDougal be in soon?"

The young man blinked at her from behind the desk, where he'd been searching for a clear spot to lay down his briefcase. "Oh! I'm sorry, I didn't introduce myself. I'm Jamie MacDougal."

Emily forgot her manners and stared. This was the lawyer Aunt Beatrice had chosen to manage her affairs? There must be some mistake. He hardly looked old enough to be out of high school, let alone law school.

A flush crept up his neck. "My father was your aunt's lawyer for many years. He passed away a few months ago, and I took over. Please don't be concerned; I am fully qualified. Passed the bar and everything."

His apologetic smile was so winsome that Emily relented. She had a soft spot for young redheads anyway—they always made her think of the children she and Philip might have had. "I'm sure you're doing a fine job, Mr. MacDougal."

"Oh, please—call me Jamie. When people say Mr. Mac-Dougal, I still look around for my dad."

Emily dimpled at him and sat down. "Jamie, then."

He opened his briefcase and fumbled inside. "Just give me a second to find the papers. . . . Here they are." He closed the brief-case and sat behind the huge desk. With his suit coat hanging off his shoulders and his shirt collar loose on his skinny neck, he looked like a second grader playing teacher. "Would you like to read the will, or would you just like me to summarize it?"

"I suppose I'll have to read it eventually, but just a summary for now, please."

"Okay." He held up a thick document, on the back of which Emily could read *The Last Will and Testament of Beatrice Worthing Runcible*.

"Some of the storefront properties in Stony Beach go to Brock Runcible under the terms of Horace Runcible's will. Then there's ten thousand dollars to Agnes Beech, Mrs. Runcible's housekeeper, and a hundred thousand to a trust for the purpose of establishing a clinic in Stony Beach. One of the storefront properties is willed to that trust also. We have a few small bequests to various charities, and then—the rest is yours."

Emily was sure she couldn't have heard correctly. Why would Aunt Beatrice have left all the rest to her? They'd had little contact beyond Christmas cards for the last thirty-five years.

"The—the rest? What is the rest, exactly?"

"Well, let's see. There's her house, Windy Corner, of course, and all her personal property. A number of beach rentals—I'll get you the list in a minute. Three blocks of storefronts she acquired after her husband's death. And, after taxes, I'd guess about"—he shuffled some papers—"six million dollars in cash and liquid investments."

"Six—*million*?"

"That's right." Jamie grinned, his eyes dancing. "You have just become a very wealthy woman."

two

The sudden acquisition of ten thousand pounds was the most
remarkable charm of the young lady to whom he was now
rendering himself agreeable.

—*Pride and Prejudice*

E mily sat back in her chair, all the wind knocked out of her.
"I can't believe it. I thought—hoped—she might have left
me her library. But all this"—she waved a hand wide to encom-
pass the immensity of her inheritance—"I can't take it in."

"It appears you were her only living relative. So it's not all
that surprising she'd leave most of it to you."

"I guess that's true. I hadn't thought about it." Her parents
were long gone; her one brother, Geoff—named for Geoffrey
Chaucer—had died a few years before, leaving no children.
Beatrice had no offspring of her own, no other nieces or nephews.
The Worthings were quickly dying out.

Emily shook her head briskly to orient herself to the here
and now. "What are my duties as coexecutor?"

"To some extent, that's up to you. I'm the other executor
and, if you prefer, you can leave most of it in my hands. All you'll
have to do is sign checks and papers. And make decisions about

what to keep, what to sell, et cetera. Of course, if you'd like to take a more active role, you certainly have that option."

Emily pictured her aunt's house as she had last seen it: a four-thousand-square-foot Victorian crammed to the rafters with books, knickknacks, keepsakes, and heirlooms. "I think going through the house is going to keep me plenty busy. I'm happy to just sign things."

"Great." Jamie's smile suggested the extra work would not come amiss. What a feeling—to be able to delegate hours of work to a lawyer and not have to worry about how much it would cost. She could get used to this.

He bustled and rustled and in a few minutes handed her several paper-clipped stacks of documents. "Here's a copy of the will and a list of all the assets—except for the miscellaneous personal property. The more valuable things—the ones she insured specifically—are listed here." He indicated one of the stacks. "You can look at these at your leisure, no rush."

She stood to receive the papers. Belatedly, he looked around for something to put them in, then handed her a battered expanding file. "Sorry, this is all I've got."

"No problem." She wedged the papers into the file and extended her hand. "Thank you, Jamie. I suppose I'll see you at the funeral?"

"Absolutely." He scooted past her and opened the door. In a moment she stood on the sidewalk, feeling like a completely new woman.

Emily Cavanaugh, heiress. She could be the heroine of one of her favorite novels—a Trollope, perhaps. *The Runcible Inheritance*. At least she was old enough that fortune-hunting suitors wouldn't be beating down her door.

She hoped.

* * *

With two hours to kill before the funeral, Emily treated herself to a leisurely brunch at the local pancake house, then made the twenty-minute drive along the marshy north shore of Tillamook Bay and up the coast to Stony Beach. Every mile brought back memories: the abandoned log cabin outside Garibaldi that she and Luke had jokingly dubbed their "dream house" and had woven whole histories about. The little tourist train that ran between Garibaldi and Stony Beach that they'd miraculously had to themselves one day. No, mustn't go there; that memory was far too strong.

On northward through the woods to the south end of Stony Beach, where Luke's family had lived. She couldn't see the house from the road—just as well. The one time he'd taken her there, his mother had turned the warm summer day to arctic winter with one glance. It had taken Emily the rest of the day and into the night to thaw Luke out after that.

Downtown Stony Beach, such as it was, had changed little. The shops and restaurants had different names, and she thought there were a few more of them. That one hotel surely hadn't been there in her day, looming on the beach side of the highway and blocking the view of the ocean from the shops. A couple of the cafés had FREE WI-FI signs, and the cars were more modern; but for that she could have believed herself back in the late seventies.

She turned east and drove up the hill a few blocks to St. Bede's, arriving at the modest, old-fashioned white-clapboard church with half an hour to spare before the funeral began. The day was fine and warm—unusual for May on the coast—so she wandered among the graves in the churchyard. Runcibles dominated the sunniest corner, where a newly dug grave gaped beneath an imposing stone carved with angels that read, HORACE RUNCIBLE, 1919–1971. BELOVED HUSBAND, RESPECTED PA-TRON OF STONY BEACH. And beside that, BEATRICE WORTH-ING RUNCIBLE, 1927– with room for an epitaph underneath.

How would that epitaph read? Beatrice had probably dictated it in her will. If not—well, then Emily supposed it would be up to her to decide. She'd known Beatrice less than most of the people in the town. It didn't seem right she should be the one to write the defining words about her life.

The sound of cars coming up the hill roused Emily to make her way inside. If she were already seated when the others came in, they'd be less likely to approach her. In the porch, out of the constant wind, she attempted to pin her wayward auburn curls back into their soft bun, but without a mirror it was hopeless. She smoothed her dark brown linen skirt (she owned no black), buttoned her peplum jacket over her cream lace blouse, squared her shoulders, and strode up the aisle, past the gleaming, flower-drenched cherrywood coffin to the front pew.

The rector, already robed, turned from lighting candles around the altar at her approach. He took in her appearance with a faint look of surprise and came to greet her. "Are you Mrs. Cavanaugh?"

"Yes." Emily shook his hand.

"I'm Father Stephen. Welcome to Saint Bede's. I'm sorry it's such a melancholy occasion. Beatrice Runcible was the heart and soul of this town. She will be greatly missed." He peered at Emily as if assessing the depth of her grief. "Were you—close?"

"I hadn't seen my aunt for thirty years. But we were close when I was a teenager. I owe her a great deal. It's hard to believe someone so full of life could be gone."

The rector shook his head in agreement. "Of course she was quite elderly, but so vital, one didn't notice. It was a shock to us all."

Emily darted her eyes toward the closed coffin. "Could we have the coffin open? I—haven't had a chance to say good-bye."

He startled and waved his hands. "Certainly—it's just— the flowers—" Wreaths and sprays covered the coffin from head to foot.

"I'll help you move them."

Together they lifted the largest spray from the head of the coffin and shifted a wreath or two, then Father Stephen raised the half-lid. The head on the pillow had a little less hair and a great many more wrinkles than Emily remembered, but it was unmistakably Aunt Beatrice: the high forehead and cheek-bones, the beaky nose, the firmly set mouth. Only the com-manding light in her eyes was missing—and the twinkle hidden behind it.

Emily crossed herself, then kissed her fingertips and laid them to the cold white hands folded across Beatrice's thin breast. "Good-bye, Aunt Beatrice," she whispered. "And thank you."

She turned to Father Stephen, who was fidgeting beside her as people began to enter the church. "All right, we can close it back up now. I just wanted to see her to convince myself it was real."

He lowered the lid, and they lifted the huge spray of lilies back into place. Emily scooted into the left front pew without turning to look at the people coming in. She hoped no one would presume to share the pew traditionally reserved for family.

In this hope, however, she was to be disappointed. Only a minute passed before a tall, dark-haired man approached and deposited himself on the pew beside her, not quite close enough to be offensive but close enough to give onlookers the impression they were together. Emily would have scooted away, but she was sitting in the corner of the pew as it was.

The man unbuttoned his well-fitted black jacket, then turned toward her and laid his arm across the back of the pew. His musky cologne overpowered even the scent of the flowers. He flashed her a toothy smile. "Cousin Emily?"

Emily started. Such presumption she was quite unprepared for. Her tone in reply was worthy of Aunt Beatrice herself. "I am Emily Cavanaugh. But I have no cousins."

He chuckled. "I admit I'm using the term loosely. I'm Horace's nephew, Brock. So that makes us sort of cousins-in-law, doesn't it?"

"I'm not aware that makes us any sort of relationship at all."

He put up both palms. "Hey, just trying to be friendly. After all, we are sharing an inheritance."

"Yes, I suppose." Perhaps she'd been too hard on him. His toothy smile was rather charming in a Gilderoy Lockhart sort of way. And his tanned face was decidedly handsome, although lined enough to make her suspect his wavy hair might need some help to stay black. "I'm sorry. This is all such a shock to me. Both her death and the inheritance."

He pulled a sad face. "I know. Such a tragedy the old girl's gone. She was something, wasn't she? But do you really mean to say you didn't know she was leaving everything to you?"

Emily shook her head. "No idea. Even when I got the lawyer's letter, I thought maybe some books. I never dreamed she'd leave me the lot."

"Well, well, well." He turned to lean back against the pew, arms crossed.

Emily wondered what that "well, well, well" meant, but the organ music was swelling to a crescendo. Apparently, the service was about to begin.

Her attention drifted as the traditional words from the old *Book of Common Prayer* washed over her. Then Father Stephen mounted the carved pulpit to give the eulogy.

"We are gathered here today to speed the passing into life of one of the Lord's most faithful servants. If not for the generosity of Beatrice Runcible, we would have no roof over our heads in this house of God. If not for her sound business acumen, many of you might lack jobs. And without her erudition and forthrightness, I know the general level of grammatical competency in our community would be much lower than it is."

A titter spread through the congregation at this, and a smile teased Emily's lips as well. Good old Aunt Beatrice, self-appointed defender of the English language against all encroachments of imprecision, error, and modernity. That, Emily thought, was the greatest inheritance Beatrice had bequeathed to her.

The rector went on at some length, praising Beatrice's piety, generosity, shrewdness, vitality, and spunk. He carefully avoided any reference to the way her more imposing qualities tended to overshadow, even smother, those on whom she bestowed her beneficence; but clearly no one in the room was ignorant of that. Emily squirmed in her seat, wondering, when she got around to reading the will, what strings she might discover attached to her inheritance. It would be quite unlike Beatrice to leave none at all.

At last the eulogy ended, and it was time to follow the coffin to its final resting place. Brock, solemn-faced, took Emily's elbow as the two of them walked first behind the coffin. Emily felt no need of support but didn't want to be rude and shake him off.

He stayed by her side at the grave as Father Stephen read the final prayers and the coffin was lowered. "Ashes to ashes, dust to dust . . ." She scooped up a handful of dirt to spread over the coffin, wondering who had chosen it and why people thought it worthwhile to spend so much on a mere box that would never be seen again and that would shortly become the site of one of nature's most revolting spectacles, a decaying body.

"It's a handsome casket, isn't it?" Brock whispered in her ear. "I hope you approve of my choice."

That answered that question. Somehow she wasn't surprised.

Only when the prayers were ended and the sexton began shoveling the rest of the dirt into the grave did Emily look up and take in the faces that surrounded her. The whole permanent population of the town must be here—but no one she could recognize after all her years away.

Then she caught sight of one weather-beaten face toward the back of the crowd, towering over most of the others. Cropped graying hair above it, a crisp khaki uniform collar beneath. Between those, an unmistakable pair of deep gray eyes that could shift in a heartbeat from laughter to longing. And those eyes were fastened on hers.

· three ·

> Eight years, almost eight years, had passed since all had
> been given up. How absurd to be resuming the agitation
> which such an interval had banished into distance and indis-
> tinctness! . . . Alas! with all her reasonings, she found, that
> to retentive feelings eight years may be little more than nothing.
>
> —*Persuasion*

Luke. Incredibly, astonishingly, devastatingly here after all
these years. And he'd recognized her. She'd have no chance
of escape.

She heard a voice in her ear, but it carried no more meaning than the distant roar of the waves. She turned to see Brock
looking quizzically at her. "Emily? Did you hear me?"

"No, sorry, I was miles away."

"I was saying, I've taken the liberty of arranging a little
reception back at the house. People expect it, and you weren't
around, so . . ."

"Oh, of course. That's fine. Thank you."

"Do you want to be the one to announce it? Since you're
technically the hostess and all."

"Oh. Everybody? Right." She faced the crowd and cleared
her throat. "Hello, everyone. I'm Beatrice's niece, Emily Cavanaugh. Thank you for coming today to honor my aunt. I hope

you'll join us for some refreshments at Beatrice's home." In an undertone to Brock, "I guess everyone knows where that is?"

He smirked. "It's kind of obvious." Beatrice's home was at least twice as large and half again as tall as any other house in town. Not to mention being the only one with a name.

Emily avoided Brock's arm this time and smiled her way through the crowd to her car. She had to be alone, if only for the space of a five-minute drive. She had to prepare herself for the inevitable: a conversation with Luke.

As she drove down the hill and turned right toward the north end of town, she debated how to receive him. Not with reproaches—that would be undignified. Certainly not with any display of the turbulent emotions one glimpse of his face had aroused in her: shock at how he'd aged, fury at all his broken promises, a jolt of desire such as she hadn't felt for years, and, most treacherously, an undercurrent of leaping joy that made it difficult to keep her foot on the pedals and her hands on the wheel. What she wanted was to run and dance and sing.

But no, surely a calm, friendly, but distant greeting would be best. Let him take the lead. He was the one with all the explaining to do. But he surely wouldn't do it in a crowd of a hundred people.

Emily drove past the last stragglers of the beachfront rentals that lined the highway on this end of town, then on another mile to the stout stone pillars that marked the entrance to Windy Corner. Beyond the open gate, tall poplars stood sentry around the sloping lawn and lined the curving driveway. Emily followed the curve, then took the fork that led to the garage, which would surely be occupied by Beatrice's own car. Thirty-five years ago it had been a venerable black Mercedes sedan; now it was probably a slightly newer black Mercedes sedan.

She was surprised to see another vehicle parked at the end of the drive—a white commercial van with GIFTS FROM THE SEA emblazoned on its door. So this "little reception" was being catered. And the whole town invited. Emily wondered what Brock would consider "big."

She parked the Cruiser, walked back to the main drive, and took the fork that circled before the front door. The house rose above her, its brick-red paint as fresh and perfect as she remembered. Cream, sage, and gold picked out the doors and windows and the gingerbread that lined the numerous gables and dormers. She dropped back a few paces to get a good view of the octagonal tower, soaring three stories into the bright-blue sky. The aerie at the top of the tower had always been her favorite spot to curl up in a window seat and read. Now she'd be able to take refuge there anytime she wished.

Anytime except now. Other cars were already following her up the drive.

She stepped up to the front door and tried the knob. Locked. Automatically, she rang the bell, then remembered the keys Jamie had given her. She was fumbling in her purse for them when the door opened and a tall, cadaverous old woman in a starched, white-collared black shirtdress glared down at her.

Emily quailed, feeling like a third grader who hadn't done her homework. "Hello," she managed. "I'm Emily Cavanaugh. Beatrice's niece."

The glare did not soften but gave partial space to a flicker of deference. "Agnes Beech. Housekeeper. Until you make other arrangements."

Emily put out her hand. The other woman eyed it as if it were something dragged in by the obese black-and-white cat that now slunk out from behind her. But at last she condescended to touch Emily's fingers in a parody of a handshake.

"Thank you so much for staying on and keeping things running. It seems we're having a reception. I hope the caterers have managed all right?"

Agnes Beech drew in a long and eloquent sniff. "Caterers!" she spat. "As if I couldn't have done it all myself with one hand behind my back, and made it worthy of the mistress's memory. But Mr. Brock would have his way." She turned on her heel and stalked off down the hall toward what Emily remembered as the kitchen.

Emily peeked into the spacious dining room and saw several white-suited young people bustling about. "Hello," she said, then repeated it louder when no one turned. "I'm Emily Cavanaugh." Blank faces. "I've just arrived, but I'm the new owner."

One woman, a little older than the rest, detached herself and came to shake Emily's hand. "We were hired by a Mr. Runcible. He doesn't live here?"

"No. He's the other legatee—I'm the one who got the house. But I couldn't get down here before today." She craned her neck around the woman to see the table, which was laden with platters and cake stands, a huge arrangement of lilies towering over all. "Is everything nearly ready? People are starting to arrive."

"Oh yes, just the finishing touches." She turned to the other workers and clapped her hands. "Finish up now, it's showtime!"

Right on cue the doorbell rang. Emily turned to answer it, but Agnes Beech was already striding down the hall. Emily hoped she'd be a trifle more welcoming to the guests than she'd been to her new employer.

The townspeople seemed to move in schools, like fish, because after the first ring they streamed in so steadily, Agnes never had an opportunity to shut the door. Within minutes all the reception rooms were packed with black-garbed guests, white-coated waiters with high-held trays slipping between them like flashes of sunlight on a cloudy day.

Too late, Emily realized she should have been standing at the door to receive the guests' introductions and condolences. Heading toward the parlor, she could glimpse Brock's tall form moving from cluster to cluster, his face as preternaturally solemn as an undertaker's, playing the host and grieving heir. She didn't know whether to be amused, grateful for being spared the role, or indignant at his presumption.

She settled on grateful. Being in this crowd was bad enough without being its focal point.

But her reprieve didn't last long. Brock spotted her and made his way to her side, then took her elbow again—what was this fascination he had with her elbow?—and guided her into the parlor. There he stationed himself beside her, and by some incomprehensible magnetism people began to flow toward the two of them, one or two at a time.

The first was a paunchy, balding man of around sixty who pumped her arm so hard, she expected to start spouting water. "Everett Trimble. Mayor of Stony Beach. Too bad about the old girl, but this town's moving forward, get it? Great to get some new blood in." He ran a handkerchief up over his shiny brow and down his scalp. "Give me a ring when you get settled. You and me gotta cooperate, get it? Get this town on the move." He shoved a business card into Emily's hand, clapped Brock on the shoulder, and headed toward the food.

Right behind him was a tall, svelte blonde in red lipstick and a red suit that burst out like a splash of blood against the black-and-white crowd. At first glance Emily thought the woman was in her early thirties, but after a glance at her neck, where a string of perfect pearls gleamed against a not-so-dewy throat, she revised the estimate up ten years. "Vicki Landau," the red lips said in a crisp, commanding alto voice. "Realtor. I'm sure you'll want to be selling some of your properties. Windy Corner, for starters." She surveyed the room with a greedy spark in her midnight-blue eyes. "Much too big for one person, don't you think? Just give me a call. I've got buyers lined up from here to Portland."

Her smile made Emily feel like a freshman in a class of graduate students. She took the business card Vicki offered and shoved it into her pocket along with the mayor's, intending never to look at either again.

More faces, more handshakes, more names she hadn't a prayer of remembering. In most cases a thin veil of solemnity overlaid avid curiosity about herself, Brock, the house, her plans; but she turned aside all questions with a smile. Jamie Mac-Dougal's freckled and grinning countenance made a welcome break from all the strange ones, but he only shook hands and moved on. His grin faded when he came to Brock, who seemed determined never to budge from her side.

She wished Brock would drop the barnacle act. Why did he persist in clinging to her? It couldn't be for the pleasure of her company; she'd said as few and as neutral words as possible, and she'd long since abandoned hope of keeping a man at her side by virtue of her feminine charms alone. She must have five or ten years on Brock, and each of those years had left her a memento of its passing in the form of gray hairs, wrinkles, and extra pounds. Amazing, really, that Luke had recognized her.

Think of the devil. There he was before her, tipping his uniform cap with his old teasing grin. "Sheriff's Lieutenant Luke Richards at your service, ma'am."

She was tongue-tied. All she could do was look at him. In fact, she couldn't stop looking at him. She willed Brock not to notice.

Luke's eyes cut to Brock for a second, then he inserted himself between them. "Don't you think it's time for a breath of fresh air?" he said to Emily, then to Brock, "You'll hold the fort here, won't you?"

Brock gaped but could hardly refuse.

Smooth, Luke. Smooth as rich dark chocolate sliding down her throat. Smooth as his kisses on her lips, her neck, her ear . . . *No. Don't go there. Don't ever go there again.*

Luke took her elbow. The same touch on the same body part, but oh, how different his touch felt from Brock's. How was it possible that thirty-five years could make no dent in the power of that touch?

But before they could move, an immense woman draped in a chartreuse-and-violet muumuu blocked their path. "Rita Spenser," she boomed in Emily's face. Her halitosis combined with her pungent body odor nearly made Emily gag, while her fuchsia-dyed hair styled à la Phyllis Diller made Emily wonder if someone had dropped acid in her drink.

"You're from Portland, aren't you?" the whale woman thundered. "What do you do there? Are you married? How long do you plan to stay in Stony Beach?"

Between Luke's touch on her elbow, so familiar and so utterly strange, and the whale woman's assault on her other senses, Emily was so discombobulated, she couldn't resist the barrage of questions. She answered most of them, truthfully but as briefly as possible, sensing Luke's growing impatience at her side. Before the whale woman released her, she heard a ring from the direction of his pocket. He answered the call, listened briefly, then swore under his breath.

He interrupted the whale woman without apology. "Emily, I gotta go. Fender bender south of town. But we have to talk. Soon."

She turned to him and saw all the turmoil he'd stirred up inside her mirrored in his eyes. She nodded, her mouth dry. And then he was gone.

four

She had never seen a place for which nature had done more,
or where natural beauty had been so little counteracted by
an awkward taste. . . . At that moment she felt, that to be
mistress of Pemberley might be something!

—*Pride and Prejudice*

B rock had melted into the thinning crowd. Emily sped the
departing guests on their way with gracious smiles and
thanks-for-comings. At last, thinking herself alone but for the
caterers cleaning up in the dining room, she fell onto a couch in
the parlor, kicked off her pumps, and put her feet up on a
cushion—only to hear Brock's voice, once again, at her elbow.

"Glad that's over. What a mob!"

She peered at him from beneath the arm flung over her
eyes. "Yes. I'll be glad to be alone." Surely that hint was broad
enough.

But no. He threw himself into a chair across from her and
stretched out his legs as if he owned the place. His black
dress shoes had looked smart and polished from above, but a
crack spread across one sole and the opposite heel was worn
to the wood.

Suppressing a groan, she pulled herself back into a sitting position. "Where are you staying?"

"Stony Beach Inn. Not exactly the Ritz, but at least they got rid of the bedbugs. I thought the Driftwood might give me a discount, but no. That's one of your properties, not mine." His voice put an edge on the words, but he flashed her a smile that took it off again. "Used to belong to the Landaus, you know. Just a bit of local history."

"I could call them and arrange something if you like." Why she should feel some obscure sense of guilt and obligation to this man, Emily couldn't fathom. Just the aura she got from him, she supposed.

"Don't bother. Of course I'd really prefer to have my old room here, but Agnes Beech seemed to think it wouldn't be appropriate." He made a deprecatory face.

"Your old room? I didn't know you'd spent that much time here."

"Oh, you know, just off and on." He waved a vague hand. "Beatrice was an entertaining character. And now I have even more reason to spend time here." He sat up and fixed his gaze on her. "Family relationships are always worth cultivating, don't you think?"

"You weren't technically Beatrice's family. And you're certainly not mine." Why was she so quick to repudiate him? She had no other family. An oily cousin might be better than none.

"Well, not blood family. But that just makes things more interesting."

Emily cut narrowed eyes toward him. What was that glint in his eye? Surely he wasn't thinking—

No. That was impossible. "I really do want the house to myself, Brock. I'm sorry to be rude, but I've had an emotionally wrenching, as well as physically exhausting, day, and I just want to curl up with a book and a big cup of tea."

He sighed and pushed himself to his feet. "Never let it be said that Brock Runcible can't take a hint when it's served on a platter. But are you sure you won't reconsider? I can be very useful around the house."

She certainly wouldn't take him for a handyman—not with those soft, elegant, manicured hands. Maybe he *was* thinking, incredible as it seemed. "Thanks, but no."

"Then I shall say au revoir." He caught her hand and raised it to his lips. "Until we meet again."

"I know what au revoir means." She wondered if he did.

He left, the caterers at his heels. At last the house was empty but for herself. And Agnes Beech.

She wondered how one summoned that august personage, or indeed if summoning was acceptable. She didn't see anything in the nature of a bellpull. But she knew well where the kitchen was; the housekeeper in the old days had been a motherly sort who let Emily and her brother, Geoff, have cookies and milk on the sly whenever they wanted them.

She was about to push open the kitchen door when it opened from the inside onto the towering figure of Agnes Beech. "Did you want something, madam?"

"Some tea would be lovely, Mrs. Beech. If it isn't too much trouble."

"The name is Agnes, and it's my job. Anything to eat? That fancy stuff those caterers brought wouldn't satisfy a fly." She said *caterers* as one might say *worm-infested feces*.

Emily realized she'd never had time for a bite of that "fancy stuff," which had looked plenty filling to her. "Something light would be wonderful, thank you."

Agnes Beech looked her over as if she could deduce her taste in food from her appearance. "An omelet. And some of my currant scones." It wasn't a question, so Emily simply smiled in reply.

"Oh, and there's no need to come to the kitchen. There's an intercom in every room. Will you eat in the dining room, or do you want a tray?"

The books down the hall rustled on their shelves, calling to her. "A tray in the library, please."

With the feeling of greeting a long-lost friend—one with far less baggage than Luke carried—Emily opened the double doors of the library. A smell of leather and lemony wood polish greeted her, spiced with the faintest whiff of ancient cigar from Horace's days. Oh, blessings on the head of dear Aunt Beatrice: it hadn't changed a bit.

The wood in this room could have built a whole cottage. Parquet floor, inlaid ceiling, and shelves covering every inch of three walls—all wood, and all gleaming with the proof of Agnes Beech's diligence as a cleaner. The fourth wall was a semicircle of windows looking down toward the sea, with a French door to the terrace at one side.

Emily made a circuit of the room, trailing her hand across the tooled and gilded leather bindings—no cheap editions for Aunt Beatrice. And nothing published after 1960. Emily chuckled. That was all right; her own library at home would make up that deficiency.

She knew from of old that the books were arranged according to the Dewey Decimal System, although no numbers marred the handsome spines or even headed the shelves. This was not a public library. The people who used it—or, for many years now, the person—knew where everything was.

Emily had always gone straight for the fiction section, housed in a queer semicircular case that bowed out from one corner into the room. She stopped there now and greeted all her old friends: Austen, Dickens, Dostoevsky, Montgomery, Sayers, Tolstoy, Trollope, Wodehouse. E. M. Forster, from whom Beatrice had borrowed the name Windy Corner for her home. Emily had known them all more intimately than she knew any but a few real people. Luke. Geoff. Philip. Marguerite, her closest colleague in Reed Lit and Lang. Only they were as vivid to her as Elizabeth Bennet, Anne Shirley, Anna Karenina, David Copperfield, Lord Peter Wimsey, Bertie and Jeeves.

The thought of Philip brought home to her with a jolt that she hadn't spoken to him all day. Could it be his presence was confined to Portland and he hadn't followed her to Stony Beach? Or did all the older voices drown him out?

Philip? she thought tentatively. *Are you there?*

I'm here, my dear. You've had quite a day, haven't you?

I know, can you believe it? I'm rich! Now we can go to Russia like we always wanted to. But touring Russia with an invisible husband only she could hear did not sound all that appealing.

She was about to ask his opinion of her new status as heiress when Agnes Beech appeared in the doorway bearing a silver tray. Emily smiled to see her old favorite tea service—white bone china with tiny pink rosebuds. As a child she'd dawdled over her tea just so she could look at the rosebuds a little longer. She'd hoped Aunt Beatrice might leave the service to her someday. And lo and behold, she had.

Agnes deposited the tray on a small table beside the deepest, cushiest chair in the room—leather spread with a tan knitted blanket. But before Emily could sit, the obese black-and-white cat she'd glimpsed earlier jumped onto the blanket and circled, then plopped sideways, his immense belly bulging. His stare dared her to try dislodging him.

"Bustopher Jones, you get off that chair this minute!" Agnes scolded. He blinked at her as if to say, *Make me.* Emily would hardly have dared, but Agnes scooped him up, and he lay cowed in her arms. The glare he shot Emily was enough to curdle the milk for her tea.

"Do you have everything you need?" Agnes asked.

"Oh, yes. And my old favorite tea service—thank you. Of course you couldn't have known, but this is the one Aunt Beatrice always used when I came to visit. I can almost see her sitting there, pouring out, asking me, 'One lump or two?' though she knew I always took two. It's hard to believe she's gone."

Agnes gave a sniff that seemed somehow expressive of grief. "She was a good woman and a good mistress. She'll be greatly missed."

"Do you know, I just realized no one's told me what she died of. Just old age?"

Agnes snorted. "Old age! That one? She was younger than most people half her years. Old age indeed! She died of acute gastroenteritis. *Not,* I'll have you know, due to my cooking. She ate *out* that night." She said *out* as one might say *at a drunken orgy.*

"Oh, I see!" Emily had been picturing a quiet end, at worst a massive heart attack or stroke that would have killed Beatrice instantly. But acute gastroenteritis—that likely meant hours of suffering, and highly undignified suffering at that. Poor Beatrice. "Was she prone to that sort of thing?"

"Only one food she couldn't eat without getting sick and that's lobster, but she was so stubborn, she wouldn't give it up for good. Apparently, that's what she ate that night. Doc said that's all it would've taken to kill her." Agnes's brow darkened like a winter storm. "I don't believe it for a minute. Mrs. Runcible was too strong to die from anything that plain disagreed with her."

Her next words sent a chill through Emily that all her logic could not dissipate. "Something poisoned her. Something—or someone."

· five ·

Lady Elliot had been an excellent woman, sensible and
amiable; whose judgment and conduct, if they might be par-
doned the youthful infatuation which made her Lady Elliot,
had never required indulgence afterward.

—*Persuasion*

Emily awoke in the room that had always been hers years
ago—the octagonal tower room on the third floor. It was
small and far from the bathroom, and the attic stairs had surely
grown steeper since she was last here. But she loved the tower's
bird's-eye view of both the ocean and the grounds. The same
lace canopy hung above her, the same birds trilled outside the
window, and for the moments stolen from eternity that hung
between sleep and waking, she believed she was still sixteen-
year-old Emily Worthing on summer vacation, free of school,
free of parents, and gloriously in love.

The illusion lasted only until she stretched and winced at
the stiffness of her fifty-one-year-old joints. Then all the events
of the last few days came flooding back. The inheritance. Luke.
And her conversation with Agnes Beech the night before.

"Agnes, you're not serious? Who'd want to poison Aunt
Beatrice?"

"There's plenty in this town'd be glad to get her out of the way. *Plans* they have. Plans she'd never have stood for."

"What sort of plans?"

"Developing." As one might say *chopping up innocent children*. "They want to make Stony Beach into another Seaside."

"Oh, that would be too bad." Seaside and Cannon Beach were the most popular getaway spots on the Oregon coast. In the summer they were overrun with vacationers—a louder, rowdier crowd than Stony Beach attracted. In July and August one could barely find beach room. Stony Beach got enough traffic to keep itself alive, but it was still a quaint and quiet place, with plenty of sand and waves for all.

"Well, don't you worry, Agnes. I have no intention of going along with any development scheme. I assume Aunt Beatrice's financial interest in this town will still carry plenty of weight, even though I'm not half the businesswoman she was."

"As long as you don't go selling out to the mayor and that real estate hussy, we'll get along all right." By *we* Emily wasn't sure whether Agnes meant herself or the town. She'd prefer to get along with both.

But the first thing to do was to gather more information. She needed to read the will, see exactly what her inheritance consisted of, and meet with Beatrice's accountant and property manager. She ought to make a tour of the town and check up on her properties in person. She wanted to be well armed when the seemingly inevitable confrontation with Mayor Everett Trimble took place.

Not that she put any stock in Agnes's poisoning theory. That kind of thing only happened in books.

Emily said good morning to Philip, who greeted her with his

usual laconic affection. She hauled her stiff bones out of the soft bed, pulled on her robe, and went to the window. The poplars that bordered the lawn bowed before their oppressor, the constant shore wind. Waves slammed against the beach, and in the distance, a gray expanse of water blended into gray sky. She knew from experience the temperature would have dropped twenty degrees from yesterday's balmy seventy-five. The weather on the Oregon coast was as unreliable as a summer romance.

After a long, hot shower, Emily dressed in yesterday's skirt with a plainer high-necked blouse, a warm cardigan, and low pumps. She'd have preferred something more comfortable, but it looked like it was going to be a doing-business day, and she needed all the help she could get to feel businesslike. If only she had an ally in this place—someone who was not only sympathetic but knowledgeable about all the ins and outs of the town. Someone she could trust.

Someone like, say, the local sheriff.

She shook that thought aside. Business and Luke could not occupy the same brain-space. Her mind still felt like a blender on CRUSH whenever he entered it.

She descended the U-shaped wooden stairway to the dining room and found the sideboard laden with silver dome-covered salvers. Scrambled eggs in one, bacon and sausage in the second, steaming fried potatoes in the third. A bowl of sliced cantaloupe and strawberries ended the row. Enough to feed a houseful. She took a modest portion from each dish, poured herself some coffee from the silver pot, and sat. Two neatly folded newspapers lay next to her napkin—the *Oregonian* from Portland and the *Wave*, the weekly that covered this section of the coast.

News of the larger world could wait. She unfolded the *Wave* and jumped to see her own face staring back at her from the front page. *Portland Professor Pockets Pretty Penny*. The story took up three full columns.

"What on Earth . . . ?" Where could the reporter have gotten that much material? No one had asked her for an interview.

She glanced at the byline—Rita Spenser—accompanied by a picture. The whale woman who had waylaid her and Luke at the reception. Emily couldn't remember exactly what she'd answered to the woman's nosy questions, but surely she hadn't said everything that was quoted here; some of it wasn't even grammatical. Added to this flight of fancy were quotations from Luke, Brock, the mayor, and several other people she'd met yesterday afternoon. The woman must have had a hidden tape recorder—or maybe a Quick-Quotes Quill. Her name was Rita, after all.

Furious, Emily slapped the paper down on the table just as Agnes appeared in the doorway. "Can't they give me even a day's peace? Good heavens, anyone would think I was royalty!"

Agnes's mouth quirked in a parody of a smile. "That's Stony Beach for you. Better get used to it if you plan to stick around." She primmed her mouth and drew herself up. "And speaking of that, madam, I'd appreciate knowing your plans as soon as possible. I've got my own arrangements to make."

"Oh! As to that—well, I've hardly had time to think about it. But I certainly won't be selling Windy Corner anytime soon, and as long as I have it, I suppose I'll need a housekeeper, whether I'm living here full-time or not." A house like this couldn't safely be left unattended. "I'd be pleased if you'd stay on."

Agnes's expression was unreadable. Had Emily said the wrong thing? "That is, if you want to. Unless you're thinking of retiring?"

Agnes gave a mighty snort. "And just what would I do with myself if I retired? Putter about some tiny cottage all day? No, thank you. I'll stay right where I am, if it pleases you. Besides, I'm the only one who can handle That Cat."

The animal in question now slunk into the room and heaved his bulk up to lean his white forepaws against the sideboard, nostrils twitching. "I have all the food I need, Agnes. Really, it's way too much for one person. Does Bustopher Jones get the leftovers?"

"That he does, madam, the ungrateful beast. But I'll make a bit less from now on, seeing as you're such a light eater." She eyed the food on Emily's plate and shook her head. "The missus, now, you'd be surprised at how much she could put away, thin as she was. Always moving, that one."

"Yes, well, I've got quite a bit of moving to do myself today. Lots of people to see, things to get straightened out. In fact, you'd better not count on me for lunch. But by dinner I should have a healthy appetite." She smiled at Agnes, who merely humphed and commenced clearing the extra food.

Emily addressed herself to her breakfast before it cooled completely. Agnes Beech might have her little ways, but she certainly knew how to cook.

If Emily stayed in Stony Beach, she'd never have to cook for herself again. Nor settle for college cafeteria food. Could any consequence of her inheritance be sweeter than that?

Emily hadn't quite finished eating when the doorbell boomed. She heard Agnes open the door, then a brisk, commanding alto voice reply. Oh, no. Not the real estate agent. She didn't lose any time, did she?

Through the open door Emily saw Vicki Landau push past Agnes Beech and into the dining room. Emily rose, expecting an apology for the intrusion; but Vicki just headed for the sideboard, poured herself a cup of coffee, and sat down. Emily was too astonished to stop her. Clearly Miss Manners was not revered in Stony Beach.

Dazed, Emily sank back into her chair. Vicki sipped her coffee, then opened her portfolio and took out a fat sheaf of papers. "I've got the contract all ready for you," she said. "All you have to do is sign." She held out a pen.

Emily kept her hands in her lap. "Contract?"

"For me to sell the house. We talked about it yesterday." Vicki's tone implied Emily's memory was not all it should be.

"I recall you mentioning the possibility, but I certainly didn't agree to it. Even if I wanted to, I couldn't sign anything until probate goes through. Legally, I don't even own the property yet."

Vicki's face froze. Her hand remained suspended, pen out. "But you will sell after probate?"

Could this woman be real? "I doubt it. I'm quite fond of Windy Corner. It holds a lot of memories. And it's the perfect getaway from city life."

"Exactly." Vicki reanimated. "Which is why I can get such a premium price for it."

"Ms. Landau, you don't seem to understand. I don't need more money, and I don't want to sell. Now perhaps you'll allow me to finish my breakfast in peace."

Vicki retracted her pen but stayed in her chair. "Some of your other properties then. Surely you don't want to be bothered with all those vacation rentals and commercial buildings your aunt owned. You being in Portland most of the year. You just name your price, and I'll make sure you get it." Her red lips curled into a smile, her slightly longer, curiously sharp canine teeth denting her lower lip.

Emily shook her head, as much in disbelief as in denial. Stony Beach might have changed since she was here last, but surely it hadn't become home to vampires. "I haven't even had a chance to find out what all I'm inheriting, let alone make any decisions about it. You really must give me more time. I'll let you know if I do decide to sell anything."

Vicki's smile vanished as if it had never been. "Oh, very well. I'll check back with you in a week or so." She gathered her things and stood. But before she turned to go, she scanned the room with its carved moldings, built-in sideboard, and the pane of stained glass in the bay window. Her eyes were alight with greed, but Emily glimpsed something else behind the greed—something even darker. Before she could pin it down, Vicki was gone.

Emily refreshed her coffee, hoping to wash out all traces of Vicki Landau. But almost the instant the door closed behind her, the bell boomed again. Aunt Beatrice must have had it made loud enough for Agnes to hear from the attic.

This time it was Mayor Everett Trimble who bustled into the room. He at least greeted her and shook her hand with a firm if sweaty grip before eyeing the coffeepot. Emily saved him from copying Vicki's rudeness by offering him a cup.

"Thank you, thank you." His shiny face beamed. "Agnes Beech makes the best coffee in town."

And if it had been intended only for him and Vicki, she'd probably have poisoned it. "To what do I owe the honor of this early visit?" Emily stressed the word *early,* but the mayor didn't seem to notice. She motioned toward the chair across the corner from hers, which Vicki had just vacated.

"Just being neighborly." He pulled out the chair next to her. "You and me, we gotta get on the same page. Between us we can bring this old town into the twenty-first century. Progress, that's what Stony Beach needs. Town's so stuck in its ways, might as well be called Sleepy Beach. Get it?" He elbowed her so hard, her coffee sloshed into her saucer. Aunt Beatrice's old-fashioned cups had their merits.

"I've always thought its sleepiness was Stony Beach's greatest charm." She glanced demurely at Trimble over the edge of her cup.

He guffawed, slapping his thigh. "You're a funny one, aren'tcha? Real joker. Greatest charm! That's a good one." He shook out an enormous handkerchief and wiped his eyes, then his bald pate.

"I'm quite serious. I'd hate to see this town change its character. Why should we be like Seaside? People who want a noisy mob can go there. People who want peace and quiet can come here. It works out perfectly."

The mayor scowled. "Now just you listen to me, young lady. You've been away from here for what, thirty years? Things happen in that time, get it? Towns change. People change. Don't you go making pronouncements on what you know nothing about."

She had to admit he had a fair point, even though it contradicted what he'd said earlier. "You're quite right, Mayor Trimble. I don't really know the town anymore, and that's why I propose to spend the next few days finding out as much as I can. I don't want my decisions to be poorly informed."

His smile beamed again. "That's the spirit, girlie. Once you've got the goods, you'll see things my way. Gotta pull together, get it? Get this cart out of the mud."

He heaved himself out of the chair and stuck out his hand again. Emily pretended not to see it. "Good day, Mayor. Perhaps I'll see you around."

"Right." He bustled out, and Emily was left free to enjoy the humor of being called "young lady" and "girlie" by someone at most ten years her senior when she herself would never see fifty again.

She finished her coffee and moved to the library, where she spread out on the massive desk all the papers Jamie MacDougal had given her. She read through the will, which was straightforward and contained little of Aunt Beatrice's characteristic acerbic voice until Emily came to the paragraphs detailing her own bequest.

To my great-niece, Emily Worthing Cavanaugh, I leave all my books, as I know no one else who would value them as I have done. As I do not wish the books to be moved, I leave her Windy Corner as well; and since the house is likely to become a money pit in its old age, I bequeath to said great-niece all the residue of my property not otherwise disposed of herein. I regret to say this is likely to include the cat Bustopher Jones, who will undoubtedly outlive me as he is far too ornery to die; however, it may be possible to palm him off onto Agnes Beech, who seems to have an unaccountable fondness for the creature.

It is my hope and belief that this sudden acquisition of wealth will not spoil Emily's character nor prove to be too great a burden; but if it does become a burden, I ask only that she shall not dispose of any of the real property in accordance with the fiendish

and underhanded plans for development of Mayor Everett Trim-
ble, nor entrust it to the agency of Vicki Landau for sale. This is a
request, not a condition, as I have every faith in Emily's intrinsic
Worthing good sense, which bypassed her father but has only
wavered in Emily once, to my knowledge, in her extreme youth.

Emily smiled as she read. She could hear Beatrice's voice in her head, could almost see her standing just there, by the French window, dictating these words to Jamie MacDougal. She winced at the final phrase, though. So Aunt Beatrice had known about Luke, though Emily had hugged the secret of their relationship to her chest like a safety blanket. Of course. Aunt Beatrice knew everything.

And if Emily did not carry out her wishes, Aunt Beatrice would know that, too, and would undoubtedly exact some awful vengeance, such as siccing Bustopher Jones on her from beyond the grave. It was fortunate Emily's good Worthing sense had already set her on the right path.

The will, to her surprise, did not specify the wording of Beatrice's epitaph, stipulating only that Emily should be the one to write it. She was touched by that. Beatrice trusted her not only to honor her memory, but to do so eloquently, concisely, and without undue sentiment. This was not stated, but Emily knew from the many times Beatrice had corrected her essays exactly what her aunt would expect.

She turned to the list of properties. A total of fifty-three rental units, including single houses, duplexes, and a couple of fourplexes, most of them in prime locations within sight of the beach. The Driftwood Inn, the biggest and classiest of the town's three hotels. Three entire blocks of downtown retail space. "Downtown" was a mere four blocks long, and the fourth block had gone to Brock. This left only a few outlying shops, cafés, and taverns to be owned by others. In addition, Emily now owned all the undeveloped property from the beach to the highway for more than a mile to the north of town, all the way past Windy Corner and up to the rocky promontory that put a parenthesis to that end of the town's five-mile-long beach.

No wonder Trimble was eager to get Emily on his side. North was the only direction the town could potentially grow. To the east, the coastal range rose too sharply to permit more building. To the south, the beach ended where the houses petered out and Tillamook Bay began. Beatrice, and now Emily, stood in the breach, single-handedly defending Stony Beach from unwelcome expansion.

She felt rather like Boadicea defending Britain from the Romans. She might fight with all her valor, but her eventual defeat seemed assured.

six

As a brother, a landlord, a master, she considered how many people's happiness were in his guardianship!—How much of pleasure or of pain it was in his power to bestow!—How much of good or evil must be done by him!

—*Pride and Prejudice*

The office of Wade Evans, CPA, occupied one corner of an unassuming building on Tillamook's main street. Evans had suggested ten thirty when Emily called for an appointment, and she was right on time.

She opened the outer door onto a reception room empty of receptionist. A bare, somewhat battered wooden desk took up one side of the room. Across from it, under the windows, stood a row of chairs that looked like refugees from a farm kitchen. The door to the inner office stood ajar.

Emily clicked across the linoleum floor, but just as she raised her hand to knock, a deep voice called out, "Come on in!"

She pushed the door open and found herself face-to-face with a white-haired man who, judging by the length of the jean-clad legs and the size of the cowboy boots slung up on his desk, must be well over six feet tall. He was leaning back in his wooden desk chair and aiming a balled-up sheet of paper at a point above her head. She dodged to the side and looked up to see a wire wastebasket suspended above the door. The paper ball found its target with inches to spare.

He smiled—not at her—then swung his legs off the desk and stepped around it to shake her hand. His spare frame must have had several inches on Luke, who was six foot two. Emily had to crane her neck to look at him.

"Wade Evans. You must be the niece."

"Emily Cavanaugh." His grip would have done justice to a blacksmith—a comparison no doubt inspired by the dozens of photographs of horses that jockeyed for wall space with book-cases and framed certificates. Most of the photos included Evans himself.

"Take a load off." He gestured to the wooden armchair, twin of his own but without the wheels, which stood in front of the desk. So far Emily had not glimpsed a square inch of fabric or upholstery in the entire place.

"So what can I do you for?"

She blinked at the colloquialism but decided that if he really meant to swindle her, he probably wouldn't advertise the fact. "I'd like to get a general idea of the state of Beatrice's pos-sessions. Well, mine now, or as soon as probate goes through. I have a list of the properties and their market value, but I'd like more detail—what condition are they in, are they profit-able, and so on."

Evans shot her a shrewd glance. "How well'd you know your aunt?"

"We were pretty close years ago. I hadn't seen her for a long time."

"Well, you should know Beatrice only dealt with the best. When she bought a place, she had it fixed up and kept up, and everything she owned brought top dollar. If a place couldn't pull its own weight . . ." He slashed his forefinger across his throat and made a *pffft* sound through his teeth.

"That would certainly be my expectation. Windy Corner is in excellent shape. I just thought it possible that with so many properties and her getting older, things might have started to slip a little."

"No way. She didn't do it all herself, mind. She used a property management firm here in Tillamook. Practically kept them in business single-handed. But she made sure they did their job right."

"I see." Emily didn't know how to ask her most pressing question, which was why Aunt Beatrice had chosen to employ Evans, who was now leaning back in his chair again and trying to balance a pencil eraser-down on the tip of his finger. Neither he nor his surroundings exuded professional efficiency. But on the other hand, he did seem straightforward—not the type to try siphoning Beatrice's money into a cozy retreat in the Caymans.

"I can give you a thumb drive with all Beatrice's records if you want to have a look-see."

Emily swallowed. That at least sounded efficient. But although she knew what a thumb drive was—only just—she had no way to make use of one nor any clue how. "I—don't have a computer with me." She held her breath, hoping not to be informed she could just use Beatrice's. She hadn't seen a computer in the house, but neither had she toured every room.

Evans raised one eyebrow and his mouth quirked. "Chip off the old Luddite block, eh? No prob. I've got old-fashioned files too." He pushed out of his chair and reached the file cabinet in two long strides. With no fumbling, he pulled out a fat but perfectly neat accordion file envelope and placed it in her lap. "That's everything but the kitchen sink. No mortgage on the sink, I promise." He winked and returned to his chair.

Emily decided Beatrice's employing Evans had not been the first sign of senile dementia after all. In fact, she might be able to trust him to give her an informed opinion on the development issue.

"I would like your advice about something. I've been approached by a couple of people who are anxious for me to either sell some properties or use them to help Stony Beach grow. I know Beatrice was dead against it, and I can't say I'm thrilled by the prospect either. What's your perspective?"

Evans leaned forward on his elbows, and his bushy brows drew together. "*Dead* against it. Funny you should say it just like that."

An invisible caterpillar crawled up Emily's spine. "Do you mean . . ." Her mouth went dry. She couldn't say the words.

"I mean, those people who've been pestering you might've taken it into their heads to put Beatrice out of the picture. Beatrice die of acute gastroenteritis? Yeah, and my prize stallion might get up and fly."

Emily swallowed. "Agnes Beech said the same thing. I thought it was just an old woman's delusion."

He shook his head. "Not much gets past Agnes Beech. Ask me, that doctor and that sheriff up there're either blind, lazy, or in the mayor's pocket. I'd bet a hundred to one your aunt was murdered."

• seven •

He was not altered, or not for the worse. . . . The years
which had destroyed her youth and bloom had only given
him a more glowing, manly, open look, in no respect lessen-
ing his personal advantages. She had seen the same Freder-
ick Wentworth.

—*Persuasion*

Emily left Evans's office in a daze. She hadn't met the
doctor—Sam Griffiths, Evans said his name was—but "blind,
lazy, or in the mayor's pocket" certainly didn't describe the
Luke she used to know. Could thirty-five years have changed
him so fundamentally?

Maybe it was time to find out.

She drove back to Stony Beach and wove through the streets
uphill from the highway, her memory betraying her as to the
precise location of the sheriff's office. At last she spotted a
black-and-white SUV parked in front of a building that looked
like an ordinary small house. But a demure sign half hidden by a
bush said COUNTY SHERIFF'S OFFICE.

She sat in the car for a few minutes, composing herself. Luke
had made it clear yesterday he had something to say to her—
some lame apology, no doubt, for abandoning her all those years
ago. She wasn't at all sure she wanted to hear it. Nor did she

want to be lured into confessing why his betrayal had mattered so much to her. She was here on business, and she would have to keep the meeting on that footing. Now that the first shock of seeing him was past, surely she could manage that.

She straightened her cardigan, patted her hair, and walked up to the door. It looked so much like the door of a private home, she hesitated, wondering if she ought to knock. No, one didn't knock at a public office. She turned the handle and went in.

She expected a receptionist or junior officer, but once again was caught off guard. Luke himself sat at the desk before her. And his effect on her was no less powerful than it had been yesterday. She kept her hand on the doorknob to steady herself.

"Emily!" He shot out of his chair and around the desk to greet her, then stopped short a couple of feet away. Confusion hung in the air between them. Another handshake would be a travesty of what they'd once felt for each other, a hug far too intimate for where they stood now.

They hesitated a fraction too long, so that contact of any kind became impossible. He opened his mouth to speak, but she forestalled him. "I want to talk to you about Beatrice's death."

His eyebrows rose halfway to where his hairline used to be. "You better sit down." She braced herself, let go of the knob, and managed the few steps to the single, cracked-vinyl visitor chair. He returned to his seat behind the desk.

"Somebody been spreading rumors?" His normally smooth voice held a hint of a growl.

"You might say that. Two people, quite separately, have told me—they don't believe her death was natural."

He gave a low whistle and leaned back in his chair. "That's a tough one. To tell you the absolute truth, I had a hard time believing it myself. But Doc Griffiths signed the certificate, no qualms, and I had nothing to go on." He leaned forward again and met her eyes. "Far as I could tell, the symptoms might have been consistent with some kind of poisoning. But they were just as consistent with acute gastroenteritis, like the doc said. And by the time she died—it took about twenty-four hours—"

Emily winced, and he stretched a hand toward her, but she was out of his reach. "By the time I started looking for evidence, there wasn't any evidence to find. She'd eaten in a restaurant that night. Everything she'd eaten out of had been washed, the whole place scrubbed to a squeak. She had lobster, which always disagreed with her, but other people at the restaurant had it too and they didn't get sick, so it wasn't the lobster's fault."

"What about . . ." Emily swallowed, ghastly images sticking in her throat. "What about a postmortem?"

"I wanted one, but the chief over in Tillamook wouldn't hear of it. Budget's tight this year. Doctor gave a certificate; that was enough for him."

Emily struggled to absorb this information, filtered as it was by her acute awareness of Luke himself. Every gesture, every turn of phrase, every inflection of his voice echoed within her memory, stirring up the same old maelstrom of physical and emotional response.

Doctor. Certificate. Poison. Evidence. She fastened onto those words. "Is the doctor honest? Competent?"

"Normally, I'd say both. Totally. No real reason to think otherwise in this case."

She peered at him. "But you do."

"I do." He gripped a pencil so hard, it snapped. "But I can't prove a dadgum thing."

Emily stood. "Where do I find Doctor Griffiths?"

"Clinic over on Fifth." He checked his watch. "But it'll be closed for lunch now. Fact, I was just about to head out for a bite when you came in." He shot her a look as tentative as a junior high boy getting up his nerve to ask for a dance. "Want to come with me?"

That look slipped under her defenses, such as they were. "Sure."

He opened the door for her, then locked it behind him. "I usually walk—okay by you?"

She nodded. He hadn't said where they were going, but nothing in Stony Beach was more than a few blocks away.

He strode down the walk and turned toward the highway, then checked himself and waited for her to catch up. "Oh yeah," he said with a lopsided smile. "Forgot. I always did have to slow down for you."

"I can't help it if your legs are six inches longer than mine." Her old riposte.

His laugh should have diffused the rising tension between them, but it only heightened it. Walking beside him, it was all she could do not to let her hand slip into his. She remembered so well how sheltered it had felt there. But that was the hand that had failed to answer her letters—had possibly crumpled them unread. How could she ever trust it again?

They headed south on the highway, a couple of blocks beyond the main downtown section of which she was now the primary landlady, and stopped in front of a shabby, shingled building, hardly more than a shack, with a crooked, inexpertly painted sign above the door: THE CRAB POT.

Luke must have read the dismay on her face. "I know it doesn't look like much, but it's clean and the food is great." He grinned. "You'll meet the Crab in a minute."

Emily was reminded of the Red Queen's sage advice to Alice: *Never eat anything you've been introduced to.* Too bad, because crab was her favorite seafood.

He pushed open the door, which creaked loudly enough to make a bell unnecessary. Over half the rickety vinyl-topped tables and most of the seats at the back counter were full, some with faces that looked vaguely familiar from the funeral. Luke stopped to greet several people and waved at others on his way to a table near the back.

They sat, and he handed her a laminated menu card from the condiment rack. "Everything's good, but the crab melt is famous."

The smells wafting from the kitchen tended to confirm Luke's assurances. Breakfast suddenly seemed days in the past. She skimmed the menu, but saw nothing to tempt her away from the crab melt.

No waiter had yet appeared. Luke, who was facing the counter, called out, "Hey, Sunny! Can we get some water over here?"

Emily heard a low grumbling, the slosh of water, then a slow, heavy shuffle approaching. The hairiest hand she'd ever seen slammed two plastic glasses onto the middle of the table. She looked up to see a wizened gnome with Einstein-like hair jutting out on either side of a weather-beaten bald stripe. The gnome's left arm, half the size of its brother, hung useless at his side, and his badly shaven face bore the unfriendliest scowl she'd ever seen outside of a gangster movie.

The gnome turned back toward the counter, but Luke stopped him with a tug on his ancient, food-stained overalls. "We're ready to order, Sunny. If it's not too much trouble." He winked at Emily.

The astonishingly named Sunny turned back with an audible growl. The scowl, impossibly, deepened. "Whaddaya want?"

Luke gestured to Emily.

"I'd like the crab melt, please." She'd intended to ask for fruit instead of the standard French fries, but her imagination quailed at the thought of how Sunny might react.

"Make that two." Luke gathered the menus and stuck them back in their place. "And a Coke for me." He raised his eyebrows in Emily's direction.

"Iced tea?"

Sunny shuffled off, trailing a pungent odor behind him.

"Good heavens! What hole did he climb out of?" she said in a low voice when he was gone.

Luke grinned. "Used to be a fisherman till he wrecked his arm. His sister owns the place, does the cooking. She gave him a job—no one else would—but he hates it, obviously. Been here twenty years, getting sourer by the day."

She shuddered, in pity as well as revulsion. "I'm surprised people still come here. He's enough to sour the food."

"We're used to him. Besides, this is the only place in town stays open all winter. We don't send tourists here, though. We want people to like Stony Beach."

Emily chuckled, then sobered, the mention of tourists reminding her of her day's mission. "Where do you stand on this whole development thing?"

Luke choked on his water. "Good Lord, don't tell me they're after you already?"

"Both the real estate agent and the mayor interrupted my breakfast this morning."

"Holy cow. Listen, if you want a restraining order or something, just say the word. Those two are a one-two punch."

"I take it you're not in sympathy with their goals, then?"

"Hell no. I like Stony Beach just the way it is. Way it's been all my life. Only thing could've made it better is you coming back—and now you're here." He gave her the full wattage of his smile.

She bit back the words, *I could have been here all along.* She'd better stick to business—she didn't want to break down in front of all these people, most of whom were already staring at the two of them with undisguised curiosity.

She lowered her voice. "You don't think those two want progress enough to . . ." When it came to the point, the idea seemed too outlandish to put into words.

"To kill for it? Don't think it hasn't crossed my mind. She had dinner with them the night before she died. I doubt they'd have the guts to kill her face-to-face. But a poison that doesn't act right away—a guy can kinda distance himself from that, y' know? Rationalize it might not work. And you don't have to be there to see the consequences. I wouldn't rule those two out." He took a long drink of water. "That is, if it was murder at all."

"Did anyone else have a grudge against Beatrice?"

"Oh, sure. You can't be as big as she was in a town like this without putting a few people's backs up. This place, for instance—she was convinced it was a health hazard, tried to get me to shut it down. But Harriet, the owner, she wouldn't hurt a fly. And Sunny—well, this place shutting down'd be a godsend to him."

He looked past her shoulder. "Speak of the angel. Here comes Harriet now."

A woman bustled up to the table, bearing two laden, steaming plates. She matched the gnome in stature, but her broad, beaming face was as unlined as a baby's under her cloud of white hair, and a spotless, brightly flowered pink apron enveloped her plump form. Emily would never have believed the two were siblings.

"Here you are, my darlings." With a flourish, she placed a platter before each of them. "That crab is fresh off the boat. Only the best for our new leading citizen." Her already broad smile stretched even wider as she stood back expectantly.

Luke took the cue. "Emily, meet Harriet Longman, best cook this side of the Cascades. Harriet, Emily Cavanaugh."

Harriet took Emily's hand and squeezed it in both of her own. "We're honored to have you. I hope Sunny didn't scare you too bad."

"If Luke hadn't been here to explain him, I confess I might've walked out. But Luke assures me he's harmless. And I can't wait to taste your cooking—it smells heavenly."

Harriet's face lit up the room. "Now, if there's anything at all I can do for you, don't you hesitate a second. Enjoy your lunch, my darlings." She bustled off.

"Salt of the earth, that one." Luke forked off a huge bite of his crab melt.

Emily crossed herself hastily and dug in. The sweet and salty crab melted in her mouth, while the Tillamook cheddar set it off to perfection. If Harriet and Agnes Beech were to hold a charity cook-off, they could raise thousands. Not that Agnes would ever condescend.

"What do you think about Agnes?" she asked when she'd swallowed the first bite. "She's a deep one, and she did get a legacy. Was she really as devoted to Beatrice as it seems?"

"I'd say so. They were a funny pair, both as stubborn as Balaam's ass, but Agnes seemed genuinely cut up when Beatrice died."

"That's what I thought. And she was the one who first mentioned the word *poison*. She wouldn't do that if she were responsible."

"Not likely. In a mystery novel, now, that'd be my cue to say 'unless she wanted us to think that,' but I really don't think so with Agnes. I doubt she has any idea what to do with her new-found wealth except save it for when she gets too old to work. Which, knowing her, will be the day she dies."

Emily nodded. Suddenly it struck her how bizarre it was that she should be sitting in a diner with Luke discussing possible suspects for the possible murder of her aunt, when far more burning personal questions of thirty-five years' standing hung between them. Not to mention the question that had set up a running static at the back of her mind since she first saw him yesterday, making concentration on any other issue almost impossible: What might the future hold?

She folded her napkin and laid it beside her plate. Luke, forking up the last of his crab melt, raised an eyebrow at her half-finished meal. "Full already?"

"I guess I'm too keyed up to eat much. It's been a roller coaster the last few days."

"You can say that again." He looked into her eyes. "We need to talk."

· eight ·

"When you have finished Udolpho, ... I have made out a
list of ten or twelve more of the same kind for you. ...
Mysterious Warnings, Necromancer of the Black Forest,
Midnight Bell, Orphan of the Rhine, and Horrid Mysteries.
Those will last us some time."

"Yes, pretty well; but are they all horrid, are you sure
they are all horrid?"

—Isabella Thorpe and Catherine Morland,
Northanger Abbey

J ust then an elderly woman shuffled up to their table, breathless. "Oh, Sheriff—little Timmy—come quick. That tree—so
high . . . I can hardly see him." She stood, wringing her hands,
her features contorted.

Luke made a face for Emily's benefit, then stood and patted
the woman's shoulder. "Now don't you worry, Mrs. Trimble;
little Timmy'll be just fine. Let me walk Mrs. Cavanaugh back
to her car, and I'll be over there in two shakes."

Mrs. Trimble looked at Emily for the first time. "Oh . . .
Mrs. Cavanaugh . . . You're Beatrice's niece, aren't you? So
sorry . . . Dear friend . . . Oh my." She fluttered as if she'd made
some dreadful faux pas.

"Thank you, Mrs. Trimble," Emily said. "We'd better get
going so Luke can get your grandson out of that tree."

Mrs. Trimble's eyes widened and her hand flew to her
mouth. "Grandson? Oh dear . . . Oh no . . ."

Luke slapped some bills onto the table. His mouth twitched as he shepherded both women out of the restaurant. In Emily's ear he said, "Little Timmy is her cat."

Emily barely kept her countenance until Mrs. Trimble was out of earshot, hurrying down a side street. "So that's how a small-town lawman spends his time—rescuing cats from trees for the mayor's wife?"

"His mother. She's not safe out, ought to be in a home, but Mayor Trimble's so fond of her, he won't hear of it. And you don't know the half—by the time I get there, the cat'll be safe on the ground, wondering what all the fuss is about." He halted. "You could just come with me."

She hesitated. Part of her wanted never to leave Luke's side; the other part wanted to run from all the feelings his nearness stirred up in her. And she wasn't ready to have that talk he kept mentioning; one subject in particular she was determined must never come up. "I think I've had enough excitement for one day. And I need to talk to the doctor."

His face fell. "Right. Catch up with you later, then." He reached down and took her hand. "Em—we really do have to talk."

"I know. But maybe we'd better wait till you're off duty." She eased her hand from his grasp before his touch could make her change her mind. "You don't need to walk me back. I'll just go straight to the clinic from here."

She headed north, then glanced back. Luke was still looking after her, his gray eyes as fathomless as the sea.

The clinic proved to be almost as well disguised as the sheriff's office, but the sign was a little more obvious. Emily entered an empty waiting room with an odd assortment of dilapidated chairs lining the two outside walls. No receptionist here, either. Tillamook County must be full of young women sitting at home doing their nails, dreaming of sitting in an office doing their nails, but unable to find anyone to employ them.

A door stood open at one end. Emily was reluctant to approach it; doctors' offices seemed more sacrosanct than accountants'. "Hello?" she called instead.

"Be with you in a minute," an alto voice answered. Perhaps there was a receptionist or assistant after all.

In less than a minute a short, squarely built woman in her late thirties appeared in the doorway. Her mousy hair was cropped short above the collar of her white coat, which was draped with a stethoscope and covered a T-shirt and jeans. She looked Emily over with a puzzled expression. "Don't think I've seen you before. Early for tourists, isn't it?"

"I'm not exactly a tourist. I'm Emily Cavanaugh. Heir to most of Beatrice Runcible's estate."

The woman's wide-set eyes flared for a fraction of a second, then her blunt features contracted to resemble a bulldog's. "That trust for a new clinic is absolutely sound. No lawyer's going to shake it."

Emily took a step backward. The woman's eyes had betrayed her—her belligerence was a cover-up for fear. But what did she have to be afraid of?

"I assure you, the thought never crossed my mind. What Beatrice left me is more than I ever dreamed of; I'm not looking for more." The woman's scowl faded, but her eyes remained wary. "Are you Doctor Griffiths?"

"Sam." She strode forward and shook Emily's hand with

a grip worthy of a man. "What can I do for you then? You look healthy enough."

"I'm fine, thanks. I wanted to talk to you about my aunt's death."

Sam dropped her eyes and brushed past Emily to the counter where a receptionist ought to be. "Busy now. Come back later."

Emily cast a pointed glance around the waiting room. "I don't see any patients."

"Paperwork. No help, as you see."

"Surely you can spare five minutes to tell me why you were so sure my aunt died of natural causes."

Sam fumbled with papers behind the counter, eyes down. "No reason to think otherwise."

"That's not what Lieutenant Richards said. He said the symptoms were consistent with poisoning."

Sam gave a scornful *puh*. "Oh, and a badge-wearing cat-rescuer knows more about symptoms than I do? He just wants a murder to solve. Got a hammer, every problem's a nail."

Emily's hackles rose. She put on her best dealing-with-a-difficult-student voice. "That is not a fair thing to say about Lieutenant Richards. He's not the type to go looking for trouble if it isn't there."

Sam looked up at her. "What do you know about it? You've been in town what, five minutes?"

"I used to be here a lot, years ago. Luke and I are old— friends."

Sam glared at her, then her face cleared and she leaned her hands on the desk. "Look. Sorry if I offended you. But there was nothing wrong about Beatrice's death. She ate lobster, which always made her sick, and then she was too damn stubborn to call me in. Agnes finally called in spite of her. I did everything I could for her, but by the time I got there, it was too late."

"You mean she died before you arrived?"

"No, but she was too weak to rally. Heart gave out. She was a strong woman, but she *was* eighty-seven years old."

Emily frowned into Sam's gray eyes. The doctor's expression was impenetrable. Emily was convinced she was hiding something, but what?

As casually as she could, she asked, "So this clinic trust—that's your baby? Did you know about it before she died?"

Sam resumed her paper shuffling. "Not to say knew. Asked her to give the money outright. Town needs a real clinic, decent equipment. Have to send people to Tillamook for anything worse than a paper cut. But Beatrice kept stringing me along. Never consulted a doctor herself, couldn't believe other people really needed to. Hinted she might do something in her will—wouldn't tell me straight out."

"I see." Emily drummed her fingers on the counter, wondering what else she could ask that would throw any light on the situation. What would Miss Marple say? Or Lord Peter Wimsey? Either of them might disarm the doctor with innocent questions, but it was a bit late for that. This sleuthing business was harder than books made it seem.

"Well, thank you for your time." Emily strode out. As she turned to close the door behind her, she caught another glimpse of naked fear in the doctor's eyes.

Her car and Luke's office were a few blocks away. He'd probably be back by now and lying in wait for her to have that talk.

She wasn't ready for it. They'd established some sort of working rapport over lunch, and she didn't want to jeopardize it by opening old wounds. She'd pursue her original plan of scoping out the town.

Fifth Street met the highway at the south end of the business district. This first block was part of Brock's inheritance, not hers, but that was no reason she should ignore it. Besides, the first door she came to was a yarn shop called Sheep to Knits. Irresistible. Having just finished the sweater she was wearing, she'd brought no knitting with her, and her fingers were beginning to itch for needles and wool.

Just inside the door was a display of cashmere-blend yarn in all the rich fall colors Emily adored: gold, pumpkin, nutmeg, cinnamon, olive, russet. They looked good enough to eat. She picked up a ball of the russet, the cashmere yielding like a feather bed under her fingers. She glanced at the price and was about to return the ball reluctantly to the bin, when she remembered: She was rich now. She could buy all the cashmere she wanted.

"That's a great color for you," came a voice from the back of the shop.

Emily smiled in the voice's direction and snaked her way toward it between tables piled with yarn. Next to the cash register, a young woman with spiky dead-black hair perched on a stool, knitting a long swath of indeterminate shape, the bulk of which seemed to be draped around her body in an endless spiral. Color swirled into color with exuberant disregard for harmony; stitch piled on stitch, shape shifted with bewildering randomness. Glimpses of black leggings and tank top peeked through the chaos on her legs and torso, while tattoos covered her arms.

The young woman gave Emily a disarming smile accented by a sparkling lip stud. "I like to try out every new yarn I get in so I can tell people about it. I'm working with some of that cashmere now." She held out her work for Emily to see. The fine maple-leaf-red yarn formed an intricate lace pattern that mimicked leafy vines. The knitting was expertly done.

"It knits up beautifully. Do you sell that lace pattern?"

"Nah, I just made it up. There's some patterns and magazines and stuff over there if you want to look." She waved a hand toward the south wall. "I'm Beanie, by the way."

"Beanie—that's an unusual name. Is it short for something?"

She screwed up her pixie face into a comical grimace. "My real name—my actual birth certificate name—is Princess Diana Spenser. Can you believe it? My mom was obsessed with her. She has the soul of a paparazzi with no one to stalk. And the really silly thing is, when Diana got to be a princess, she wasn't even Spenser anymore. But lucky for me, my brother nicknamed me Beanie when I was little 'cause I had this beanie I wore *all* the time."

Beanie held up her knitting, considered it, then turned the long strip and starting picking up stitches down the side. "And my brother—you really won't believe this—my brother's name is Prince Charles. He goes by Chuck, but when I want to wind him up I call him 'the brother formerly known as Prince.'"

Emily allowed her mouth to quirk. "The two of you together could almost be Bonnie Prince Charlie."

Beanie scratched her nose with the point of a free needle. "You know, that's a thought. Next Pirate Day Ball, he can be Prince Charlie, and I'll be a bonnie lass."

"Pirate Day? When's that?"

"Fourth of July weekend. We get a real mob here then. You gonna stick around?"

"I have no idea. I just came for my aunt's funeral, but things are getting a little more complicated than I planned for."

"Oh right, you're old Beatrice's niece, aren't you? Mrs. . . . Cavanaugh, was it? I saw my mom's article about you in the paper."

Spenser. The penny dropped. The soul of a paparazzi, indeed.

"And you knit. Wow, I hope you do stick around—you could keep me in business." She cast a professional eye over Emily's cardigan. "That's an awesome sweater. Did you make it?"

"Just finished it a few days ago." Emily was rather proud of this cardigan, with its intricate Aran cabling and the shaping she'd designed herself to echo that of her suit jacket: peplum, shawl collar, puffed sleeves. The yarn was a lightweight taffy-brown tweed.

"May I?" Beanie reached out a purple-nailed hand and fingered the edge of the peplum. "You do great work. Hey, wanna make some models for me? I'd give you the yarn at cost if you let me show a piece for a month or two. People want to see the yarn made into normal sweaters and scarves and stuff, and I just can't stand following patterns, y'know?"

Emily was reluctant to commit herself to anything that long-term, but before she could voice her objections, Beanie cut her off. "We can start with that cashmere. What were you thinking—shawl? Socks? Scarf and hat?"

Emily held up her free hand, palm out. "Whoa there, Nelly! I don't even know how long I'll be in town. And I can afford to pay full price for the yarn. What do you say I just buy it for now, and if I'm still here when I finish my piece, I'll let you have it for a while."

"Fair enough. Have to admit I can use the money. That new guy, what's-his-name, he's threatening to raise the rent."

"Brock?"

"Yeah. Is he like your cousin or something?"

"No real relation. Beatrice's late husband was his uncle."

"Good. I don't want to diss a relative of yours, but even if I hadn't already been sorry to see Beatrice go—which I was—having him for a landlord is enough to make me want to dig her up and bring her back. She'd make a pretty wicked zombie, don't you think? Put him in his place, for sure."

Beanie chuckled, then her eyes lit. She dropped her knitting, grabbed a notebook and pen from the counter and scribbled furiously, then closed the notebook and put it down with a contented sigh. "There. Got the plot for my next novel. Zombie Beatrice terrorizes Stony Beach. Course she'll only attack the bad guys. The development gang. Though that'll leave her hungry, 'cause they don't have any brains to eat."

The amusement that had been building in Emily since Beanie first spoke finally exploded. She laughed until tears came to her eyes and she had to prop herself with one hand on the counter, the other pressed to her breast.

Beanie looked at her, bemused. "Okay, I guess it'll be a comedy. Black comedy." She hopped off her stool, poured water from a liter bottle into a mug, and handed the mug to Emily.

Emily waved a hand, gasping. "Don't mind me. It's been a crazy couple of days. That picture just set me off. Zombie Beatrice." She drank the water gratefully. "So you don't approve of development? Even though it would help your business?"

"No way. I like Stony Beach just the way it is. I need peace and quiet for my writing. Between the shop and my book sales, I make enough to get by."

"Oh, you're published?"

"Self-published. I put out a new e-book every couple months in the off-season. Zombies, werewolves, demons, you name it. People eat that stuff up."

Emily's mind reeled. She'd heard about the paranormal craze—she'd even seen a copy of *Pride and Prejudice and Zombies* in Powell's, her favorite bookstore, and nearly ran shrieking in horror—but the idea that people were churning out such books and making at least a partial living off them boggled her. She'd stick with her beloved classics.

And her classic knitting. She considered the ball of yarn in her hand. A shawl would be perfect for chilly evenings curled up by the library fire. "I left all my knitting supplies in Portland. I'm going to need some needles and whatnot."

Beanie pointed her needles toward the south wall. "All over there by the patterns."

Emily collected a lovely lace shawl pattern, a couple more balls of yarn, fine circular needles in three sizes in case her gauge was off, and a fabric bag with a cute little sheep appliquéd on it to keep her work in. She'd take a chance on finding basics like scissors and measuring tape at Windy Corner.

As Beanie rang up her purchases, Emily said, "I'll see if I can have a talk with Brock. Maybe I can get him to see reason about the rent." She wasn't sure how she'd do that, but his behavior last night suggested she might have some influence with him.

Beanie smiled so wide, her lip stud clinked against her nose ring. "That would be awesome. *You* are awesome, Mrs. Cavanaugh."

"Call me Emily. I think we're going to be friends."

· nine ·

Elinor looked at him with greater astonishment than ever. She began to think that he must be in liquor;—the strangeness of such a visit, and of such manners, seemed no otherwise intelligible.

—*Sense and Sensibility*

Emily visited a few more shops and made it back to Windy Corner without encountering Luke again. It was five minutes to four when she pulled her Cruiser up in front of the garage door.

Agnes met her in the front hall. "Madam always had tea punctually at four o'clock," she said with a hint of reproof.

"That sounds like a wonderful tradition. Tea in the library, please, Agnes." She wouldn't insult the woman by asking for a little something to eat. *Tea* in this case undoubtedly meant the meal, not just the beverage.

She was not disappointed. No sooner had she hung up her purse and sweater in the vestibule and carried her knitting supplies into the library than Agnes appeared with a wooden tea trolley loaded with enough sandwiches, cakes, muffins, and scones to feed half of Stony Beach.

"Good heavens, Agnes! Surely my aunt didn't eat this much every day?"

Agnes drew herself up. "Not knowing your preferences, madam, I made a bit of everything."

"So I see." Fortunately, Emily's peregrinations had left her with an appetite. "I'll sample as much as I can and let you know. But all your cooking is so delicious, I suspect it'll be hard to choose."

Agnes did not smile, but her features readjusted themselves to suggest gratification. "Will you have scallops or rack of lamb for supper?"

Both were favorites and rare treats, but Emily's stomach quailed at the thought of tackling lamb after this enormous tea. "I think scallops, thank you. Assuming the lamb can wait until tomorrow?"

Agnes inclined her regal head and left the room.

Emily nibbled at everything and savored it all. When Agnes came in to clear away, Emily said, "As I suspected, everything was delicious. I really can't choose. Did Aunt Beatrice have any particular favorites?"

Agnes's mouth quirked. "Like you, madam, she liked most everything I made. But her favorite thing in the world was something I never would make. Turkish delight."

"Goodness, I can't stand the stuff. Way too sweet. But why wouldn't you make it?"

"She only liked the rosewater kind. I'm allergic to roses."

"Really!" Now that she thought about it, Emily hadn't seen any roses near the house, which seemed odd in Oregon, where roses grew so well. "So did she buy it from somewhere or just do without?"

Agnes snorted. "She'd sneak it into the house when she thought I wasn't looking. Figured if I didn't see it, I wouldn't smell it. All it takes is the smell to set me off. One good whiff and I sneeze for a week."

"Well, no worries with me. Like I say, I can't stand the stuff. Your strawberry shortcake is plenty sweet enough for me."

Agnes cleared the tea things, and Emily settled down, happily replete, to begin knitting her shawl.

Knitting was an excellent aid to ordering her thoughts, or would be, once she got the project well underway. The preliminary steps of setting the gauge and learning the stitch pattern required all her concentration. She was just finishing her first gauge swatch when Agnes appeared in the doorway and announced, "Mr. Brock to see you, madam," as if she were announcing the FBI, the IRS, and the KKK all embodied in one man.

Brock swept past her into the room and bent over Emily as if to kiss her hand. His musky cologne nearly overpowered her. Pure pheromones. Good thing she was postmenopausal and less vulnerable to such things.

She kept a firm grip on her needles. "Good evening, Brock. What can I do for you?"

He straightened, covering his foiled attempt by using his outstretched hand to smooth his already perfectly smooth hair. "Ask not what you can do for me, dear lady, but what I can do for you. I came to invite you to dinner at Gifts from the Sea. Their salmon is to die for."

Agnes stood in the doorway, glowering at Brock's back with such loathing, Emily expected to see red laser-light stream from her eyes and incinerate him on the spot.

"Thanks so much, Brock, but I'm sure Agnes already has my

dinner well in hand. Her cooking's to die for too—I couldn't let it go to waste." Agnes gave a curt nod, her glare abating slightly.

Brock flashed his hundred-watt smile at Agnes. "Oh, well, in that case, we can talk over dinner here. Set another place, Agnes, there's a dear."

Agnes's glare ought to have been registered as a lethal weapon. "There is only one serving of the scallops, madam. They don't keep."

Emily wouldn't have crossed Agnes at that moment if her entire inheritance had depended on it. "Too bad, Brock. If you want to invite yourself to dinner, you'll have to do it earlier next time."

His smile morphed into a petulant scowl so quickly, Emily was left breathless. "Oh, fine, then. Can a guy at least get a drink?" Without waiting for an answer, he strode to the side table in the bay, filled a brandy glass to the brim with Harveys Bristol Cream sherry—the only available option—and downed it in a gulp. Then he filled the glass again and plopped onto the window seat.

A spitting yowl of unearthly proportions rocketed him back to his feet. Bustopher Jones dug all twenty of his claws into Brock's backside, then launched himself off from there and stalked out of the room, tail high. Emily began to feel the cat might be a kindred spirit after all.

Not even from students had she heard the equal of the volley of curses Brock sent after the cat as he fingered the holes in the back of his suit.

"Windy Corner doesn't seem to be a very healthy place for you today, Brock. Perhaps you should go."

He slammed his glass down on the table, yanked a handkerchief from his breast pocket, and swiped at the sherry sloshed on his tie. "Go? Yeah, right. I'll go when you pay my cleaning bill. Better make that the cost of a new suit—that devil's torn this one to shreds."

Emily stood and drew herself up almost as tall as Agnes. "I refuse to take responsibility for the perfectly natural indignation of an animal that has been sat upon. Or for stains caused by the greediness of an oaf who would guzzle Harveys Bristol Cream. You will go *now*."

Brock folded and replaced his handkerchief, ran a hand over his hair, and straightened his jacket, adjusting his face along with it. The petulant overgrown child vanished as quickly as it had appeared, and the suave man of the world materialized in its place. Emily watched the transformation, fascinated.

"My dear cousin—no, sorry, you don't want to be my cousin—dearest Emily, do forgive my outburst. I was so looking forward to dining with you, my disappointment got the better of me. If I promise to be good, will you let me stay and talk to you until Agnes is ready to serve your incomparable meal?"

The guilty-puppy expression took years off his slightly seedy good looks. Emily relented. After all, there was no real harm in him. "Very well. Pour me a glass of sherry—a normal-size one—and I'll forgive you. But don't let it happen again."

He filled one of Beatrice's Waterford sherry glasses a proper two-thirds full and handed it to her with a flourish. She resumed her chair, and Brock, after checking for four-legged intruders, sank back onto the window seat.

"Now, what is so important that you have to talk to me about?"

He took a decorous sip before replying. "Nothing earthshaking. I just thought we ought to get on the same page about the property. We're sort of co-owners now—we should put up a united front, don't you think?"

Emily raised one eyebrow, her standard response to a student remark that was not properly thought through. "I don't see that we're co-owners any more than we're blood family. I own one part of Stony Beach; you own another. Or we will once probate goes through."

He waved his free hand. "If you want to be technical. But that property's always been managed as a unit. Don't you think it'd be better for the community if it stayed that way?"

Emily had about as much faith in Brock's community spirit as she had in his self-control. "What exactly did you have in mind?"

"I've been talking to Mayor Trimble. Great guy, don't you think? Forward-looking. Has a fantastic vision for this town."

Fantastic in the sense of unreal, Emily thought. But she let Brock ramble on, curious to see how deep a hole he would dig himself into.

"If we join forces, we can put this town on the map. Double the size of the place, double the property values. Then in a couple of years we can sell out and make a real killing."

"But I'm not interested in making a killing. I only want to make a living, and my share will cover that quite nicely as it is."

His nostrils flared. The scowl threatened to return, but with visible effort he subdued it. "Your share, sure. Mine's not quite so lucrative." The scowl leaked out in his tone.

"Perhaps not, but you have some other means of support, surely? You've gotten by so far. That suit wasn't cheap, and neither was your car." She'd caught a glimpse of his bloodred Porsche as he'd left after the reception the night before. "You must have some profession?"

"Oh, sure. I'm an actor. Maybe you caught me on *Abbott* back in oh-five? I was the murderer. Pretty clever, too." He downed the last of his sherry and eyed the bottle, turning his glass in his hands. "Acting's fickle, though. It's not every day the right part comes along. I can't cheapen myself by taking just anything."

That sounded suspiciously like her father claiming he couldn't lower himself to teach high school, when in fact he'd been turned down or fired by every high school in the state—after he'd exhausted all the colleges.

"I'm sorry to disappoint you, but I have no intention of falling in with Mayor Trimble's plans. I like Stony Beach just the way it is, and I plan to use my influence to keep it that way."

His full, almost feminine lips curved into a sneer. "So you're going to step into Beatrice's sensible shoes, huh? The benevolent dictator, pulling everybody's puppet strings. Never mind half the town lives below poverty level."

Emily bristled. She doubted that was true, and if it had been, Brock was the last one to care. "If I can make life better for the people who live here, I will. But I won't clear the way for expansion. That wouldn't profit the poorest people anyway, only the few who're already at the top of the heap."

Even as she said it, Emily wasn't entirely sure that was true. Development would create jobs—mostly low-paying menial jobs, but any jobs would be better than none, if in fact a significant number of residents were now unemployed. She'd have to find that out from Luke.

When people dreamed of a sudden access of wealth, they never considered all the responsibility that went with it.

Brock finally left when Agnes announced that Emily's dinner was served. She had plenty to think about during her solitary repast. Brock's behavior, for one. His attitude toward her was baffling, to say the least. If he was an actor, either he was a singularly poor one or he hadn't decided which role he wanted to play with her—fellow mourner, affectionate cousin, would-be suitor, disappointed rival for the inheritance, or bitter antagonist. One thing seemed clear, though: he wasn't satisfied with his portion under Beatrice's will.

When Agnes brought her after-dinner coffee into the library, Emily detained her. "Brock said something yesterday about his 'old room' here. Did he visit Aunt Beatrice often?"

Agnes gave a disgusted sniff. "Never saw hide nor hair of him till a year ago. Then he started turning up every month or two. Madam seemed to find him amusing."

"Did he stay long?"

"Two days, sometimes three. Till her patience started to wear thin, then he'd go."

"Which room did he sleep in?"

"East room, across the hall from hers. Madam wanted him where she could keep an eye on him."

"Was he here when she died?"

"Left a few days before. Came back like a shot as soon as he heard she was gone."

That sounded suspiciously like an attempt to establish an alibi. Time to do some sleuthing.

Emily finished her coffee, then mounted the U-shaped stairway that rose from the paneled reception hall, admiring the gleaming woodwork of the banisters. Carving like this could hardly be bought nowadays, even with a fortune like Beatrice's.

In the second-floor hall she stopped to orient herself to the maze of closed doors that surrounded her. To the left, facing the drive, were two formal guest bedrooms she'd never seen used.

Before her was Beatrice's room, largest and best in the house. At the far end of the hall were the bathroom and the small room where Geoff had slept in the summers, and to her immediate right the east room that Agnes said had been Brock's—and years ago, her father's, when he swept through on the occasional weekend visit between interviews.

She opened the door, half expecting to see the clutter of books and papers that had followed her father wherever he went and that he warned the housekeeper on pain of death never to touch. But the past was not that tenacious, nor would Agnes have been so easily intimidated. The room was spotless and, compared to the rest of the house, rather bare.

Emily made a circuit of the room, opening each drawer of the heavy walnut bureaus and checking every shelf of the tall mahogany wardrobe, so dark and forbidding, she expected it to lead not to Narnia but perhaps to Charn. It held no fur coats, however, nor indeed any personal possessions of any kind. Either Agnes or Brock himself had been quite thorough in eradicating all traces of his habitation.

At the bed Emily paused. A memory teased at the back of her mind. Herself about ten, Geoff twelve. Exploring the house, pretending to be Edmund and Lucy from the Narnia stories. Their father was away, and they'd snuck guiltily into this room against his strict prohibition. The wardrobe yielded only old clothes, and the medallions on the mantel failed to open any secret passageways. But the headboard of the bed had seemed promising with its depth and elaborate carvings of vines and fruit.

They tried the pear, the peach, the cluster of grapes. No joy. Then a hand reached out to the forbidden apple, hanging so temptingly from the peak of the triangular headboard. But whose hand was it, hers or Geoff's?

Too small for either. A pudgy, grubby little hand with bitten nails. Eustace.

It was Eustace who found the apple. Their little cousin— not really a cousin, but they thought of him that way for convenience—the six-year-old nuisance they called Eustace so often they forgot his real name. Horace's nephew, Horace who was then still alive. They couldn't shun the child because he had more right to be there than they did, but he was a brat and a pill, and they could at least annoy him by calling him Eustace, which he didn't understand because he hadn't read any of the right stories.

But he was the one who found the apple. And, of course, his real name was Brock.

The grown-up Brock, sleeping in this bed, would undoubtedly have remembered. Emily pushed the apple, but nothing happened. No, it wasn't a push but a downward pull, as if one were picking the apple. She gave a gentle tug, and the panel swung noiselessly open.

Wary of spiders, she peered inside. Neither the fading twilight from the east-facing windows nor the dim glow of the overhead bulb could penetrate the shadow of the dark velvet hangings that framed the bed. She checked the nightstand drawer and blessed Stony Beach's occasional power outages—each bedroom was always equipped with candle and matches. She lit the candle and held it up to the secret compartment.

For one mad moment Emily thought she'd entered a time warp. When the three of them first found the compartment, it had dashed all her romantic hopes by revealing only a slender pint bottle of vodka and a shot glass. It might have been the same bottle and glass she saw there now, only these were free of dust. And her father would never have left the two fingers' worth of vodka that remained in the bottle.

Emily slumped on the bed, fighting tears, just as she had done all those years ago. Eustace snickering, Geoff barking at her to "quit sniveling" only made it worse. At age ten she'd hardly understood what the bottle was; but she had known it for her enemy. Brock's pint was nothing but a letdown.

She looked again, unwilling to accept failure, and saw a darker shape behind the bottle. She pushed the bottle aside and drew it out. A book with the typical leather binding of the Windy Corner library.

Why would Brock hide a book? Beatrice was protective of her books, but not so much that she wouldn't allow a guest to read them. Emily turned it over.

Strong Poison by Dorothy L. Sayers. Emily's heartbeat accelerated. The murder method in that mystery was arsenic— one of many poisons that would cause such symptoms as Beatrice had undergone.

But as Lord Peter Wimsey so cleverly deduced, the murderer in *Strong Poison* had built up an immunity to arsenic over months, then shared a poison-laced meal with his victim. Brock couldn't have done that; he'd been out of town for several days before Beatrice grew ill.

So it seemed unlikely this book would have given him ideas. And if it had, it wouldn't make sense for him to hide the book here; he could have simply returned it to the library to sit in all innocence on its appointed shelf. If someone had killed Aunt Beatrice, he or she had been clever enough to conceal the true nature of the crime. It wasn't likely such a killer would leave incriminating evidence lying around—even in secret compartments.

Anyway, she couldn't take Brock seriously as a potential murderer. He lacked the requisite resolve for such an act. But why had he never alluded to their previous acquaintance? He'd been young; perhaps he didn't remember any more than she had at first. Yet somehow he struck her as the type who would never forget a grievance, but would nurse it until it ripened into hatred. Should she disarm that hatred with an apology for her youthful unkindness? Or would it be better to let sleeping dogs lie?

She couldn't answer that question tonight. She restored the book to its hiding place, intending to show it to Luke later in case it might be significant, then blew out the candle and returned it to the drawer. She'd had enough of sleuthing for one night. All she wanted was a book and a hot bath, then bed.

Back in the library, she pulled out an old favorite— *Persuasion*. If Anne Elliot and Captain Wentworth could get back together after so much water under the bridge, perhaps there was hope for her and Luke as well.

· ten ·

The party . . . soon found themselves on the sea-shore; and
lingering only, as all must linger and gaze on a first return to
the sea, who ever deserved to look on it at all.

—*Persuasion*

The sun streamed in through the southeast window of the
tower at five thirty in the morning, waking Emily from a
fitful dream in which Luke and Brock dueled on the beach
with starfish for weapons, while their seconds—Mayor Trimble
for Brock and Sunny Longman the unsunny waiter for Luke—
cheered them on, with Dr. Griffiths standing by to mop up the
blood.

Between the sun and her screaming bladder, Emily knew
she'd never get back to sleep. The sky was clear, and breakfast
was hours away. She slipped into chinos and a wool sweater
and headed to the beach.

The lawn of Windy Corner sloped gently downward toward
the water but ended abruptly in a rock-faced cliff about ten feet
high. A rough wooden stairway intersected the rocks. At the
bottom, a short stretch of low dunes gave way to a broad expanse

of smooth, packed sand. The difference in tides here was dramatic, and the tide was currently near its low ebb.

The beach was public, but only rarely did walkers from town venture this far north, and never at this early hour. Emily had the beach to herself. She stood for a moment, feet planted shoulder-width apart and arms raised in a V, soaking the cold salt-laced wind in through her pores. At Windy Corner she still felt somewhat like a visitor, but here on the beach she was home.

She strolled aimlessly, stopping to peer at shells and stones and driftwood, loading her pockets with smaller pieces but having no real idea what she would do with them. She skirted a flock of gulls, startling them into flight, then followed a line of paw prints up near the high-tide mark, nose down like a tracking dog. The paw prints led her into loose sand, then abruptly turned and looped back. She stopped and looked up.

The prints had led her to the mouth of the Sacred Cove. A tiny cove—more of a cave, really—no more than ten feet across, the opening much narrower, and high enough on the beach that the tide rarely reached it. This was where she and Luke used to come to be alone. *Say it straight, Emily*—this is where they had come to make love.

Memories washed over her, irresistible as an undertow. They'd worked together at the ice-cream stand on the beach downtown. He'd won her with hardly a word—a smile from those teasing eyes was enough. That, and telling her she was beautiful. She'd never heard that word from anyone else, never thought it could possibly apply to her. It brought her down like an ax on a young fir.

She'd loved him so much she could taste it. It tasted like the sea and the sand and the mingled sweat of their bodies and the old wool blanket he spread out in the cove when they made love. It tasted like freedom and adventure and possibility, like all the endless things she could become by only pointing her finger and saying, *That one.*

Would that sixteen-year-old girl have pointed to a safe, slightly boring tenured professorship and a marriage based more on companionship than passion? The mature Emily doubted it. Those choices had come only later, when so many other possibilities had been washed away in the tide. Along with Luke himself.

But now he was back in her life. Or seemed ready to be if she wanted him. Would the moving finger point his way? She called to mind the words of the *Rubaiyat*—"The moving finger writes; and having writ, moves on: nor all thy piety nor wit shall lure it back to cancel half a line, nor all thy tears wash out a word of it."

No, the past could never be rewritten. Whatever the future might hold, they would have to build it from the ground up. And this time they had better not build on sand.

Emily fortified herself with another of Agnes's admirable breakfasts and changed into her "business" clothes, reflecting that she was quickly running out of things to wear. She asked Agnes about doing some laundry, but Agnes replied, "I regret to say, madam, that the washing machine is broken. I hope to have it repaired tomorrow morning."

Emily was on her way to her car when a man came around the corner of the house, a hoe over his shoulder, whistling. His girth so nearly equaled his modest height that he rolled more than walked, his feet serving merely as rudders. A thin fuzz of white hair sprang up above the smooth, round, ruddy face of a Dickensian philanthropist, but his garb—a clean and smartly pressed blue jumpsuit—somewhat spoiled the impression.

His roll and his whistle came to an abrupt halt when he saw her. He swept off a nonexistent cap and bowed to her. "Billy Beech, at your service, ma'am. Gardener, handyman, and general factotum. As employed by your late aunt, God rest her soul, and I presume to hope by your kind self as well."

He even spoke like something out of Dickens.

"Emily Cavanaugh." She shook his proffered hand. "Beech. Are you related to Agnes?" Had any other two people been concerned, she might have asked if they were married; but it was impossible to imagine the dour Agnes married to this smiling beach ball.

"My late lamented brother was Agnes's husband, and a better husband never walked the earth, though I say it. I do my best to look after her, as Bobby would have wished, but I'm sorry to say my efforts are not always accepted in the spirit in which they're meant. She's an independent old girl, is Agnes." He chuckled, setting his several chins and massive belly aquiver.

"I haven't seen you before. I take it you don't work here every day?"

"Three days a week, ma'am: Monday, Wednesday, Friday as a rule, though I did take Monday off out of respect for the dead. You may have glimpsed me among the mourners, ma'am, but I wouldn't presume to introduce myself at that most distressing time."

The vision of Billy in full Victorian mourning gear, complete with top hat draped in black crepe, nearly set Emily aquiver herself, but she controlled herself with an effort. "Well, Billy, everything seems to be in good order here as far as I can see, so I guess you may as well carry on as you have been."

"Thank you kindly, ma'am." He swept his hand to the ground, folding his spherical girth in half in a way that suggested it was filled with something more compressible than fat and organs—marshmallow, perhaps, or memory foam. "I shall endeavor to give satisfaction." He straightened, and the marshmallow foam instantly regained its spherical shape. He rolled off, whistling, toward the flower beds that lined the drive, and Emily proceeded to her car.

eleven

Every morning now brought its regular duties;—shops were
to be visited; some new part of the town to be looked at.
—*Northanger Abbey*

E mily decided to start at the north end of what passed for downtown and work south, visiting every business along the way. The northernmost shop was called Cash and Carry. Its window displayed brightly colored beach towels, lewdly leering crab statuettes, and T-shirts with witty sayings like MY MOM & DAD WENT TO STONY BEACH AND ALL I GOT WAS THIS STUPID SHIRT.

Emily wrinkled her nose and went in. The door had barely closed behind her when a booming bass voice greeted her. "Hey there, little lady! Welcome to Cash and Carry! I'm Joey Cash, and if you can carry it, we sell it."

A tall sixty-something man stepped out from behind the counter, dressed entirely in black. Black Stetson, black Western shirt with a black bolo tie, black jeans, black cowboy boots. The tie clasp and the outsize belt buckle were silver, molded in the same intricate design—a florid JC.

"Ask me if I'm any relation to the great Johnny Cash, and I'll tell you if I'm not, I oughta be. I'd be his reincarnation except he died after I was born." When Joey shut up for a second, Emily could hear "Folsom Prison" playing in the background.

"Emily Cavanaugh." When he didn't respond she added, "Your new landlady."

That took a second to sink in. Then he grabbed her hand in both of his. "Glad to know ya, glad to know ya! Great to see some new blood around the place. Gotta get this dinosaur out of the mud, eh, little lady?"

Joey was beginning to sound suspiciously like Mayor Trimble. "So I take it you're in favor of development?"

"Absolutely. Onward and upward! No point in standin' still, eh? Keep movin' forward!"

Joey and the mayor had clearly attended the same night classes in "How to Speak Cliché." She wondered whether either of them was capable of dealing in simple facts. "What benefit do you expect for the town from further development?"

He grinned, showing uneven tobacco-stained teeth. "Money, little lady. That's what makes the world go 'round, ain't it? Lots more money."

"For whom, exactly?"

That took him aback. "Why, for the town. The business owners. You and me." He gave her a repellent wink. "For people who know a good thing when they see it."

"I see. So you don't actually expect the town as a whole to benefit? The people who work for you, for example. Will you pay them more? Give them more hours, better benefits? Hire more workers?"

His grin faltered and his eyes narrowed. "Whatchou gettin'

at? You some kinda socialist? You believe in this 'of the people by the people' bull?"

"Mr. Cash, you are quoting President Abraham Lincoln. He, like our founding fathers, wanted this country to have a government of the people, by the people, and for the people."

"Government, okay. But those guys weren't talkin' 'bout money. They had more sense. Money is of, by, and for the people who know how to get it. And how to keep hold of it. To him who has, more shall be given. Jesus said that." He shoved a horny finger in her face.

Emily drew herself up. "He also said, 'Give, and it will be given to you: good measure, pressed down, shaken together, and running over. For with the same measure you use, it will be measured back to you.' How much do you give to this town, Mr. Cash?"

She left him gaping as she turned and walked out of the store.

Next door to the Cash emporium was a bookshop called, with refreshing directness, Stony Beach Books. Emily pushed open the door and paused to take a deep breath of thoughtful, well-educated air.

From somewhere far up in that air, a pleasant male voice floated down to her. "Can I help you find anything?"

"Just looking around," Emily said, suiting the action to the word in search of the voice's source. At last she spotted a ladder in the far corner with a pair of chino-clad legs perched several rungs up. "Actually, I was hoping for a book on local history."

"Sure, I can help you with that." The legs descended, revealing a tall slender male figure and a young mocha-colored face of remarkable ascetic beauty. The man could have posed for an angel in an Ethiopian icon. With a diffident smile, he led Emily to a table near the front of the store. "Not much in the way of comprehensive history, but we've got lots of specialized stuff—lighthouses, pirates, legends, marine life, whatever floats your boat. Of course, if you're not interested in anything nautical, you may be out of luck."

Emily flipped through several of the volumes and chose one on local legends as covering the most ground. Then she wandered through the store, noting an eclectic mixture of subject matter in books old and new. A couple of racks up front contained a selection of "beach reads," but apart from that, most of the books seemed more appropriate to a university town than a tiny tourist community.

She took her selection to the counter and introduced herself.

"Ben Johnson," the young man replied. "So you're my new landlady? I hope you're not planning to sell to some out-of-towner. I'm afraid my store might not look like a big profit-maker to a developer."

"No, at this point I'm not thinking of selling. Though I have to admit, I'm a bit surprised you can keep going with a shop like this in this location. Do people really buy books on German philosophy and Russian music in a place like this?"

He dipped his head. "To tell you the truth, I sell more on-line than I do in walk-ins. I tend to buy what I like more than what I think will sell. Except for the front racks, of course." He punched the book's price into a manual cash register. "But you'd be surprised what locals do sometimes buy. Like the other day, Mayor Trimble bought a big illustrated book on the Borgias along with a volume of Machiavelli. I'd never have pegged him for a history buff."

"Nor would I." Why would a small-town mayor want to read about the most famous family of poisoners in history? What else could he want it for but professional advice?

Ben's eyes took on a wistful look. "You've got a great library up there at Windy Corner. I don't suppose you'd be interested in selling any of it?"

"I doubt it. That library is the most precious part of my whole inheritance to me. But if I do run across anything I know I'll never read, I promise you'll be the first to know."

A smile lit up his face. "Thanks. You just made my day." He put a bookmark in her book and slid it into a paper bag. "So, how are you liking Stony Beach?"

"I think I'm going to love it. I've only been here a few days, but I've met a lot of interesting people."

"Have you met Beanie yet? In the yarn shop?"

"I was in there yesterday. She's a hoot."

Ben sighed, looking wistful again. Emily didn't probe, but filed the information away for future reference: Ben was pining after Beanie. Perhaps he was too conservative for her taste—or maybe just too shy to make a move.

Emily paid for her book and said a reluctant farewell.

"Thanks for coming in," Ben said. "And thanks for not asking me if I play basketball."

Emily grimaced. "You get that a lot, huh?"

"All the time. I haven't shot a hoop since high school PE, but in most people's minds, tall black man equals basketball player. Even if he's running a bookshop."

Emily's next stop was the Friendly Fluke coffee shop—a welcome respite for her parched throat and sore feet. With some trepidation she ordered a cappuccino and biscotti, unsure whether Stony Beach could produce a proper espresso drink.

But the waitress came back with a steaming mug on top of which a whale's fluke design floated in a layer of fine foam—worthy of her favorite coffee place in Portland.

Emily introduced herself again, glad of an opportunity to talk to an employee rather than a business owner. The waitress's name tag read JESSICA, and she looked about eighteen.

"How's the job market in Stony Beach?" Emily asked. The café was empty of other customers, so with a gesture she invited Jessica to sit down.

"Not bad, at least in the summer. Winters, I haven't even tried. I'll be going off to Oregon State in the fall."

"What about your parents? What do they do?"

"My dad's a fisherman. Mom's a teacher in Tillamook. Summers she works in the kitchen here." Jessica indicated the back room with her chin.

"Do a lot of people work in Tillamook, then?"

"Yeah, pretty much. Stony Beach kind of closes down in the winter."

Emily sipped her cappuccino. Its taste lived up to the promise of its presentation. "Have you heard about the whole development thing?"

Jessica rolled her eyes. "Who hasn't?"

"What do you think? Would it make life better for the people here?"

She shrugged. "I don't see how. There'd be more summer jobs, I guess, but it wouldn't change anything the rest of the year. We already have all the fishermen the place can support, and there's nothing else here but the tourist industry. Probably get a bunch of students coming in to work summers, taking jobs away from people who live here. I don't see the point."

Emily nodded. Jessica had just confirmed her own thoughts on the matter. "Thank you, Jessica. That's very helpful."

"Sure thing." The girl went back to her station.

Emily savored her cappuccino and biscotti, then went to the counter to pay. "Boss says it's on the house," Jessica told her. "Seeing you're our new landlady and all."

"That's very kind." Emily had already taken a ten-dollar bill from her wallet, so she dropped it into a stoneware jar labeled JESSICA'S COLLEGE FUND. "But next time I insist on paying full price."

The next block was dominated by an antique shop called Lacey Luxuries. Like the bookshop, this one would have drawn Emily even if she hadn't been on a fact-finding mission. The window held an enticing array of vintage linens and china set out on dainty tables as if ready for ladies in sweeping skirts and wide-brimmed, flower-decked hats to sit down for tea.

Inside, the shop was set up as a series of miniature open-fronted rooms, each created around a different color, period, or theme. Emily wandered blissfully from room to room, fingering filmy laces and peering into delicate boxes of inlaid wood. There was nothing in the shop she needed but a thousand things she would love to own.

She paused in front of a large watercolor painting of a Victorian mansion. The colors and surrounding vegetation were different, but she could swear the house was Windy Corner. She peered at the signature. The artist's name was unreadable, but the date was 1912. That would have been shortly after the house was built.

This was a piece of history she couldn't pass up. This painting needed to hang in its rightful home.

A voice came from behind her: "You look like you belong here. I should hire you for a live diorama."

Emily turned to see a woman of about her own age, dressed similarly in a long flared skirt and high-necked blouse. Her thinning gray hair, however, was cut short in a modern style.

"Veronica Lacey," the woman said, extending her hand. "And you are Emily Cavanaugh. I saw you at the funeral."

To Emily's relief, Veronica's handshake was firm and dry. "I could easily live in this shop. You have some marvelous things, and your displays are lovely."

"That's quite a compliment, coming from the owner of Windy Corner. Your own house is full of treasures. I must admit, I'm a bit disappointed you're an antique lover—I had some hopes of picking up a few bargains at an estate sale. Your cousin hinted at the possibility."

"Brock isn't actually my cousin. He's on Horace's side; I'm on Beatrice's. You mean he thought he might get the house?"

"It sounded that way. But on balance, I'm glad it went to you. Brock might have sold it to some outsider who'd tear it down and build condos. That would be a terrible loss."

"So you don't favor development? Even though it would help your business?"

Veronica hesitated. "Well, I wouldn't mind if the town grew some. Things are a bit hand-to-mouth here. But Mayor Trimble and his followers want to take it too far. We need to preserve what we have and build on it, not raze it and start from scratch."

Emily had to admit that was a sensible attitude. "Are there others here who think as you do?"

"A few. But most of the town council is polarized—the

Troubles with Trimble versus Beatrice's Bootlickers. They've been at a stalemate for months. Of course Beatrice wouldn't budge an inch, and not much can be done without some of her property being made available for building. Your property, I should say."

Emily, who had nearly doubled over at the epithets Veronica applied to the warring factions, recovered herself and said, "Thanks for being straight with me. I'll give this some serious thought."

Veronica twinkled at her. "Not too serious, I hope. In Stony Beach you have to either laugh or go mad."

Veronica's attitude reminded Emily of Marguerite, her closest friend in Portland. She was overcome by a sudden desire to share with Marguerite all the events of the past few days and get her unique, always forthright perspective. Maybe it was time for a brief trip home.

Emily turned back to the painting. "This is Windy Corner, isn't it?"

"Certainly is. It was done by the architect who built the house. His great-grandson sold it to me. I thought Beatrice would want it, but she died before I could show it to her."

"It definitely needs to come home. How much?"

Veronica named a price. It was high, but Emily thought the painting was worth it for the sake of its history. She could afford to indulge a whim here and there—and it was her duty to support the local businesses.

It was only after Veronica had wrapped the painting and helped her load it into the back of her car that Emily thought to wonder where in Windy Corner—whose walls were already optimally full of beautiful art—she'd find to put it. Oh well. It was a big house. She'd find a space somewhere.

· twelve ·

"In repassing through the small vaulted room, however, your eyes will be attracted towards a large, old-fashioned cabinet of ebony and gold. . . . At last, however, by touching a secret spring, an inner compartment will open."

—Henry Tilney to Catherine Morland,
Northanger Abbey

By this time it was past noon, and Emily treated herself to lunch at the Crab Pot, half hoping to run into Luke. But he wasn't there. Across from the table where she'd sat with him before—which she already thought of as "their" table—sat Mayor Trimble and Vicki Landau.

Emily almost walked out. Then she thought again and approached them.

The mayor saw her first. He scrambled to his feet, catching his napkin as it slid off his lap, and swiped at his greasy mouth. "Well, well, if it isn't our local heiress! Come to talk business finally? Have a seat, take a load off." He motioned to the empty chair next to Vicki, who bared lipstick-smeared teeth at her in a rather frightening imitation of a smile.

Emily smiled sweetly. "Thanks, I won't intrude. I just wanted to say how pleased I was to hear from Agnes that Beatrice shared her last dinner with you. So good to know she was among friends right up to the end."

The mayor swayed on his feet, while Vicki choked on the mouthful of coffee she'd just drunk. Trimble steadied himself on the chair and put on a smile. "That's right, among friends. We had a real good discussion that night. Beatrice was starting to come around to our way of thinking, wasn't she, Vic?"

Vicki nodded through her coughing fit.

"Oh, was she? Of course, she had no idea that meal would be her last. And neither did you, I'm sure."

The mayor waved his hands, blustering. "Course not, how could we? Beatrice shouldn't've eaten that lobster, is all. She knew it wouldn't agree with her, get it? She even said so, didn't she, Vic?"

Vicki recovered enough to say, "She certainly did. 'I'm an old woman and I'll eat what I like. No point in being careful at my age,' that's what she said. Almost as if she did know."

"But neither of you ate lobster, right?"

"Don't care for it. Never have. I'm a meat-and-potatoes man." Emily cast a skeptical eye at the half-eaten crab melt on his plate. "And Vicki here, she always goes for chicken. No matter how fancy a restaurant we go to, it's chickie-Vicki every time."

Vicki silenced him with a glare. "For pity's sake, Everett, keep your voice down."

"Don't be silly, Vic, everybody knows you and me got lots of business together. We're the movers and shakers in this town, get it? Just trying to shake up everybody else and get them moving too." He gave Emily a wink.

"Speaking of moving, I'll be moving along to my own table now. But thanks for this chat. It's been very—illuminating."

She resisted the temptation to look behind her as she moved to the opposite side of the restaurant. But after she sat, she glanced back over the top of her menu to catch Vicki's venomous glare just sliding away from her. What had she done to merit that?

Back at Windy Corner, Emily asked Billy Beech to bring the painting in and leave it in the front hall while she found it a home. She walked through the downstairs rooms but found nothing she wanted to move or replace to make space. Besides, the painting's colors didn't blend in well here; they were more pastel. Perhaps it would fit better upstairs.

Reluctant to trespass on the sanctity of Beatrice's room, Emily turned to the formal guest rooms. Both had lovely proportions but were made gloomy by high-Victorian flocked wallpaper and burgundy velvet hangings. The painting would clash horribly here. She turned to Beatrice's room.

This room had been forbidden to her and Geoff as children (though, of course, they'd violated the prohibition once or twice), and even now Beatrice's spirit seemed to hover over it, threatening trespassers with her grave displeasure. Yet Emily doubted her aunt had cherished any skeletons in the room's ample closets; she simply wanted one room in the house where she could be sure of being alone. *Do the dead care about privacy?* she asked Philip. She took his silence for a no.

At this hour, the room was flooded with light from the west-facing semicircular bay, which echoed that of the library beneath. No dark hangings or wallpaper here: the walls were painted a pale yellow, and only the finest of lace curtains hung at the windows. Beatrice had placed her writing desk in the bay facing the ocean, a chaise longue to one side of it. Her large

canopied bed stood against the south wall; a fireplace occupied
the opposite corner. Several small ornaments stood on the mantel, but the space above it was bare. The painting would just fit.

None of the ornaments greatly appealed to Emily. She
cleared them from the mantel and piled them on the dresser,
intending to take them to the attic. But a wooden bird sculp-
ture slipped from her arms and fell in front of the fireplace.

When she bent to retrieve it, she noticed something peek-
ing out from the ashes in the grate. Agnes must have cleaned
this room thoroughly—it bore no signs of Beatrice's death
agony—but she might not have expected Beatrice to have used
the fireplace in May and therefore had not swept it. Emily
leaned in to grasp a fragment of brown paper such as one might
use to wrap a package. Adhering to it was a bit of clear tape.

As she pulled it out, she heard a noise behind her and
turned, hastily shoving the paper into her pocket. In the doorway stood Brock, eyeing her with drawn-in brows.

She stood and faced him, struggling not to look furtive.
After all, this was her house—he was the intruder. "Brock! What
are you doing here?"

His expression mutated into one of boyish innocence. "Me?
Oh, I just came by to pick up something I left in my room. Last
time I was here."

"And when was that, exactly?"

"Gosh, I don't know, a while ago. Let me see . . . I think I
left on the seventeenth. I'd been here about a week."

Emily did some quick calculating. Beatrice had died on
the twenty-second, so she must have gotten sick the evening of
the twenty-first. Brock's story matched Agnes's, which put him
in the clear—provided he'd really left the area as well as the
house.

"I'd prefer you not wander around the house by yourself. If you need anything else, ask me or Agnes to get it for you."

Brock put up his hands, palms forward. "Whoa there, Nelly. Nothing to get excited about. Just retrieving my own personal property."

"And did you find it?"

"Yup, got it right here." He patted a bulge in his coat pocket. Emily eyed the bulge. About the right shape for the pint of vodka she'd found in the headboard.

"Then I presume you'll be going."

He pouted. "You're not going to invite me to tea?"

"Not today. I have things to do." She wasn't sure just what, but she'd find something.

"All right then, I'll go." He stepped back from the door as if to let her go out first, but she stood her ground. At last he slouched off toward the stairs.

Emily watched him out of sight beyond the landing, then set her hand on the knob of the room he claimed to have visited. It did seem slightly warm.

She went in and looked around. Nothing looked different from the last time she'd visited the room.

She went over to the bed and examined the headboard. A sliver of deeper darkness rimmed the leading edge of the center panel. Someone had opened it recently, and it hadn't been properly closed.

She pulled on the apple, and the panel swung open. Both the bottle and the book were gone.

The morning's cloud cover had burned off to leave the day clear and warm. Emily asked Agnes to serve her tea on the terrace, which opened off the library and overlooked the sea. She had a good appetite this afternoon and made quick work of the cucumber sandwiches and strawberry shortcake Agnes had prepared. Only then did she turn her attention to the mail Agnes had brought out to her on a little silver tray.

Two white window envelopes. One from the funeral home and one from the caterer. Bills.

Both were made out in her name, and both amounts took her breath away. Brock had clearly had no compunction about spending her money. He might not be a murderer, but at best he was no better than a cheap con man. Anger sent her pulse racing, but she talked herself down. If some comparatively small portion of Beatrice's money went to honor her memory, that was only fitting—never mind that it could have been done well for half the price. She set the bills aside to pass on to Jamie. They would have to be paid out of the escrow account.

When Agnes came to clear away, Emily detained her.

"Agnes, would you tell me exactly what happened the day Beatrice got sick?"

"Like I told you, she went out to dinner with those people, the mayor and that Landau woman. She came home about nine and went straight to her room. By ten thirty she was sick as a dog. She wouldn't let me call a doctor, and I thought she'd be better in the morning. I wasn't feeling so good myself, sneezing my head off all night, couldn't figure out why. But by morning she was worse. She got weaker all day till finally I up and called Dr. Griffiths on my own. She got here around five o'clock, but it was too late to do anything. Miss Beatrice was dead by six."

"But what about earlier the day before? What did she do? What did she eat and drink? Did anyone come to see her?"

"She was here all day, puttering around, working in her office, telling Billy what to do in the garden. She had her regular breakfast, lunch, and tea, nothing unusual. Bustopher Jones and I ate the same, no harm done. Before she went off to dinner, she had a sherry out of that same decanter you've been drinking from. No visitors until the mayor came to pick her up for dinner."

At that moment Emily caught a movement out of the corner of her eye. She turned her head and saw what looked like a man disappearing behind the toolshed. "Wait a second, Agnes. I just saw someone."

Agnes turned to look, but by now there was nothing to see. "Billy, no doubt. Putting his tools away."

"No, this person had dark hair. And he wasn't big like Billy. Could've been Brock."

"What would Mr. Brock be doing sneaking around the garden? He could just come up and talk to you."

"I know. That's what makes it so strange." Emily stole across the grass to a point where she could see beyond the shed, but she saw only Billy crouched over a flower bed.

"Billy, did you see someone go by here just now?"

"No indeed, madam, but my attention was on the sweet woodruff."

"I saw somebody sneaking around. Would you have a look, please?"

Billy bowed. "Your wish is my command. I shall secure the premises forthwith."

Emily went back to her chair and said, "From now on, Agnes, don't let Brock in without my express permission. I found him wandering around upstairs on his own this afternoon. He has no business being here, and I'm tired of it."

Agnes nodded. "Just as you say, madam. He's no loss to me, I assure you."

Before she finished speaking, the telephone rang. For a crazy instant Emily thought Agnes had turned into Gerald McBoing-Boing, who spoke in noises instead of words. Then Agnes closed her mouth and went into the house.

She came out a moment later. "Telephone for you, madam."

"I'll take it in the library." Ooh, she felt just like a character in a British Golden Age mystery saying that.

Luke's voice greeted her. Hearing his disembodied voice gave her almost as much of a jolt as had seeing him again for the first time at the funeral.

"Oh, Luke, I'm glad you called. Brock's been behaving very strangely." She detailed to him the events of the last twenty-four hours.

"What a weirdo. Want me to get you a restraining order against him?"

"Oh, I don't think that'll be necessary. I'm sure he's harmless. You might want to keep an eye on the mayor, though."

"Why's that?"

"I hear he bought a book on the Borgias a few days before Beatrice died."

"Huh. That's a strange one. What kind of book—a how-to on poisoning, or just history?"

"I don't know for sure. Ben Johnson in the bookstore mentioned it, but I didn't want to seem too curious."

Luke laughed shortly. "Yeah, that's my job. I'll see what I can find out. But fascinating as all this is, it's not why I called. I wanted to ask you to have dinner with me tomorrow night."

Her first impulse was to jump at the offer, but a second,

stronger impulse held her back. She cast about for an excuse. "Tomorrow? I'm afraid I can't. I have to go back to Portland for a couple of days. Things to take care of—I hadn't planned to stay this long."

"Oh."

He sounded crestfallen, and she regretted her second thoughts. She never could bear to disappoint him. "How about tonight?"

"Can't. I'm on duty."

"I'll take a rain check, then. For after I get back? I'm only going to stay overnight."

"Fair enough." His voice brightened. "Hey, we can celebrate our birthday together. I'll take you to Gifts from the Sea."

One of the eerie coincidences they'd fastened onto when they were first falling in love—as proof they were destined for each other—was the fact that they shared a birthday: June first. Saturday. "I'd like that."

As soon as she hung up, Emily regretted giving in. Wasn't it only that morning she'd concluded that the past could never return? But she was committed now.

· thirteen ·

Fanny was almost stunned. The smallness of the house, and thinness of the walls, brought every thing so close to her, that, added to the fatigue of her journey, and all her recent agitation, she hardly knew how to bear it.

—*Mansfield Park*

E mily had always loved her snug mock-Tudor brick house on Woodstock Boulevard, just a few blocks uphill from Reed. Its steep front-facing gable swooped down to shelter the heavy oak front door, while the cute little eyebrow dormer of the second-floor bathroom blinked above the living room bay. The rooms were cozy and few, but just right for the needs of a couple with no children and two cats.

But now, when she pushed open the door with her empty suitcase, and her sleek gray cats, Levin and Kitty, came running to meet her, the living room struck her as cramped and dingy with its fraying upholstery, faded drapes, and threadbare rugs over hardwood floors badly in need of refinishing. The air was stale from unopened windows and unchanged litter, plus a whiff of milk left too long in the fridge. Emily felt as though she'd traveled the world and been gone for months, instead of driving a couple of hours and being gone three days.

How quickly she'd grown accustomed to the trappings of wealth.

First things first. She put down her suitcase and scratched the heads of both cats at once, filled their water dish, then opened a can of Tasty Treats and split it between their two bowls. They yowled insistently throughout the process, volume and urgency intensifying the closer the food got to its destination. But the cats were overdramatizing; remnants of the food she'd left out for them still clung to the sides of the bowls.

That done, she threw open all the windows and changed the litter, then made a pass through the fridge for dead food and took out the garbage. Now at least she could breathe freely.

She flipped through the mail on the mat: bills, catalogs, ads. Nothing urgent, but she went ahead and paid the bills just because she could. Nothing here on the scale of the charges Brock had incurred in her name. Her temper sizzled again at the thought of it.

Business taken care of, she stared around at the home that had become so suddenly and unaccountably unfamiliar. She felt restless, like a guest left on her own and afraid to touch her hosts' things in their absence. Her unquiet feet led her upstairs. Surely her own bedroom would welcome her? But no; the bed, which she'd left unmade, the open drawers and closet doors from which she'd hastily extracted random articles of clothing, all stared at her resentfully, as if to say they'd been getting along quite nicely without her, thank you very much, and if she couldn't even take the trouble to care for them properly, why should they care for her?

She had to get out of here. She fled back down the stairs and called Marguerite. "Margot, you've got to save me! For God's sake, take me to lunch."

Marguerite was free, and they met at the Beanery, a favorite student hangout that was blessedly quiet during the summer months. The sight of petite, chic, brunette Marguerite cheered Emily beyond measure and regrounded her in her Reed-centered life.

"Where have you been, *chérie*? I have been trying to call you for ze past three days." Marguerite could speak perfect, unaccented English when she wanted to, but she felt the slight French lilt made her more exotic.

"Would you believe Stony Beach?" Emily told her about the inheritance.

"You are an heiress? *Mais, chérie, c'est magnifique!* Now we can travel the world together, yes? I can show you Paris. The Louvre, the Bois de Boulogne in the rain, my favorite café. You will eat a real croissant. You will buy the clothes that fit. You will meet a handsome Frenchman and stay in Paris forever!"

Emily laughed. "Well, there are a few snags in that plan." She told Marguerite about Luke and their suspicions regarding Beatrice's death.

Marguerite ignored all hints of murder and zoomed in on the far more important hints of romance. "So you are living the French proverb, *On revient toujours a son premier amour.* You are feeling how?"

"Wonderful. Terrible. Confused. Honestly, I don't know which way is up."

"And he? How does he feel?"

"I haven't a clue. Except he did seem to be glad to see me. He keeps trying to talk seriously to me, but something always gets in the way. And I'm not sure I want to talk. What's the point of dredging up the past?"

Marguerite gave Emily her trademark one-eyebrow-up

glare, the one that inevitably daunted BS'ing students into admitting they didn't know what they were talking about. "What is the point of gaining for yourself some peace of mind? What is the point of fanning a spark of old passion into a flame that could warm your remaining years? What, after all, is the point of love? *Non,* it is too inconvenient, too risky, too ruffling to your oh-so-smooth feathers. Better to be miserable and alone and spend the rest of your life wondering what might have been." She sat back and crossed her arms. QED.

Emily had to admit Marguerite had a point. When it came down to it, what was holding her back but fear?

"It feels kind of—disloyal to Philip. He's only been dead two years."

"And what is two years? Perhaps a tenth of the time you have left to live! Surely he would not demand more than that? And, at any rate, Luke has the prior claim, *n'est-ce pas?*"

"He forfeited that when he broke my heart."

"But perhaps he is sorry! Perhaps he has some explanation. Do you not owe him the chance to make it?"

Emily was running out of arguments. "Well, I did agree to go to dinner with him when I go back."

"*Eh bien,* you see? You agree with me yourself. So stop arguing and talk to the man."

Emily sighed. "All right. If it happens, I won't run away. But listen, I'm going back tomorrow. Will you take care of Levin and Kitty for me? And forward any important mail? I have no idea how long I'll be—could be days, could be weeks. I might end up spending the whole summer there."

"I am happy to feed *les petits chats,* but if you will stay so long, why not take them with you?"

Emily grimaced. "I doubt they'd stand a chance against

Bustopher Jones." Levin and Kitty were naive indoor cats who'd never done more than playful kitten sparring with each other. A cat like Bustopher would reduce them to quivering masses of neurosis if he didn't kill them outright.

Marguerite regarded her with her shrewd black eyes, which could tease or flirt or command or cajole, but never under any circumstances missed a trick. "You have not been happy teaching since Philip died."

"Of course I haven't been happy. I've been grieving for my husband. Whom I loved."

Marguerite waved an elegant hand. "Grief is grief. I am talking about your career. You have lost the love, yes? You only go through the motions."

Emily squirmed in her chair. Why did she have to choose a friend who saw through all her self-deceptions? And who had no qualms whatever about calling her to account?

"It's true. It all feels so—pointless, somehow. I mean, I still love literature, I still want other people to love it, but—I just wish they'd get on with it. Without me."

Marguerite gave a crisp nod. "You need a break, *chérie*. Perhaps a sabbatical. Perhaps even to retire? You can afford it now."

Retirement was a thought Emily had not yet permitted herself to entertain. Suddenly a future without teaching stretched before her—not bleak and empty, as she would once have expected, but tantalizing and full of possibilities. Almost the way it looked when she was sixteen.

Maybe it really was time to write that book. Or travel. Or spend an entire year doing nothing but walking on the beach.

She leaned over the table and kissed Marguerite on the cheek. "You are a genius, Margot. I might do just that."

Energized by this prospect, Emily went back to the house and gave it a thorough cleaning, then packed a large suitcase with an assortment of clothing and toiletries that would get her through at least a month. She also threw in some basic knitting supplies and her prayer book and journal. That done, she made a hodgepodge dinner out of leftovers and produce that would otherwise go bad before she returned, then settled down to while away the evening with the copy of *Persuasion* she'd brought from Windy Corner.

But even her beloved Jane and the company of two over-affectionate cats could not keep restlessness at bay. Her thoughts kept drifting to Windy Corner—to her tower room, her claw-foot tub; to Agnes and Billy and even Bustopher Jones. She tried to picture Agnes going about her evening chores, but could see only vague indeterminate shapes, as if her imagination were a television with poor reception. A feeling nagged at her that all was not right there; her presence was needed. If it hadn't been dark already, she would have headed back that night.

It wasn't only her new wealth that had spoiled her. Windy Corner had recaptured her heart.

Emily left Portland early the next morning and drove as fast as she dared, propelled by that persistent feeling that something was wrong. As she crested the pass on Highway 6, the clouds began to gather. In Tillamook the wind picked up and a drizzle spotted her windshield. By the time she reached the southern outskirts of Stony Beach, a summer storm flung rain horizontally against the glass, nearly blinding her, as if determined to drive her back. But she pressed on, half expecting to see Windy

Corner in ruins like Manderley or Thornhill, Agnes stranded on
the rooftop, bravely going down with her ship.

But the house was intact, not even a tree down across the
driveway. Emily stopped the Cruiser in the drive opposite the
front door, pulled her jacket over her head, and ran for cover in
the porch. She rang the bell, waited, knocked and waited again,
but there was no response. She fumbled in her purse for the
keys she had not yet had occasion to use and at last wrestled
the door open, her hands shaking in trepidation. It was conceivable Agnes couldn't hear the bell or her knocking over the
storm, but it seemed unlikely. Agnes had never failed to hear
before.

"Agnes?" she called, stopping only to hang her sopping jacket
in the vestibule before hurrying toward the kitchen.

The kitchen was dark and cold and eerily silent against the
howling from outside. Agnes was not there.

"Agnes? Where are you?" Emily ran through the other
rooms on the main floor, then sprinted up the stairs and checked
the bedrooms. No Agnes. Up the attic stairs, into her own tower
room and finally the storage rooms. Rain pounded the windows,
wind shrieked through the chimneys, but Agnes was nowhere
to be found.

Slowly now, dread and exhaustion dragging at her feet,
Emily descended and knocked at the one door she'd missed,
Agnes's bedroom off the kitchen. No response. Could Agnes
be sick in bed? She cracked open the door and peeked inside,
but the bed was empty and neatly made.

Bustopher Jones yowled from the kitchen, and Emily turned
back there once more. This time she turned on the light and
noticed that the door to the cellar stairs stood open. Bustopher

crouched opposite the doorway, baleful eyes fixed upon it, the tip of his tail twitching.

Emily padded up to the doorway. An odd smell rose to meet her, the dankness of dirt and mold mixed with a whiff of last year's apples, overlaid with a stench like meat left out too long in a hot room. A subtler odor she puzzled over, finally identifying it with the smell left on her hands after counting a jar of pennies.

Steeling herself, she stepped onto the landing and looked down. Two steps from where she stood, jagged edges of broken boards stuck out where the tread should be. At the bottom of the flight, a dark shape loomed.

Emily held her breath and flipped the light switch on. Nothing happened. She reached up to touch the bare bulb—it was loose in its socket. She tightened it, and a white glare flooded the stairway.

At the bottom of the stairs lay Agnes Beech, legs doubled up and arms flung out to her sides, her head twisted in a way no living head could be. As Emily stared aghast, a fat fly alighted on one sightless eye.

· fourteen ·

"A man does not recover from such a devotion of the heart
to such a woman!—He ought not—he does not."
—Captain Wentworth to Anne Elliot,
Persuasion

Emily had read enough detective stories to know one must never disturb a possible crime scene. But even if she hadn't, nothing would have induced her to go down those stairs and take a closer look at Agnes's body. She rushed to the powder room, grateful she hadn't taken time for breakfast, then staggered to the library to call Luke.

In five minutes he was at the door, and in five minutes and ten seconds she was in his arms, incoherent and weeping. She managed to convey that Agnes was in the cellar. Luke helped her to a sofa in the library and poured her a glass of sherry, then grabbed a blanket off a chair and tucked it around her shivering shoulders.

He knelt before her, a hand on her knee. "Can you tell me what happened, Em?"

She gripped her glass and tried to breathe deeply. "I came home and she was nowhere. I looked all over. Came back to the kitchen. The cellar door was ajar. I turned on the light, but nothing. I screwed the bulb in, and that's when—I saw her." She forced the gag reflex down.

"Did you notice anything else? Any sign of anyone being there?"

The picture rose vividly in her mind. "One of the steps was broken."

"Good girl." He stood, keeping a hand on her shoulder. "Is there another way into the cellar?"

She scoured her childhood memories. Sneaking in for apples—so much more fun than asking, although the house-keeper would have given them all they wanted. "There's an outside door. Around the back."

Luke left the room, and she heard him speak in a low voice to his officers at the front door. Then he was back, kneeling be-fore her. "I'm gonna have to leave you now and check it out. You be okay?"

She nodded, though she was by no means sure she would; but she couldn't keep him from his work.

She heard noises from the cellar—muted voices, thumps, taps. Then a new voice at the front door—Dr. Sam Griffiths. The officer on duty sent her around to the back. She must be standing in for the medical examiner. But surely Dr. Griffiths ought to be a suspect? What if she declared it was an accident?

Long minutes passed. More people arrived. From the li-brary window Emily could see them tromping through the steady rain back to the outside door: a man sheltering a large camera, a woman lugging a heavy case full of God knows what. The crime scene team, no doubt. And a little later, a couple of paramedics with a gurney.

She waited for what seemed forever. She poured another

sherry, lay down on the sofa and tried to rest, got up and paced awhile, then collapsed by the window again. The macabre procession repeated itself in reverse: the paramedics wheeling a gurney that bore a body bag, the crime scene people, the doctor, the uniformed deputy from the back door. And finally, Luke himself.

He came in through the French window off the terrace, sat beside her on the sofa, and took her hands. "Looks like it was planned," he said.

She nodded. The loose bulb had told her that.

"That broken stair—it'd been half broken and stuck back together. The nails barely held it in place. One step on that'd send anybody straight to the bottom."

"What killed her exactly?"

"Broken neck. Would've been quick, at least—she didn't lie there and suffer."

"Doctor Griffiths didn't say it was an accident? I don't trust her, Luke. She was so shifty when I talked to her about Beatrice. I wish you'd had some other doctor on this."

"Doc said it looked like an accident, but she just meant it happened in the fall. Not for her to say if the fall was planned or not. I say it was."

"You didn't—let her near the evidence?"

He dropped her hands and sat back away from her. "Course not. What do you take me for? I don't get a lot of murders on my beat, but that doesn't mean I don't know my job when I do."

Oh great, now she'd offended him. Her book-learning versus his street smarts had always been a sore point between them. "I'm sorry, Luke, I didn't mean that. Of course you know your job. I'm so keyed up, I don't know what I'm saying." She let her guard down, and the shivers returned.

Luke wrapped the blanket tighter around her. "Don't mind me. Sorry I snapped at you."

She snuggled into his arm. "I knew last night something was wrong. I just felt it. I should have come back then."

"Em, she's been dead at least twenty hours, maybe twenty-four. You would've been too late. This is not your fault. There was absolutely nothing you could've done to prevent it."

She digested this. Maybe she couldn't have prevented it by being there, but . . . "This is connected to Beatrice, isn't it?"

"I can't say for sure just yet, but my gut tells me yeah."

"We were talking about Beatrice's death the other day. Agnes and I. The day before I left for Portland. But then I saw somebody in the garden and cut her off." She looked at Luke with horror. "What if that was the killer? What if he heard something that made him think she was onto him? Though I don't know what it could have been. Nothing she said clued me in."

"That's possible, but it still doesn't make it your fault. And sorry as I am Agnes was killed, it does give us something to go on for both her and Beatrice." He paused and looked sideways at Emily. "I'm gonna ask for an exhumation and autopsy on Beatrice. You okay with that?"

She shuddered. "I hate the thought of it, but I guess it's the only way."

He nodded. "We'll get him now, Em. We'll get him before he can do any more harm."

The rain had abated, and as the others were leaving, Billy Beech arrived. Luke met him at the back door and brought him into the library. When he saw Emily, he removed his ancient cloth hat and held it in both hands.

"What is the difficulty, sheriff? The driveway was so full of vehicles, I could barely get through."

"I have bad news for you, Billy. I'm afraid Agnes is dead."

Billy's face went as white as his hair. "Agnes? Dead?" He passed a hand over his face. "What was it, a heart attack?"

"She fell down the cellar stairs and broke her neck. Looks like she was meant to."

Billy stared, his lip quivering. "*Meant* to? What villain would want to harm our Agnes?"

"That's what we have to find out. I need to ask you some questions, if you're up to it." Luke pulled a chair from the library table and waved Billy into it. "When did you last see Agnes?"

Billy swallowed. Emily poured him a glass of water from the carafe on the sideboard, and he gulped it. "Wednesday. It must have been Wednesday. I bade her farewell when I left, as usual. Around five."

"Did you go into the cellar for anything?"

"No indeed, I had no occasion to that day. I did, however, remove the padlock from the cellar door in preparation for a visit from the washing machine repairman on Thursday." He shot an apologetic grimace at Emily. "Although my skills are numerous, I fear the mysteries of modern washing machines fall outside my purview."

"Washing machine repairman?" Luke's voice was sharp. "You mean Trimble?"

"Our honorable mayor himself. Is it not admirable that even in the glory of his high office, he still performs such humble work to earn his bread? A true man of the people."

Luke snorted as he scribbled in his notebook. "But you weren't here when he came."

"Alas no, Thursday is my day to tend to our local park."

"Did you expect him to lock the outside door when he left?"

"No indeed, for the padlock was safely stowed in my toolshed. I planned to lock it myself this morning."

Luke frowned at him. "Isn't that kind of risky, leaving it open overnight?"

Billy's eyebrows shot up. "The cellar contains little of value. Agnes always locks—" He held his hat to his heart, eyes to heaven. "I mean to say, she always *locked* the door to the kitchen stairs."

Luke drummed his fingers. "What time did you take off the padlock?"

"Just before my departure at five o'clock. I saw Mr. Brock Runcible off the premises first, then removed the padlock and stowed it in the toolshed, which I locked. After that, I said good-bye to Agnes and made my way home."

"You actually saw Brock drive away?"

He nodded emphatically, his chins quivering.

"All right. I think that's all for now, Billy. You'll be around the rest of the day?"

"I shall." He stood and turned to Emily. "My apologies for my late arrival, madam. The rain made it impossible to work in the garden, so I waited until it cleared." Billy made his improbable squished-marshmallow bow and exited through the French doors.

Luke hunched over his notes, tapping his pen against the table. "So far that's three people who had easy access to the cellar."

"Three?" Emily asked. Her mind wasn't working clearly yet.

Luke ticked off on his fingers. "Billy himself, if he's holding something back. Trimble, obviously. And Brock could easily have stopped by the road, waited till he saw Billy leave, and come back. So three—or, if you want to look at it that way, three thousand. Anybody could've walked in, though they wouldn't likely have known it'd be open."

"Anybody including Dr. Griffiths. I'd be willing to bet she knows how to swing a hammer."

Luke huffed. "Why do you keep harping on Sam? She's a doctor, for pity's sake. It's her business to save lives, not take them."

"I know, but she wanted that clinic awfully badly, and she was so evasive about Beatrice's death. She must have known Agnes was suspicious—maybe she thought Agnes had some kind of proof."

"Well, I won't rule her out. But the other three are a lot more likely."

"I think we can eliminate Billy, don't you? He'd have no reason to hurt Agnes. Or Beatrice, for that matter."

Luke chewed his bottom lip. "There's more to Billy than you might think. You know he had a brother?"

"Bobby. Best husband in the world, if Billy does say so himself."

"That's a matter of opinion. Bobby worked here before Billy. Beatrice fired him for pilfering. Agnes sided with Beatrice, and a week later Bobby hanged himself in the garage."

Emily stared. Such drama, right here in sleepy Stony Beach. "How long ago was that?"

"Three, four years."

"Even if Billy were the vengeful type—which he doesn't seem to be—why would he wait so long to take his revenge?"

Luke shrugged. "Could be Agnes or Beatrice said or did

something, brought it all up fresh. And, of course, he'll get Agnes's money now, assuming she hadn't made a will; she didn't have any other family. That could be a motive for both murders: kill Beatrice so the ten grand goes to Agnes. Wait the hundred and twenty hours for survivorship, then kill Agnes and get the ten grand."

"But there again, why wait till now?"

"Maybe he's just now run into money problems. I can check that out."

Emily couldn't cast Billy in the role of murderer no matter how she tried. "Even so—Billy? If he needed ten thousand that badly, Beatrice probably would have lent it to him."

"You never know. What if it was a gambling debt? She wouldn't lend money for anything she didn't approve of."

"True. I guess you have to check it out. But my money's on either Trimble or Brock." Emily hesitated, trying to be fair to two of the people in Stony Beach she most disliked. "I guess the mayor's probably handy with a hammer if he's a repairman. Somehow I can't see Brock doing anything as practical as rigging a broken stair."

"Well, we'll know in a week or two. Couldn't get any fingerprints, but we did pull a hair out of that tread. Sent it off to the lab for DNA. I'll get samples from all the suspects too. But I want to solve this thing faster than that. God knows what he might try next. And if I don't get an arrest quick, they'll call in somebody senior, state police even. I want to nail this bastard myself."

"It takes a week or two to get DNA results?"

"Around here, with our budget, yeah. I know on TV they get 'em right away, but that's TV. DNA's useful for conviction, but as far as an arrest, we're on our own."

He sighed and pushed himself to his feet. "Better get going and interview those two. We still on for Saturday night?"

"Absolutely. But couldn't I come with you? I'm starting to get into this whole sleuthing thing."

Luke frowned, hands on hips. She swallowed. That position of his took her back thirty-five years.

"I can see three good reasons why not. One, it's not proper procedure to have a civilian along. Two, they might not talk in front of you. And three, I'm starting to be afraid for your safety. I'm thinking maybe the less you know from here on out, the better."

Emily deflated like a balloon. "It can't be dangerous for me to know what you know. Couldn't I listen on a hidden intercom? Watch through a two-way mirror or something?"

Luke barked a laugh. "Emily, you've seen my office. Intercom? Two-way mirror? You're thinking TV again. Besides, I don't want to put the wind up them yet. I'm going to talk to them wherever I find them."

She sidled up to him and ran her hand down his arm. "Oh, come on, Luke. Can't you swear me in as a temporary deputy?" She gazed at him from under her lashes. "Please?"

The muscles tensed along his jaw, and his breath came short. "Emily, don't do this to me. It's not fair."

She took a step back and dropped her arm, her face hot. "You're right. I'm sorry."

He ran his hands over his face. "The thing is—I might actually be able to do that, except that technically speaking, you ought to be a suspect."

"A suspect! But I wasn't even here when she died. Either of them."

"No, but neither was the murderer, far as I can tell. You

profit the most from Beatrice's death—anybody who didn't know you would at least want to check you out."

"But why would I kill Agnes?"

"Maybe 'cause she knew something damaging. Just like with the real murderer."

Emily was shocked to her core. That anyone—especially Luke—could even think of her in the same sentence with the word *murder* . . .

She had just tried to cozy up to a traitor.

She turned her back on him. "I think you should go now."

"Emily—" She felt his hand on her shoulder and shrugged it off. "Em, please. I didn't say I *do* suspect you—it's just you're in a position relative to this case where I can't involve you on an official level. It's not my decision. It's policy."

She maintained a stony silence.

"*I* know you'd never kill anyone. Or even think about harming them. Hell, do you think I would've fallen in love with you—would still be in love with you—if I thought you capable of that?"

His words rocked her to her foundations. Her voice came out small and high. "You're—*still* in love with me?"

"Damn straight I am. You didn't know?"

She shook her head, then slowly turned to face him. "Go, Luke. Go interview your suspects. I'll find something useful to do while you're gone." She put her hand up to his cheek. It flamed under her touch.

He pulled her palm to his lips and kissed it. "I'll be back as soon as I can."

· fifteen ·

"There is always something offensive in the details of cunning. The manoeuvres of selfishness and duplicity must ever be revolting."

—Anne Elliot to Mrs. Smith,
Persuasion

Emily had no idea what useful thing she'd find to do in Luke's absence, but she wasn't left to wonder long. The sound of his engine had barely faded down the drive when she heard another car approaching.

To be precise, a van, ocean blue, with THE WAVE painted in an inexpert wavy shape across the side. From the driver's side emerged a young man with a camera. He went around to the passenger side and assisted in extracting the beached whale woman from her seat trap.

Emily shut the door behind herself and stood at the top of the porch steps. Rita hauled her bulk toward her. "I hear there's been another murder," she bellowed. "We're here to get the scoop."

Luke had not instructed her on how to handle a media assault. She fell back on her usual model of behavior: fiction.

"No comment," she said. "You'll have to talk to Lieutenant Richards."

"Oh, come on," Rita boomed. "You can at least confirm that Agnes Beech is dead."

"No comment."

"Rick, go get a picture of the cellar." The young man with the camera headed toward the side of the house.

"The cellar is a sealed crime scene. No one is allowed to enter."

Rick paused. "Go on, Rick. Don't listen to her."

"Mrs. Spenser, you and your tame cameraman are trespassing on private property. There is nothing for you here. Now please leave before I call the sheriff."

"You go ahead and call your tame sheriff. He's just the man I want to talk to. About why he hasn't already arrested *you*!"

Emily felt the blood rush to her face. Her fists clenched of their own accord, and her pulse throbbed in her ears. She, so long a mistress of words, could find no words scathing enough to express her fury with this human scourge.

She was saved from spontaneous combustion by the appearance of Billy Beech from the back of the house. He advanced on Rick and Rita with all the authority of a cannonball. Even Rita quailed before him.

"Away with you forthwith, you poisonous worm! Go! Begone! Leave my mistress in peace!" He shooed them back into their van like so many chickens. He gave the van a slap on the rear bumper, and it bolted like a frightened horse.

"Billy! I didn't know you had it in you. Thank you."

"I am ashamed to say, madam, that female snake is my cousin and the bane of my existence. It was a pleasure and an honor to dispatch her from your presence." He bowed—just an inclination this time, not a full-fledged marshmallow fold—and rolled back the way he'd come.

Emily divided the next couple of hours between prayer and sleep. She hated herself for sleeping at such a time, but her body demanded it after the adrenaline depletion of the morning. Yet every time she dropped off, she was awakened by Bustopher Jones's piteous howls from the kitchen. She'd tried giving him food and water, even attempted to pet him, but he rebuffed all her advances. He preferred to be alone with his grief—though he wanted all the world to know about it.

Late in the afternoon Luke returned. He sank into Bustopher's favorite chair—currently unoccupied—and lay back, exhausted. Emily offered him sherry, but he asked for coffee instead. She was about to call for Agnes when she remembered. She went to the kitchen and made the coffee herself. When she returned, Luke was dozing in the chair.

She stood over him, tracing in memory the lines of his youthful face, now hidden beneath the coarsening of maturity. He'd kept in good shape, but he hadn't kept out of the sun and wind. She laid the coffee tray on an end table and ran one finger lightly around his hairline and down his jaw, reacquainting herself with the feel of him. Then she bent down and lightly kissed his brow.

He didn't stir. She hated to wake him, but he must have so much yet to do. "Luke?" she said softly.

His eyelids fluttered, then abruptly he sat up straight, looking about as though he had no idea where he was. He turned to her and focused again.

"Did I fall asleep?" He scrubbed his face with his hands.

"Just a little. I brought your coffee."

"Thanks." He took the cup from her hand. She'd added one sugar but no cream. He sipped it and smiled. "You remembered."

She felt herself flush. "I remember lots of things."

He set the cup down. "We better save that for later, okay? Got to stay focused on the case. You understand, don't you?"

"Of course." She took the chair opposite him. "What did our two suspects have to say?"

"Talked to the mayor first. He was easy to find, in his office. Insisted he didn't know a thing about it. I took him through it. He got here around ten A.M. Thursday. Came to the back door to check in with Agnes. She told him to go in from the outside, which he did. Asked if he noticed anything funny—nope. Looked at the stairs—nope. Must've fixed the washer with his eyes closed, practically. Agnes didn't come down; he didn't go up. He was done in half an hour and went out the way he came, leaving the door latched but not padlocked, like Billy said. Went to the back door again and handed Agnes a bill."

"So that's the end of that?"

Luke rubbed the back of his neck. "I don't know. I took him through it a couple of times. His story didn't slip, but he was jumpy as a cat the whole time. He sounded innocent, but he looked guilty as hell."

"Hmm. What about Brock?"

"Took me a while to run him down. Tried the Stony Beach Inn; they said he'd checked out Wednesday night around seven and hadn't come back. Asked around all the restaurants and taverns, found out he'd had lunch at the Friendly Fluke at one o'clock today. Nobody'd seen him in between. Finally found him on the beach, said he was waiting around till three P.M. to check back in at the Stony."

"Did he have any explanation for lurking around my yard?"

"Said he'd lost a cuff link in the grass and was looking for it. Claimed after Billy ran him off, he'd driven straight back to town, gone to the Beach Brew for a couple of beers and a pizza, then decided on a whim to drive to Portland. Said his agent'd got him an audition for a stage play. Had the audition Thursday, but it didn't pan out, so he came back this morning."

"Do you believe him?"

"He's as plausible as an abbey full of monks, but I don't trust him. Still, I followed up on everything he told me, and it all checks out. That is, all except him driving straight to town after Billy threw him out—bartender at the Beach Brew remembers him coming in but had no idea of the exact time. So there's nothing to say he couldn't have snuck back into the cellar while you and Agnes were inside and rigged that tread."

"Seems like we would have heard something."

"What were you doing between five and six?"

"I was in here, reading. Agnes was making dinner—come to think of it, she had the radio on pretty loud. I could hear it in here. But that would be awfully bold, to be jimmying a stair just a few feet from the kitchen door with Agnes on the other side of it."

"There's also the chance he could've come back later, after you were both in bed. Brock stayed with a lady friend in Portland. She said he got there at nine, but it wouldn't surprise me a bit if she was lying."

"Good point. I'd certainly never hear anything from the third floor. Agnes sleeps—slept—right off the kitchen, but I think she used earplugs to block out the sound of the sea. I like it myself, but it bothered her."

"So Brock's still in the running. I asked him—before I'd said anything about the cause of death—whether he'd ever done any carpentry, and he said he didn't know one end of a hammer from another. I put one of the boys onto a full background check to see if that pans out. Should know by tomorrow."

He sat, slumped, his elbows on his knees, hands dangling. He looked like he had as much energy as a marionette with no puppeteer holding the strings.

"You're exhausted, Luke. Why don't you go home to bed?"

"Can't. Still got a ton of paperwork." He eyed the coffeepot. "Any more in there?"

She poured him another cup and stirred in the sugar. He drank the lukewarm coffee in two gulps, then pushed himself to his feet. "I'll see you tomorrow. Dinner's still on, no matter what." He gave her a weary smile.

She stood on tiptoe and kissed his cheek. "No matter what."

Hunger finally caught up with her after Luke left. She went to the kitchen, hoping to find something she could nuke for supper. But not only were there no convenience foods and no leftovers anywhere in the kitchen, there wasn't even a microwave. No short-cuts for Agnes.

But Emily did find eggs and cheese in the fridge and a couple of scones in the pantry, so she made herself a quick-and-dirty omelet. Bustopher Jones had given up howling and now crouched under the kitchen table, staring at Emily as if he held her personally responsible for Agnes's absence. She tried speaking to him, but he only glared the more balefully.

She ate her supper in the library, which had always felt cozy to her before but now seemed huge and empty, the house around it stretching out into indifferent infinity. She washed her few dishes and then toured the house, making sure all the doors and windows were fastened and locked, before plodding up the stairs to bed. Even her tower room could not comfort her. The sea pounded, distant and uncaring, almost threatening, beyond her windows. She crawled under a pile of blankets and shivered.

Philip? she said tentatively, but he did not reply. Even Philip had deserted her—perhaps because of what had happened with Luke. Never in her life had she felt so alone.

In the morning she cooked more eggs and washed more dishes, feeling like a bumbling intruder in her own kitchen. Bustopher Jones still sat under the table, his food and water untouched. She was beginning to worry about him. He wasn't a young cat; prolonged fasting couldn't be good for him. But try as she might, she could not coax him out.

The house's silence thundered in her ears. She had to get out of here, do something—but what? The investigation, such as it was, seemed to have reached a stalemate. She would have liked to do something for Agnes, but Billy had insisted he had the funeral under control, knew exactly what Agnes would have wanted and was well able to pay for it out of the legacy that would now pass to him.

The weather was uninviting—gray skies with a lackadaisical drizzle, hardly more than a mist—but she decided to go for a walk nevertheless. She wouldn't accomplish anything sitting in the house. If she walked into town, she'd have at least a chance of picking up some useful tidbit. She threw a rain slicker over her chinos and sweater in case the drizzle decided to buck up and act like a real rain.

The mile and a half to downtown felt like three, so she treated herself to a latte at the Friendly Fluke before moving on. Several people she hardly knew stopped by her table to offer curiosity disguised as condolences about Agnes's death. Following Luke's instructions, she implied it was an accident without saying anything specific.

Since her booth here offered no refuge, she finished her latte quickly and moved on, heading vaguely toward Luke's office—not with any real purpose, just drawn there by the magnet of his presence. Passing City Hall, which she'd expect to be deserted on a Saturday, she caught movement through one of the windows and decided on a whim to go in.

The door was not locked, but the receptionist's desk was unoccupied. The inner door to the mayor's office showed a crack of light.

Acting on instinct, she padded silently up to the door, paused, then pushed it open. Mayor Trimble and Vicki Landau had their heads together in front of a table by the far wall. They sprang apart when they saw her; then, in a move that looked rehearsed, both turned and leaned their backsides against the table, blocking Emily's view. But in the instant before they closed ranks, she glimpsed something that looked like an architectural model.

Emily cast about for an excuse to give for her presence— something that would both disarm them and force at least one of them to move away from the table, if only momentarily. "Oh, hello—I was just passing and saw the light, so I thought I'd pop in and ask a favor. I'm going to need a new housekeeper. I thought one of you might know someone, or at least know how I could go about advertising. Is there a community job board or anything?"

Vicki merely glared at her, but Trimble licked his lips, eyes darting about the room. "I, uh—I might know someone. I'll get in touch with her and give you a call, get it?"

"Couldn't you call her right now?" That would require him to cross over to his desk and leave the table unguarded.

"Uh, no, not now. Wouldn't be home, get it? She—uh—she works on Saturdays."

"But if she has a job already, why would she want to be my housekeeper?"

"No, no. No job, just—busy, that's all. Busy. Call her tomorrow."

"What about you, Vicki? Do you know of any prospects?"

Vicki crossed her arms and tapped her red-lacquered fingernails against her elbow. "Anyone who'd want to keep house for *you*? No. Not likely you'll find anyone around here who wants to be stuck in that mausoleum a mile from town. Especially with Agnes likely haunting it. You'd be much better off selling."

Emily had a fleeting vision of Agnes's ghost hovering over the new housekeeper's shoulder, short-sheeting the beds and making her cakes fall. But this was no time for either spookiness or levity.

She spotted the current *Wave* on the mayor's desk, which stood under the window at right angles to the mysterious table. "Mind if I check your want ads? Just in case." She headed toward the desk.

The mayor darted forward as if to head her off, then leaped back to shield the end of the table that faced toward the desk. Vicki slid over to take his previous position, blocking both sides of the corner from Emily's view. But in the shuffle, Emily caught a glimpse of the whole model.

It showed a stretch of coastline that looked just like Stony

Beach. But at the north end of town, where her property—the greenbelt and then Windy Corner—should have been, she saw what looked like a huge hotel surrounded by a golf course, tennis courts, condos . . . the works.

Emily called on all her drama training from high school to act as if she'd seen nothing. She turned to the desk, unfolded the *Wave,* and paged through it, pausing at the classified section but not taking in a word of it. She took a deep breath to steady herself, then turned back. "Nothing there. Well, I'll hope to hear from you tomorrow, Mayor Trimble. Thanks for your trouble. I'll let myself out." She strode from the room without looking back.

Safely outside the building, she leaned against the shingles, her breath coming in short gasps. So this was what they had planned! Not just opening up property for anyone who might want to come in and build, but a full-scale luxury resort. On *her land.* That model—and the preliminary architect's work it was based on—must have cost a pretty penny. How could they make an investment like that without even a reasonable hope that the property would ever be theirs?

Only one answer to that. They must have believed they had a reasonable hope.

Emily fairly ran up Third Street to Luke's office. She shoved open the door to see one of his young officers at the front desk, staring at a computer screen. "I have to see Lieutenant Richards," she blurted, and made for the inner door, ignoring the young man's protests.

Luke was similarly engrossed at his computer but stood when she burst in. She leaned her hands on his desk, panting. "You won't believe what I just saw."

"Here, sit down. Take your time." He pushed a chair up

behind her and poured her a glass of water. She sipped and then told him between gasps.

Luke frowned. "That's motive if I ever saw one. And plenty of opportunity, both for Agnes and Beatrice. But where's the goddamned *proof*?" He thumped his fist on the desk. The papers that littered it jumped, and so did Emily.

"No joy on the background checks and whatnot?"

"None so far. But we've mostly been working on Brock. This puts our fine mayor in the lead as far as I'm concerned."

Emily chewed her lip. "Maybe we should have dinner at the same place they all ate the night Beatrice got sick. See if anybody remembers anything they might have overlooked before."

"That's where I was planning to take you anyway. Only four-star restaurant in the county. But I didn't want it to be a working meal."

"There is no real off duty until the case is solved. Isn't that what they teach you in sheriff school?"

"No such thing as sheriff school, but yeah. Only it shouldn't have to apply to you."

"Are you kidding? I'm in this up to my topknot. I won't be able to relax until we nail this killer, whoever he is."

sixteen

Her heart was affectionate, her disposition cheerful and
open, without conceit or affectation of any kind—her manners
just removed from the awkwardness and shyness of a girl;
her person pleasing, and, when in good looks, pretty.
                                            —*Northanger Abbey*

E mily arrived at Windy Corner at about eleven, and ten
minutes later the doorbell rang.

On the porch stood a young woman—hardly more than a girl.
Her thick brown hair was pulled back from her fresh, pretty,
un-made-up face. She bit her lip and rocked from foot to foot.

"Mrs. Cavanaugh? I'm Katie Parker. I heard about Agnes
Beech—I'm so sorry—and I'm sorry to burst in on you like
this—but I was wondering if you'd be needing a new housekeeper?"

Emily was taken aback. Had the mayor acted so quickly
after all? Or was this girl's appearance a blessed coincidence?
"Come in, won't you?"

Katie stepped over the threshold and stood there, looking
around her. "Wow," she said in a breathless voice. "I've never
been in here before. I knew it was big, but I didn't realize it was
so— Wow."

Emily's mouth quirked. "Do you still want to apply for the job? It is rather a lot of house to take care of, but then there's only me living here, and I'm not too demanding."

Katie whipped her head around to face Emily. "Oh, I want the job. I need the job. I'm young and strong and I'm careful; I won't break anything. I'm a good cook, too. And I learn fast. I can learn to do anything you want me to do."

Emily hesitated. "So—are you saying you don't have any actual experience as a paid housekeeper?"

"Well, not exactly. I've worked as a maid at the Driftwood, and I did one summer as a waitress at the Fluke. I'm the oldest of seven, so I always had to help my mom a lot at home."

"I see. I really hate to cook for myself, so I'd need you here from about seven in the morning till seven at night, say six days a week. You wouldn't be busy every minute, but you'd need to be mostly here. Are you willing to put in those hours? It wouldn't leave you much time for a social life."

"Oh, I don't care about that. In fact"—Katie bit her lip again—"well, I was kind of hoping I could live in. Like Agnes did."

"Don't your parents live locally?"

"Yeah, but like I said, there's seven of us, and it's pretty crowded. And besides . . ." Katie paused, wringing her hands. From somewhere outside Emily heard a muffled cry.

Katie's face contorted. "Oh shoot, I was hoping she'd stay asleep. The thing is—I have a baby."

"A baby! Where is she?"

"I left the stroller up against the porch. I was hoping to get you to say yes first, and then I was going to ask if it was okay to bring her with me."

"You can't leave her alone down there. Bring her up here right now."

Katie scurried across the porch and down the steps, then climbed back up holding a bundle of blankets. She parted the blankets, and Emily looked down at the sweetest little face she'd ever seen—deep blue eyes just beginning to widen in wonder at the world, skin so fair as to be translucent, and a curly fuzz of pale reddish hair.

"Oh, she's adorable! But she's tiny—what, a couple of months old?"

"Seven weeks."

"Seven weeks! Are you sure you're ready to go back to work?"

"I don't have a choice. Her dad's . . . not in the picture, and my parents . . ." She blinked and swallowed. "My parents won't let me stay any longer. They kicked us out." Her lower lip wobbled along with her voice.

Emily put an arm around the girl's shoulders. If things had gone differently for her years ago . . . But that was beside the point. Katie needed her help.

"What's her name?"

"Elizabeth. I call her Lizzie."

"Lizzie." Emily stroked the baby's downy-soft cheek with one finger. "Just like Lizzie Bennet."

"Yeah, that's who I named her for. I love Jane Austen. I've read all her books three times."

Emily's heart swelled almost to bursting. A kindred spirit. "I've read them all more times than I can count. But then, I have quite a head start over you."

She stepped back to look Katie in the eye. "You and Lizzie are welcome here. You can move in today and start work as soon as you're ready."

Katie's eyes lit up, sparkling through her incipient tears.

"Oh, thank you, Mrs. Cavanaugh! You're an angel, an absolute angel. Not even in disguise."

"Did you bring your things with you?" Emily looked around for a car, but the drive was empty.

Katie shook her head. "I don't have a car. We walked up here from town."

"Well, let's go get your stuff then. Do you have a car seat for Lizzie?"

"Yeah, my cousin gave me her old stroller and the top part lifts out for a car seat."

"Bring it and let's go." Emily grabbed her purse and headed to the Cruiser. She had to do this quickly before her sensible Worthing side got the upper hand and convinced her she was insane to take on a teenager with a baby.

Katie directed Emily to the far south end of town, where small dilapidated houses huddled on tiny lots. Emily offered to help carry things, but Katie said, "If you wouldn't mind just staying in the car with Lizzie, that would be great." So Emily opened the hatch and watched as Katie brought out two suitcases, half a dozen boxes, and a bag of disposable diapers.

"That's all you have? What about a crib?"

"I don't have one. She's been sleeping with me at night. For naps I put her in the stroller."

"That won't last long. Pretty soon she'll be rolling over, sitting up." Emily was foggy on just when these things happened, but she'd seen enough babies at church to know they were bound to happen in the first year of life.

"Do you know a lot about babies?" Katie asked, her eyes almost worshipful.

"Nothing at all, I'm afraid. I never had one of my own." Emily's throat clenched on the words.

"Oh. Well, I've taken care of six younger siblings, so I guess I can cope."

"Don't your parents have a crib you can use?"

"My youngest brother's still using it."

"I see. Maybe we can find a crib in the attic." Beatrice and Horace had never had children, but at some point in the last hundred years, someone must have been born at Windy Corner.

Katie refused to let Emily help carry her things into the downstairs bedroom. Instead Emily carried in a sleeping Lizzie in her car seat and then realized she hadn't yet cleared the room of Agnes's things. She made a quick call to Luke to ask whether it was all right to move them.

"Nah, it's fine," he said. "We searched it yesterday. Didn't find anything significant, but I didn't expect we would. Say, that's quick work getting a new housekeeper. Just couldn't stand to cook for yourself, huh?" he teased.

"I didn't go looking—she came to me. She needed a place to stay, so I said she could start right away." She couldn't bring herself to mention the baby.

He laughed. "That's my Emily—taking in all the waifs and strays. You sure she's reliable? Check her references?"

Emily swallowed. Her sensible Worthing side shook its finger in her face. "Actually, she didn't offer any. But if you saw her . . . She's just a kid, Luke. It's obvious there's not a dishonest bone in her body. And anything she might lack in skill she'll make up for in enthusiasm."

She could almost hear him shrug. "It's your funeral. At least, I hope not. That just slipped out. Oh God . . ."

"I know. Too many funerals lately. Speaking of which, will Agnes's body be released in time for a funeral on Monday? That's what Billy's planning."

"Oh yeah. Cause of death was pretty obvious—no need for a full autopsy. She's on her way to the funeral home now."

"That's all right then. Any other news?"

"Not yet. We're still plugging away. Fact, I better get back to it. Pick you up at six?"

"Sounds good."

Irrationally cheered by the conversation, Emily began clearing Agnes's closet and drawers. Agnes had remarkably few possessions—three dresses, all similarly drab, in the closet; a week's worth of serviceable, much-mended underwear in the dresser; a folded flannel nightgown under the pillow, dressing gown and slippers by the bed. A worn leather Bible on the nightstand next to a pair of reading glasses, watched over by a framed photograph of someone who looked like Billy's younger, shiftier twin. A few neatly filed papers in a desk drawer, a stout hairbrush and a jar of pins atop the dresser.

These few things were all that was left of Agnes Beech. And yet her personality had been large enough to fill all of Windy Corner. Emily's knees buckled, and she sat down hard on the bed. This seemed sadder even than finding Agnes's body. That had been horrible, but this was heartbreaking.

After a few minutes Emily pulled herself together, fetched a couple of vegetable crates from the back porch, and piled everything into them. She found some clean sheets in the closet and was beginning to pull the blankets off the bed when Katie came in with her last load.

"What are you doing, Mrs. Cavanaugh? That's my job!"

Emily stopped mid-pull. "Oh. I guess it is. I'm still not used to having a housekeeper, you know? I was thinking in terms of getting a room ready for a guest."

Katie threw her arms around Emily. "You are the sweetest thing." Emily cleared her throat, blinking. She could see it wouldn't take much for this girl to get under her skin.

"Well, I guess I'll leave you to it then. I'll go see what I can find in the attic."

Emily had not yet ventured into any of the rooms on the third floor except her own. Frankly, she was a little afraid to. She was not at all fond of spiders, dust made her sneeze, and if she happened to see a rodent, she would probably faint. She took a deep breath and opened the first door off the hall.

She needn't have worried. Agnes's fanatical cleanliness had extended even to the attics. Not a speck of dust or a thread of cobweb could be seen. Neat metal shelving lined the walls, filled with taped and labeled boxes and a few larger items sitting on their own. Under the dormer window stood a few pieces of furniture—a straight chair with a broken leg, a floor lamp with a frayed cord, and an antique cradle.

Emily knelt before the cradle, tracing the carved teddy bear on the headboard. She gave it an experimental rock—no creaks. She pushed on the little mattress; the wood beneath it held firm. But the mattress itself was lumpy and hard in the middle.

She pulled it up off the cradle bed. There underneath the mattress sat an ancient, rusted can about three inches in diameter and an inch tall, with a pry-open lid. Unrusted dents in the lid and scratches in the rim of the can suggested it had been opened recently and clumsily, perhaps with a flat-end screwdriver. The label was so worn, she couldn't make it out.

Emily reached out to pick up the can, then pulled her hand

back. This could be evidence, which meant she ought not to handle it. She'd better call Luke.

She hurried down the attic stairs and into Beatrice's bedroom to use the extension. But Luke wasn't in. The officer on duty said he'd driven over to Tillamook to pick up the exhumation order for Beatrice's body. Would Mrs. Cavanaugh care to leave a message? No, there was no point. She'd wait till he came to pick her up for dinner.

She went down to the kitchen, but Katie wasn't there. She found her nursing Lizzie in their bedroom. "I'll get your lunch in just a minute," she said. "Lizzie woke up starved."

"No problem. I can make a sandwich or something."

"There you go, trying to do my job again! I'll be ready in a minute. Do you know what you'd like?"

"I don't really know what we have in the house. Just not eggs, please—I had those for dinner and breakfast."

"I'm sure I can come up with something. Then maybe one of us should go shopping. How did you handle that with Agnes?"

"I personally didn't. I was only here with Agnes a few days. I know she never went out—I don't think she knew how to drive—and I certainly didn't buy any groceries myself. Most of the produce probably comes from the garden. I think she must have had other things delivered, or maybe Billy shopped. I'll take a look at the accounts and see if I can figure it out."

At least she knew where the accounts were kept—in the little nook of an office off the front hall. An old clerk's desk with dozens of cubbyholes, augmented by a couple of tall filing cabinets, nearly filled the small space. Emily rifled through the cubbyholes until she found a receipt from the local fish market and another from a large chain grocery store in Tillamook. That store would never deliver; maybe Billy had gotten a list from Agnes and done the shopping there. If there wasn't enough food in the house to get by till Monday, she'd do some shopping herself.

A noise like a back-alley catfight sent her running to the kitchen. Katie cowered in the doorway, while Bustopher Jones, made twice his normal size by his fur standing on end, hissed and spat at her from the center of the floor.

Katie turned bewildered eyes to Emily. "He . . . doesn't seem to like me much. I didn't see him under there. All I did was set something on the table, and he . . . just exploded."

Emily squeezed her shoulder. "It's not your fault. He was very attached to Agnes, and this room was Agnes's domain, much more than her bedroom. I'll see what I can do."

She went into the library and grabbed the blanket off Bustopher's favorite chair, along with a catnip mouse she'd occasionally seen him bat around. "Here." She handed the mouse to Katie. "Dangle this in front of him while I make him a bed, then see if you can lead him into it."

Emily folded the blanket and placed it in the farthest corner, where it wouldn't be in Katie's way. Katie, dangling the mouse at arm's length, crept around the room, Bustopher following as if pulled against his will. Finally she dropped the mouse onto the blanket, and Bustopher pounced.

Katie leaned against the counter, shaking. "Whew. Usually I get along fine with cats, but that one . . ."

"We're going to have to give him some time. Hopefully, in a couple of days he'll come around."

Katie pulled herself together and turned to the fridge. "I was going to make you a salad. Is that okay?"

"Sure. Oh, I found a cradle upstairs, but it'll have to wait a bit before we bring it down. I think"—she cast about for an excuse—"I think it's going to need a new mattress."

"No prob. We've gotten along without one so far. Why don't you go relax somewhere? I'll have this done in a jiff."

"I'll be in the library. I usually have a tray in there."

After lunch, while Lizzie continued her nap, Emily showed Katie around the house. "I don't use most of the rooms much. Agnes liked to serve breakfast and dinner in the dining room, but I don't really care when I'm alone. I mostly use the library, the second-floor bathroom, and the tower bedroom. The other rooms you'll only need to dust once in a while."

"Don't you want to do any entertaining? This house would be so perfect for it."

"Maybe someday." Maybe after the murders were solved— but she couldn't say that to Katie. It wasn't common knowledge there had even been a murder. "After you get into the groove of things. I don't want to make too much work for you up front— with the baby and all."

"That's sweet of you, Mrs. Cavanaugh, but you've hired me to keep house, and I intend to do my job." In the tower room Katie noticed Emily's pile of laundry. "Like the laundry, for instance. Where's the washer and dryer?"

Emily gulped. Luke didn't want the cellar disturbed, but again, she couldn't say why. "They're on the fritz right now. Billy'll take care of it on Monday. I can get by till then."

Emily was knitting to relieve the stresses of the day when the doorbell rang. Katie answered it and ushered Dr. Sam Griffiths into the library. Sam was wearing an ill-fitting black skirt suit, and her cropped hair had been bullied into some semblance of an actual style.

Emily stood to greet her. "Doctor Griffiths! What brings you here?"

"Sam. Want to talk business with you. If you have time."

The doctor's brusque manner brought out the full measure of Emily's Victorian courtesy. "Certainly. Would you like a cup of tea? I know I would."

Sam produced an indeterminate rumble. Emily said to Katie, "Tea for two, please."

Katie almost managed a solemn-servant face, but her eyes were dancing. "Yes, ma'am."

Emily sat and indicated a chair for Sam. "Now, what can I do for you?"

"It's about the clinic." Sam's heavy brows drew together. "Been pricing stuff. Beatrice's money won't be enough."

"A hundred thousand dollars? Not enough?" Emily knew medical equipment was expensive, but she would have thought a basic small-town clinic could be quite adequately outfitted for that amount.

"Barely do for the equipment, but gotta hire a nurse. Gotta build up the practice before I can pay her out of what I take in."

"Isn't it customary for doctors setting up practice to borrow what they need? Like any other business?"

"Sure, but then I'd have to charge what other doctors charge. People around here, fishermen and whatnot, don't all have insurance. Can't afford eighty-five bucks for an office visit. Want to be able to treat them for what they can pay."

"I see." That was a worthy goal, and Emily certainly wouldn't miss the money. But she still wasn't completely convinced Sam didn't want this clinic badly enough to kill for it.

She temporized. "How much more do you need?"

"Fifty thousand."

Emily saw her way out. "I will give this serious thought, Sam. I'm all in favor of people getting local medical care they can afford. But I can't spend on that scale until Beatrice's will clears probate." *Or until I know you didn't kill her.* "And of course you'll have to wait for that anyway, won't you? The clinic trust won't be funded till then."

Sam slumped in her chair. Katie came in with the rose tea set on a silver tray and placed it on a low table in front of Emily.

"Milk or sugar?" Emily asked as she poured the first cup.

"Neither." Sam fairly grabbed the saucer from Emily's fingers and tipped the scalding tea into her mouth. Then she put the cup down and stood. "Gotta go. Thanks for the tea. Let me know when you decide." She turned and strode out without waiting for Emily's reply.

· seventeen ·

"Dare not say that man forgets sooner than woman, that his love has an earlier death. I have loved none but you. Unjust I may have been, weak and resentful I have been, but never inconstant."

—Captain Wentworth in a letter to Anne Elliot,
Persuasion

After Sam left, Emily drank her tea in a civilized fashion, then decided to take her time pampering herself before her dinner with Luke. She ran a hot bath, dumped in way too much bubble bath, buffed her feet, knees, and elbows, and soaked until the water turned tepid. Then she let the water out and washed and conditioned her hair under the shower.

She found some scented body lotion of Beatrice's and slathered it on until she smelled like a walking flower garden. Back in her room, she gave herself a manicure and massaged a firming night cream into her face and neck. She hadn't groomed this thoroughly since Philip died. And yet, she told herself firmly, the agenda for this evening was dinner and nothing more.

In anticipation of the evening, she'd brought her favorite dress from Portland—ivory linen in an Edwardian style with a slightly raised waist and A-line skirt, antique lace trimming the deep tucks on the bodice and edging the sleeves and hem. The color set off her fair complexion, while the cut disguised her menopausal belly and accentuated her still firm bust—the one benefit of never having babies. By the time she'd put up her hair in an elegant chignon and touched a bit of makeup to her face, she felt younger, prettier, and more feminine than she had in years.

Luke arrived promptly at six. Katie was busy with Lizzie, so Emily let him in.

This was the first time she'd seen him out of uniform. He wore a charcoal gray suit, a pale blue shirt, and a conservatively patterned tie—not an imaginative outfit, but one that showed off his muscular shoulders and brought out the flecks of blue in his gray eyes. Those eyes widened and warmed as he took in her appearance. A slow smile spread across his face.

"You look fabulous. Emily Worthing, you are one classy lady, and I am honored to be going out with you."

She let the name slip pass—hardly noticed it, in fact. The last thirty-five years might never have happened.

"You look pretty sharp yourself." She moved close to him and pulled a tiny fleck of lint from his lapel. He held her with his eyes as if he might kiss her there and then.

She pulled back. Too early for such shenanigans. Besides, they had a bit of business to attend to before they could leave.

"I tried to call you this afternoon, but you were out. There's something I need you to see. It's in the attic."

She led the way up the two sets of stairs, burningly conscious of his eyes on her as they climbed. At last she stopped by the cradle and pulled the mattress back. "I found this right here. What do you think of that?"

He squatted beside the cradle. "You didn't touch it?"

"No, Lieutenant. I know better than to handle the evidence."

"Dang, I wish I had my kit with me." He took out his cell phone and snapped a picture of the can where it lay, and another of the position of the cradle in the attic. Then he pulled a handkerchief out of his coat pocket and gingerly lifted the can by its edges, wrapped the handkerchief around it, and dropped it in his pocket. "I'll stow it properly when we get to the car."

"What do you think it is?"

"Can't read the label, but I'd lay odds it's rat poison."

Emily's hopes deflated slightly. "I guess it makes sense to keep rat poison in an attic."

"Yeah, but not hidden in a cradle. There's something fishy about this, for sure." Her hopes puffed up again.

"That it?" He smiled at her. "No more revelations?"

"No more revelations. Can you carry the cradle downstairs for me now that the evidence is taken care of?"

He cocked an eyebrow. "You gonna use it for a cat bed, or what? Personally, I don't think Bustopher Jones deserves that kind of pampering."

Then she remembered—she hadn't told him about Lizzie.

She put on a casual air. "Oh, didn't I mention? My new housekeeper has a baby."

He gaped at her for a moment, then broke into a laugh. "I should've known. You fell for a sob story, didn't you?"

Emily felt her cheeks grow hot. "Sort of, I guess, but Katie really does seem like she can handle the job. I think it's going to be fine."

"Whatever." He hefted the cradle and made for the door. "Then let's go eat. If we don't get there quick, they'll give our reservation away."

✿ ✿ ✿

Gifts from the Sea outdid any of the restaurants Emily fre-
quented in Portland, both in ambiance and in menu. She sat on
an ebony chair in the sparely decorated, Japanese-themed
dining room and looked over a bewildering variety of dishes
with ingredients she'd never heard of, like agridulce, za'atar,
and pomegranate molasses. At last she settled on an innocent-
looking seafood fettucini.

Luke ordered lobster. "I don't know how you can," she said
to him after the waiter had gone. "That's what Aunt Beatrice ate
the night before she died."

He shrugged. "Yeah, but lots of other people ate lobster here
that night, and she's the only one who got sick. It wasn't the lobster that killed her. Maybe her reaction to it, if we've been
wrong all along, but not the lobster itself."

"I guess. It's just the associations. I couldn't do it."

When the young waiter brought their salads, he looked at
Luke more closely. "Hey, aren't you the sheriff who came around
a week or so ago asking about Mrs. Runcible?"

"That's right. Was it you I talked to?"

"You talked to the manager, I think, but I was the one who
served her party that night. I remember exactly what they all
had: Mrs. Runcible had the lobster Béarnaise, Mayor Trimble
had the filet mignon, and that other lady had the chicken cor-
don bleu. And they all had death by chocolate for dessert." He
grimaced. "We changed the name to triple chocolate decadence
after that."

"You have a good memory—what was your name again?"

The waiter smiled all over his fresh young face. "Jake."

"Good memory, Jake. Maybe you remember something else

about that night. Like how they all acted with one another. Were they friendly? Nervous? Hostile?"

Jake screwed up his eyes in concentration. "I didn't hear a lot of their conversation, 'cause people tend to shut up when the waiter comes by. But just from looking at them—the mayor was doing most of the talking. He seemed to be trying to impress Mrs. Runcible or talk her into something, but she wasn't going for it."

"Did Mayor Trimble get angry at all?"

"He didn't raise his voice, if that's what you mean. But his face was pretty red by the time dessert rolled around."

"Did you see any of them do anything that looked odd or suspicious to you?"

Jake's eyes widened. "Are you thinking maybe she was poisoned?"

"Let's just say we're not entirely satisfied her death was natural."

The boy's color heightened. "Wow. Yeah. Now that you mention it, I did see something funny. When I served the coffee, Mrs. Runcible asked if we had any saccharine. We have just about every other sweetener you can think of, but not saccharine; hardly anybody wants it anymore. Then the mayor took a little packet out of his coat pocket and handed it to her. She took it without looking at it and stirred it into her coffee."

Jake leaned forward and lowered his voice. "I picked up that packet when I cleared the table. It wasn't labeled 'saccharine.' It was just plain white with no label at all. And the end looked like it could've been glued by hand." He straightened with a triumphant smirk.

Luke drummed his fingers on the table. "That's very interesting, Jake. You didn't save the packet, by any chance?"

"Uh, no." His triumph faded. "I didn't think too much of it at the time. It didn't occur to me till just now there might have been something else in that packet besides saccharine." He lowered his eyes. "Are you gonna arrest me for obstructing justice?"

Luke frowned at the boy. "I guess not this time. But you better watch your step from now on. I'm going to have my eye on you."

Jake slouched off, stricken.

Emily gave Luke's wrist a slap. "Shame on you! He was only trying to help."

"Cheeky devil, he deserved it. Giving us a tip like that with no way to follow it up. God knows if it even happened. He'd'a made up anything just to feel like he was involved." He grinned at her. "Anyway, that's enough about Beatrice's death. That trail's cold." He lowered his voice as he closed his hand over hers. "I've got something much more interesting in mind."

Emily felt her cheeks flame. She stared at the tablecloth. Then his hand withdrew and she looked up, puzzled.

"Eat first."

After all that, she'd be lucky to get anything down for wondering what awaited her afterward and how she would get out of it. She picked at the salad; then Jake brought their entrées, and she picked at that. Luke cleaned his plate, then cocked an eyebrow at her half-full one.

"You don't seem to have much of an appetite. At least when I'm around."

"I can't eat when I'm in suspense."

He grinned. "All right, I'll put you out of your misery so you can enjoy your dinner." He reached into his lower coat pocket and pulled out a small box wrapped in gold paper. "Happy birthday."

"Oh, Luke! I didn't get anything for you."

"I bought that a long time ago, so it doesn't really count as a birthday present. Open it."

She fumbled the paper off and saw a square velvet-covered jeweler's box. Her breath drew in as a sharp gasp before she could control it. It couldn't be—a *ring*?

"Come on, open it. I promise it's not a bomb."

Blood whooshed in her ears and her hands shook. At last she managed to pry open the box.

Nestled in white satin lay a gold heart-shaped locket engraved with the entwined initials L E. She pushed the catch, and it opened to reveal, on the right, a miniature photo of the two of them as teenagers and, on the left, a braided lock combining his chestnut and her copper hair.

Her eyes misted, but she couldn't tear them away from the locket. "Oh, Luke . . ."

"I had that made for you at the end of our summer. I wanted to give it to you before you left, but it wasn't ready in time. Then I was gonna mail it, but you never answered my letters. I couldn't hardly send it then, could I?"

She looked up at him at last. "You wrote?"

"Sure I wrote. I wrote to tell you I was leaving for the army. I wrote from boot camp to give you that address. And then I wrote again when I got posted. But I never got an answer." He lowered his eyes, and his voice dropped to a mumble. "Not one."

"But I never got your letters!" His head came up again, hope dawning in his eyes. "We moved, we didn't end up where I thought we were going. I wrote to tell you the new address." No need to go into what else that letter contained. That part of the past, at least, could stay buried. "You never got my letter?"

He put his hand over his eyes. His voice croaked. "Ma never

did approve of you. Of me and you, I mean." His voice went high and singsong. "'A boy from South Stony Beach has no business with a girl from Windy Corner. Don't get above yourself.'"

A snort escaped Emily's nostrils. "That's a laugh. If she could've seen the way we lived the rest of the year, she'd have said you had no business dating trailer trash."

"Not trash. Never trash. Not my Emily."

His voice went soft on the last words. Her heart melted at the sound and threatened to pour out her eyes.

He reached out and gripped her wrist, holding her eyes with his own. "If you had gotten my letters . . . would you've kept writing? Or was yours a *Dear John, sorry it was just a summer fling*?"

She hesitated. Apparently, the last thirty-five years had been one long lie. They needed truth from now on. At least, up to a point.

"I would've kept writing. And writing and writing. Till there was no need to write anymore."

They had coffee and dessert—triple chocolate decadence—but Emily hardly tasted it. She felt as if all her memories of Luke had been restored to her, no longer polluted by her perception of his later betrayal. Those memories bore her high on a cloud of elation. She kept touching the locket at her throat as a talisman against crashing back to Earth.

They talked of their lives since they'd parted. He'd done his stint in the army, then come back to Stony Beach. "I did get up my nerve to go see Beatrice when I got back, ask for your address. But she told me you were already engaged."

She'd waited five years in the hope of hearing from him. Agonizing to think she'd given up just a little too soon.

Army training got him a job with the sheriff's department, and he moved up fast. He married a girl who'd always had a crush on him, but it didn't work out; she knew she wasn't first in his heart. They had one son, who was now grown up and living in California. After that he knew better than to try marriage again. The first in his heart would always be Emily.

She told him about college at Reed, where she met Philip; they married between college and graduate school, then took a few short-term teaching posts before both achieving tenure back at Reed. He was never a hot-blooded man and was satisfied with the affection and companionship Emily always had to give in plenty to anyone she cared about. She would have liked children, but it didn't happen, so she contented herself with her career—until Philip's death two years before had made everything in her life feel so pointless.

They talked till the restaurant emptied and neither of them could hold another sip of coffee. Unwilling to part but, in Emily's case at least, unready to pursue the evening to what might seem its logical conclusion, they lingered by the car, looking at the stars. The clouds had burned off in the afternoon, and the sky was brilliantly clear.

"Look over there," she said, pointing. "I don't know what constellation that is, but it makes me think of a hooded monk." The word *monk* triggered another recollection. "You know, Brock told me he played the murderer in an episode of *Abbott*. I got the impression that was the highlight of his whole career to date."

Luke turned to face her. "He played a murderer?"

"A pretty clever one, he said."

"I think we better watch that episode. It might've given him ideas. Maybe it'll give us some too."

"How? You have an all-night video rental place around here?"

His mouth quirked. "Yeah. It's called Netflix."

She knew Netflix was something to do with movies and computers, but that was all she knew. "What's that?"

When he got over laughing, he said, "It's a membership website where you can either rent DVDs or watch movies streaming right on the computer or a digital TV. They have lots of old TV shows. I bet you another dinner they'll have *Abbott*."

"I don't doubt you, but I'll take you up on it anyway. Just for the sake of having another dinner with you."

He bent down and kissed her, quick and light, on the lips. "Let's go."

Luke lived in one of the newer houses on the east side of town, nestled up against the hills. "Wanted to get as far from the office as I could," he told her as he let her in. Inside, everything was clean and bright and new-looking, though as bare of ornament as bachelor pads are wont to be. A TV screen dominated the living room, covering most of one wall.

"Good heavens, Luke, this is a regular movie theater!"

"Home theater, that's what they call it. Have a seat, and I'll get set up. Want some wine?"

"Sure." That might be unwise, but she was buzzing from all the coffee.

He disappeared into the kitchen, then returned holding two large glasses of red wine, a laptop tucked under his arm. He handed her a glass, took a swig from his own, then opened the computer and clicked around for a while. "You don't know the name of the episode, I guess?"

"No, but he said it aired in oh-five."

"Okay, I'll just search by his name." More clicks. "Here it is.

'Mr. Abbott and the Absent Assassin.'" He cocked an eyebrow at her. "That's pretty interesting right there."

He punched some buttons, and the TV screen came to life. Emily had never seen *Abbott* before, though she'd heard about it from colleagues. At first she was so taken with the eccentric detective himself, she forgot to pay attention to the plot. But when Brock appeared on-screen, she sat up and took notice.

"He looks a lot younger, doesn't he?"

"Well, this is eight years ago. Plus they can do an awful lot with makeup and lighting."

She sat back. Luke pulled the age-old maneuver of stretching to get his arm around her shoulders. She laughed at him and snuggled in.

The plot unfolded. Brock played a famous and extremely arrogant politician. The victim had been the politician's lover and had pestered him to divorce his wife and marry her. The scene cut from them discussing this to her lying dead.

Brock's character produced the ultimate unbreakable alibi: at the time of the woman's death, he'd been in China. He had all sorts of testimony and film footage to prove it. Abbott, with his amazing powers of observation and deduction, eventually figured out that the politician had drugged the woman, then rigged up an ingenious Rube Goldberg-type device that would kill her many hours later, after he was out of the country. The device was triggered by a large package being left on her doorstep—a package Abbott managed to trace back to the politician.

"Well, that didn't have anything to do with poison," Emily said.

"No, but it did show it's possible to commit a murder without being on the scene. Or anywhere near it."

"You think he might have mailed her something?"

"Possible. You'd think Agnes would've mentioned it, though."

"It's conceivable she didn't know. Or didn't think it was important." Emily's mind went back to the afternoon on the terrace when she'd caught Brock eavesdropping. "He could've killed her before she got around to figuring out it was important enough to tell me."

"Which makes it pretty damn near impossible to prove."

"What about the post office? Or UPS or whatever?"

"If he was smart, he'd've used parcel post so it wouldn't be trackable. We'd be relying on somebody's memory that's already ten days old. You'd be surprised how much people don't remember after a day or two."

"And even if we proved the existence of a package, we couldn't prove who sent it or what was in it."

"That's exactly right."

"So we're back where we started."

"Just about."

Emily frowned at the credits, chewing at her newly manicured nails. Then she sprang up. "Take me home. Now."

Luke looked up at her in consternation. "What the heck? I didn't even get fresh with you. Yet."

She shook her head. "It's not that. I've just remembered something. It might be important."

"Whatever you say, boss." He collected his coat and keys.

Emily leaned forward throughout the five-minute ride as if by so doing she could get them there faster. The minute he pulled up to the door, she jumped out and ran into the house and up both flights of stairs to her room. She fumbled in her closet till she found her brown linen skirt, then shoved her hand into the right-hand pocket and pulled out the fragment of brown wrapping paper she'd found in Beatrice's fireplace.

Luke stood in the doorway. "I don't enter a lady's bedroom without an invitation."

Emily felt a deep flush spread up her neck to her face. She wasn't ready to issue an invitation that might prove difficult to retract.

She went up to him and held out the paper. "I found that in Beatrice's bedroom fireplace."

He whistled. "That's a beauty, that is." He fumbled in his pocket and found a tissue, which he held out for her to drop the paper into.

"Oh. I guess I shouldn't have touched it."

"Woulda been better, but we can always eliminate your fingerprints. Chances of the sender's being on this particular fragment—and being clear and liftable—aren't that great anyhow. But we'll give it a shot."

He grinned at her as he stuck the improvised parcel in his pocket. "You're shaping up into a pretty fair detective, Emily Worthing."

"Why, thank you, Lieutenant Richards."

He took her hands. "I notice you didn't invite me into your bedroom."

She bit her lip. "I'm not ready for that, Luke. Not yet. Not while everything is so—unsettled."

"I understand." He tipped her chin up and kissed her, a real kiss but not too deep. "I'll take a rain check on the rest."

He turned and skipped like a kid down the attic stairs. She stood, her hand on the doorjamb, watching him, feeling his kiss on her lips and feeling the years and the heartache ravel away—up to that one hard-felted knot that could never come undone.

eighteen

"Will not your mind misgive you when you find yourself in this gloomy chamber—too lofty and extensive for you, with only the feeble rays of a single lamp to take in its size—its walls hung with tapestry exhibiting figures as large as life, and the bed, of dark green stuff or purple velvet, presenting even a funereal appearance? Will not your heart sink within you?"

—Henry Tilney to Catherine Morland, *Northanger Abbey*

On Sunday, Emily wanted nothing more than to relax with a good book and forget about murder. She brought *Persuasion* downstairs with her, intending to have breakfast and then hole up in the library for the entire day.

Breakfast, however, was not ready. Katie had just started the coffeemaker when Emily poked her head into the kitchen.

"I'm so sorry, Mrs. Cavanaugh. Lizzie had a bad night, and I just got her settled down. I'll have your breakfast ready in a jiffy."

As Katie set the frying pan on the stove, Emily heard a doleful wail from the bedroom next door.

"Oh no . . ." Katie took a step toward the bedroom, then turned back to the stove. She broke an egg into the pan, then, "Oh shit, that was for the bacon!" She turned to Emily, a hand to her mouth. "Sorry . . . I just can't think when she's crying."

"Is she hungry?"

"I just fed her."

"I'll see to her. Just relax and take your time."

Emily tiptoed into the bedroom and up to the cradle. Little Lizzie's perfect face was red and contorted; her tiny fists beat the air. Emily leaned down and picked her up, one hand behind her head, as Helen at church had taught her to do with her baby, Emilia, who was Emily's goddaughter. Emily held the baby against her shoulder, rubbing her back and swaying as if to inaudible music. The wail subsided to a whimper.

Emily walked a slow circuit of dining room, foyer, parlor, library. By the third round, Lizzie's featherweight was beginning to feel like lead, and Emily vowed the first chance she got to scour the attic for a rocking chair. She ducked her head and saw that Lizzie's eyes were closed, her mouth making sucking motions as she slept. Maybe Emily could risk sitting down.

She stopped in the dining room and gingerly lowered herself into one of the hard chairs. Lizzie slept on. Emily felt a peace and contentment steal over her such as she hadn't known in years, along with a rush of deep affection for the tiny bundle of humanity in her arms.

She kissed the baby's downy red head, then leaned her own head against it and closed her eyes. In an instant she startled to see Katie laying a plate of bacon and eggs in front of her. A steaming mug of coffee followed the plate.

"Wow, I can't believe she went to sleep for you!" Katie said softly. "I'll take her now so you can eat."

They made the transfer as delicately as if the baby were a ticking bomb. She stirred but did not go off.

"Thanks so much."

"It was a pleasure. Truly."

Emily ate her breakfast, then, out of old habit, took her

dishes into the kitchen. Bustopher Jones sat in his corner, glaring with deep hatred at the world that had deprived him of his Agnes.

"He hasn't eaten?" she asked Katie.

"Not a bite. I've tried tempting him with all sorts of goodies, but he'll have none of it."

Emily stooped and put out a cautious hand to the cat. He sniffed at it, then turned his head away. She gave his head a tentative scratch; he suffered her touch but did not respond.

She would have to do something about him soon—but what? Her knowledge of abnormal cat psychology was nil; her own two had always been remarkably well adjusted.

Marguerite was an expert on cats. She'd know what to do. Emily went to the phone in the library and called her.

"*Chérie,* do you know the time? Only for you do I answer so early on a Sunday. Do not tell me you have discovered another body?"

"Believe it or not, yes. My housekeeper. But I was actually calling you about her cat." Emily described Bustopher's normal personality and his current behavior.

"Ah, *c'est difficile, le* grief *d'un chat.* There was no one else he cared for besides this—how do you call her—Agnes?"

"Maybe Aunt Beatrice, but she's gone too. He wouldn't have anything to do with me."

"Sometimes a shock, you know, a big change in the life, such as perhaps another animal in the house. You could bring in Levin and Kitty—he is too low to attack them, *n'est-ce pas*? And perhaps they might bring him around."

"That sounds drastic. I hate to uproot them and then throw them in with Bustopher on top of that."

"They are pining for you, *chérie.* When I went to feed them yesterday, they were heartbroken that I was not you. If you are not careful, you will have three *chats désolés* on your hands."

Emily's heart sank at the prospect of another trip to Portland—and then a trip back with two caged animals crazy with fear. Levin and Kitty hated traveling.

"I don't think I'm up for coming to get them right now. Maybe in a few days."

Marguerite put on her wheedling voice. "Perhaps I could be persuaded to bring them to you. If, you know, I were invited to stay a few days in your oh-so-*riche maison sur la plage*."

"Oh, Margot, of course! What a terrible friend I am. I've been so preoccupied, I hadn't even thought of that. But by all means, come down with the cats—if you can stand to drive with them—and stay as long as you like."

"*Bon.* I will arouse myself and be there this afternoon, and you will see what a little feline company will do for your Bustopher Jones."

Emily went in search of Katie. She didn't want to use the intercom for fear of waking Lizzie, and anyway, Katie didn't seem the intercom type.

Katie was washing up in the kitchen. She turned at Emily's approach. "Lizzie's asleep in the cradle. She loves that thing. I'm so glad you found it."

"So am I. Next I'm going to look for a rocking chair. But meanwhile, I've just invited a friend from Portland to stay for a few days. She's bringing my two cats with her. We'll need to fix her up a room."

Katie laid the last pan in the drainer and dried her hands. "Sure. Which room did you have in mind?"

"That's a bit of a problem. Why don't you come up with me and help me decide?"

They stood in the upstairs hall and looked around. "Of course Beatrice's room is the nicest." Emily pointed toward its closed door. "But I don't feel right putting anyone in there just yet. Not till . . ." What Emily meant was, *not till I've solved her murder,* but she didn't want to involve Katie in her suspicions. "Not till I've gone through her things."

Katie turned to the right and glanced into what had been Brock's room and the nursery at the end of the hall—the one sterile, the other shabby. "These two aren't very appealing."

She turned back to the front of the house and opened the doors of the two imposing guest rooms. "Boy, these rooms could be in a museum," Katie said. "Hey, you know what they make me think of? The red-room where little Jane Eyre is shut up and then faints."

"Oh, you've read *Jane Eyre?*" Emily was pleasantly surprised—a lot of young women were reading Austen these days, but it was less common to find one who knew the Brontës.

"Oh yeah. Loved it. Especially that part where Jane hears Rochester's voice from clear across the country. Gives me the chills."

"That's my favorite bit too." The two exchanged the smile of kindred spirits. "These rooms always reminded me of the red-room too. I was terrified of them as a child." Emily went into the right-hand room and turned in place, taking in the dark mahogany wardrobe, tallboy, and desk, the burgundy velvet window drapes and bed-curtains. The only thing in the room that wasn't dark was the pink-and-blue Aubusson rug.

She strode to the windows and pulled open the drapes, flooding the room with sunlight. "Marguerite might not mind too much. She's French—she kind of likes all that old-world magnificence."

Katie moved to the bay, whose western angle allowed a glimpse of the sea. "At least she could see the ocean from here. And I could bring in some flowers, cheer it up a bit. Any chance the bed-curtains could come down?"

"Absolutely. And I'll bet I could rustle up a prettier coverlet for the bed."

"The first thing to do is air it out. Nobody can be cheerful without fresh air." Katie opened the windows, then pulled a stool up to the bed and began removing the drapes from their hooks.

Emily went to the linen closet in the hall for fresh sheets and found a cream crochet-lace coverlet with matching pillow shams buried on a high shelf. She passed these to Katie, then climbed to the attic and poked around in a garret she hadn't yet visited. She found a couple of brightly embroidered throw pillows, as well as a rocking chair in reasonable condition that she felt un-equal to negotiating down the stairs on her own.

When Emily reentered the guest room, Katie had finished remaking the bed and had placed a couple of vases of fresh flowers on the mantel and desk. She appeared to have a gift for flower arranging. Emily added the pillows, which picked up the colors of the rug, and the room was transformed.

"Hey, we make a good team," Katie said. "You know, we could really fix this place up nice with some new wallpaper and stuff. It'd make a great B and B." She darted a look at Emily. "I mean, if you wanted to. But you'd probably rather have your privacy."

Emily was surprised to find a corner of her mind—or per-haps her heart—warming to this idea. "I am a pretty private person, and I certainly don't need the income. But it does seem almost a crime to waste all these rooms." She imagined a young honeymoon couple lounging in the lace-covered four-poster and gazing out on the lawns and the sea as they sipped Katie's coffee—the girl did know how to make coffee—and nibbled at a flaky *pain au chocolat.* "I'll give it some thought."

Marguerite arrived just in time for tea. She left her Peugeot in the drive, doors open, as she hefted a cat carrier in each hand. She set the carriers down in the hall to embrace Emily in continental fashion with a kiss on each cheek. *"Chérie,* you did not tell me you were living in a château! *C'est magnifique!"*

Emily knelt to release Levin and Kitty from their prisons. They blinked up at her and let out welcoming mews. First Levin, then Kitty stepped cautiously out, and the two began to sniff their way around the hall.

Emily wondered if these could really be her own cats. "How on Earth did you keep them so calm? I thought they'd be basket cases after that drive."

"A little pheromone spray works wonders. And I put their blankets in the carriers to smell like home. You should take them out and put them wherever you want *les chats* to sleep."

"I'm sure they'll end up in bed with me, but let's put the blankets in the library for now. That's where I spend most of my waking time."

They set the blankets side by side on the window seat where the afternoon sun streamed in. Levin and Kitty, however, were still occupied in exploring the parlor, whiskers twitching as the cats crept around the perimeter of the room and checked out each piece of furniture. Emily and Marguerite stood in the open double doorway to the library and watched them until Levin, who had taken the shorter route, emerged from behind a sofa to face the door.

He stopped, nostrils working frantically. Then his hackles rose, and he backed up behind the sofa again. "He must smell Bustopher," Emily said. "Bustopher used to sleep in here a lot, though he's been holed up in the kitchen since Agnes—" She stopped, seeing again that indelible picture of Agnes sprawled at the bottom of the stairs.

"Pick Levin up and bring him in. Show him it is safe," Marguerite said. She did the same with Kitty, who had reached the door with similar results.

The cats quivered in the women's arms as Emily and Marguerite carried them around the room. "It's all right, Levin, see? Nobody here but us," Emily crooned, scratching the sleek gray fur in Levin's favorite place behind his ear. She gave Bustopher's chair a wide berth as she moved toward the window seat and deposited Levin on his blanket. Marguerite set Kitty down on hers. The two circled their respective beds, then sat and began grooming each other with intense concentration.

"They will do for now," Marguerite said. "Let us see to this Bustopher Jones in white spats."

But just then Katie came in with a trolley loaded with tea set, sandwiches, petit fours, and scones. "That can wait till after tea," Emily said. "Katie, how did you manage all this so quickly?"

"Well, I did find the scones and petit fours in the pantry. They were wrapped up tight. I hope they're not too stale."

Emily spoke sternly but silently to the lump in her throat, reminding it that Agnes had not died of poison, and even if she had, she would hardly have put it in her own scones. "I'm sure they'll be fine."

Over tea, Emily updated Marguerite on recent events.

"*Mais, chérie, quelle aventure!*" Marguerite exclaimed. "Fate snaps its fingers, so, and you have wealth and romance and mystery all *d'un seul coup.* If I could be in your shoes!"

Emily grimaced. "I wish you were. You might find they pinch a bit. Any one of those things alone would be as much as I care to cope with. It's no joke, Margot—the wealth is a huge responsibility; most of the town depends on me in one way or another. You'd think the romance would be all good, but you can't imagine how it's shaken me, knowing what really happened back then. And as for the mystery"—she put down her half-eaten scone and pushed her plate away—"more people's lives could be at stake. We don't know for sure why Beatrice and Agnes were killed, and therefore we don't know how many other people the killer might think are in his way." She rattled her teacup into its saucer. "Me, for instance."

At last Marguerite's pixie face registered concern. "You, *chérie?* But why? You have had no time to make enemies."

"I've stepped into Beatrice's place, and I've let it be known I intend to carry on in her tradition. Whatever motive led to her death—unless it was something strictly personal, like with Billy, which I really can't swallow—could equally well apply to me."

Marguerite waved an elegant hand. "Bah! I do not believe it. He would not be so bold. These two old ladies, he makes it look like an accident, *non?* Like natural. They are old; old people die, no one thinks twice. But you, *chérie,* in the prime of your life, with you it would not be so easy. And besides, now he is on his guard; he knows he has not fooled *les gendarmes* with this second murder."

"But that's just it. Unless it's one of the people Luke's already questioned, he might not know. Luke's letting the public think

Agnes's death was an accident. And nobody knows we're suspicious about Beatrice."

Marguerite threw up her hands. "So we tell the world! We drop a few discreet hints, and soon the whole town knows. Is not that the way of it in a little village like Stony Beach?"

"We can't do that! I'm sure Luke has his reasons. He knows his job, Margot. I'm not going to work against him."

"Phoo, you are too compliant." She reached for another petit four. "Where is the excitement in a romance if you always do what your lover tells you to do?"

"In this case, he's not my lover; he's the law." Emily felt her face catch fire. "And anyway, he's not my lover at all. Not now."

"I speak in the old sense, like your revered Jane Austen. A lover is one who loves."

One who loves. The words traveled through Emily's veins and warmed her from head to foot. *One who loves.* Present tense. Just when she'd thought everything good and joyful and promising lay in her past, buried along with old secrets. Secrets she'd yet to share with Luke.

But the present wasn't entirely rosy by any means. It held a number of problems, the least of which—but perhaps the most manageable—was Bustopher Jones. "If you're finished, maybe we should go take a look at Bustopher."

Marguerite popped the rest of her petit four into her mouth and licked her fingers sensuously, her pink tongue flicking out to grab the last crumbs and then the whole finger drawn slowly through pursed red lips, her eyes closed in mock ecstasy. Really, it was a pity no man was around to watch. "*Bon.* Lead me to this so-morose cat. We shall see if we can snap him out of his depression."

nineteen

"There are two odious young men who have been staring at me this half hour. . . . They are not coming this way, are they? I hope they are not so impertinent as to follow us. . . . And which way are they gone? One was a very good-looking young man."

—Isabella Thorpe to Catherine Morland,
Northanger Abbey

Katie was working in the kitchen, Lizzie asleep in a sling on her back. Bustopher still crouched under the table, paws invisible beneath him. He shot them a baleful glare from unblinking eyes. A slice of chicken and a mound of tuna lay untouched in his bowl.

"I've tried offering him treats, but he's not interested," Katie said. "He growls if I get close. I guess he needs some time to get used to me."

"He would tolerate you better in any other room but this one," Marguerite told her. "He associates this room with his old mistress. You are an interloper. He may even blame you for her absence."

Seeing Katie's stricken look, Emily put in hastily, "I doubt that. Katie didn't show up until the day after Agnes died. Bustopher was already pretty much catatonic by then."

Marguerite shrugged. "Well, no matter, we will soon put

him right." She knelt, poked her head under the table, and waggled her fingers. "*Allo,* Bustopher Jones. *Moi, je suis Marguerite, l'amie de tous les chats. Voici ce que j'ais pour toi.*" From her pocket she pulled a mouse toy complete with fur and a long leather tail. "*C'est un souris de cataire. Tu aimes beaucoup la cataire, n'est-ce pas?*"

Over her shoulder she said to Emily, "*Les chats* always respond best to *le français.* And to catnip."

She dangled the mouse in front of Bustopher. His nose twitched, but he didn't move. She moved the toy closer, and his whiskers went into a frantic dance. His agony was palpable, as his longing to pounce warred against his firm resolve to play dead with these Wrong Humans.

Marguerite crooned to him. "*Tu sais que tu le veux,* Bustopher. *La cataire, c'est fraîche comme un souris nouveau-né.*" She pulled the mouse back a few inches. "*Saute-toi,* Bustopher! *Avant qu'il s'échappe!*"

At last the catnip won. Bustopher pounced, all claws extended, and tore the mouse from Marguerite's fingers, narrowly missing tearing her flesh as well. Emily watched, amazed and rather alarmed, while the cat fought the toy as though it were a living mouse. At one point the mouse shot across the floor toward the doorway. With all four paws, Bustopher leapt onto it and carried the battle into the hall, then into the dining room.

Marguerite brushed her hands together. "You see, he responds, he is out of the kitchen. He will go crazy for a while until the catnip loses its freshness, then he will be himself again."

Emily quailed to think what that would mean for her own cats. "Maybe we'd better shut him in the dining room for the time being. I don't want him meeting Levin and Kitty in this condition."

Luke phoned as Emily was helping Marguerite get settled in the guest room. (*"Mais c'est charmant, chérie!* All it needs is a little furniture more light, more delicate. Louis Quinze, *peut-être*. You can afford that now, *n'est-ce pas?"*)

Emily took the call in Beatrice's room and stopped Katie with a raised palm as she was about to head back downstairs.

"Hey there, beautiful." Luke sounded just like his teenage self, using his old name for her. "Got some news for you."

"Just a sec." She covered the mouthpiece and whispered to Katie, "Can we handle another person for dinner?"

Katie's eyebrows shot up, but she nodded.

Emily spoke into the phone. "Come tell it to me over dinner. I've got a friend here I want you to meet." As soon as she said that, she regretted it. What was she thinking, introducing her beloved to the most accomplished seductress she knew? But Luke wasn't Marguerite's type. She liked her men suave and continental. More like Brock—or at least like Brock's facade.

"I'd love to come to dinner, but my news is kinda confidential—you know, about the case."

"I'm afraid I've already told Marguerite about the case. I didn't see how it could hurt—she's from Portland. She doesn't know any of the people involved. Except me, of course."

Luke gave an exaggerated huff. "Some assistant! I can't leave you alone for a second without you going blabbing to the first stranger who walks in."

Emily bit back the self-justification that sprang to her lips. If Luke were standing in front of her, she'd see the teasing light in his eyes, the quirk at the corner of his mouth. "You left me alone for most of a day. I had to talk to somebody."

"Well, shame on me. I guess I should be thankful your friend's a woman. But I have been pretty busy. Tell you when I get there."

Marguerite was waiting on the landing when Emily hung up. "That was the lover, *non*? It is written all over your face. When do I get to meet this man who can make my old friend light up like a bride?"

"He's coming to dinner. And none of your tricks, understand?"

"*Moi?*" Marguerite laid her hand over her heart. "I will be more innocent than a child of ten."

"I'll believe that when I see it. I'm going to change."

Emily fixed herself up as well as she could without seeming overdressed for a dinner at home, praying Marguerite would dress discreetly. But when they met downstairs, Emily's heart sank at the sight of Marguerite in a knee-length, boat-necked, form-fitting black silk sheath with a string of pearls, looking far more like Audrey Hepburn than any middle-aged woman had any right to look. Luke would have to be love-blind indeed not to notice how far Emily was outclassed.

"Innocent, you said. A child of ten, you said."

Marguerite spread her hands. "*Mais, chérie,* what did you expect, the pigtails and the pinafore? This is the most innocent dress I have."

That was probably true. Inwardly, Emily cursed the impulse that had led her to invite Marguerite into the vicinity of this fragile relationship, so new and uncertain although it was so old. But she couldn't get out of it now.

Luke arrived punctually at seven, dressed in a crisp dress

shirt and jeans, bearing a bouquet of yellow roses. Emily opened the door to him herself so they could have a moment before she introduced Marguerite.

Looking into his eyes was like seeing love spark there for the first time so long ago. She put up her face to be kissed, and came to only when a thorn pricked her arm.

"We're squishing the flowers," he murmured into her ear.

She buried her face in the blooms and inhaled. "You remembered." Yellow roses had always been her favorite.

"I remember everything." The look he gave her boosted her confidence that it could be safe to introduce him to Marguerite after all. She took his arm and led him into the library.

She watched him carefully as she made the introductions. He certainly noticed Marguerite—he was a man, after all—but his glance didn't linger. He turned back to Emily as soon as courtesy allowed.

"So how do you two know each other?"

"We're in the same department at Reed. Marguerite teaches French. We've been friends for—"

"My whole career," Marguerite finished for her. The real number would give away Marguerite's age, which was a secret more closely guarded than any Emily had ever held.

They made small talk over sherry. Marguerite behaved with admirable restraint, her usually mobile face giving nothing away.

In a few minutes Katie announced dinner. Luke gave a start when she came in but didn't say anything. Emily filed that away to ask him about later.

She was relieved to see that Bustopher had fled the dining room at some point while Katie was preparing it for the meal; Levin and Kitty were closeted in the library, safe from potential attack. Dinner was simple—roast chicken with red potatoes and steamed asparagus—but the chicken was moist, the potatoes subtly flavored with garlic and rosemary, and the thin stalks of asparagus cooked barely to tenderness. And Katie had pulled this off with a baby to tend to. Yes, Emily thought she would do.

When Luke had taken the edge off his appetite, she asked him, "So what about this news?"

He wiped his mouth and took a drink of sauvignon blanc. "Finished up that background check on Brock. Slippery devil. List of jobs long as the Oregon rainy season between acting gigs. Different names here and there—just for fun, apparently, 'cause he's got no criminal record at all. Long and short, he did work as a carpenter or an odd-jobman more than once. So we know he lied about that, anyway."

Emily chewed this information with her chicken. "He lied. But that doesn't necessarily mean he fixed that stair."

"Nope. He's the kind'd lie just to keep our eyes off him. Naturally sneaky. Still, it's suggestive."

Marguerite had listened in uncharacteristic silence, picking at her food but taking long drinks of wine. She refilled her glass for the third time, then looked up at Luke through her impossibly long dark lashes. "*Very* suggestive."

Luke raised an eyebrow, and his mouth quirked.

Emily shot Marguerite a look calculated to set fire to all that wine. "He's sneaky, but he may still be *innocent* of murder." She put an unnatural stress on the word *innocent*. Marguerite wrinkled her nose at her.

Luke cocked his head at Emily, a crease between his brows. It wasn't like her to restate the obvious. She gave him a dazzling smile to distract him. His slow smile in response suggested her diversion had been successful.

Katie brought in dessert—ice-cream sundaes in tall glasses with long spoons. Emily quailed. She'd seen Marguerite eat ice cream. The woman could get a lot of mileage out of her agile pink tongue and full red lips.

Well, Emily's lips might not be quite as full or red as Marguerite's, but she still knew how to use them. And she had a potent memory on her side. Ice cream had been involved the first time she and Luke made love.

She spooned up a bite dripping with sauce and closed her lips around it. She'd expected caramel, but Katie had outdone herself—the sauce was flavored with Grand Marnier. She closed her eyes in ecstasy, then opened them to see Luke gazing at her, his spoon at his lips. The memory had visited him, too.

Emily had no doubt Marguerite was putting on quite a show across the table, but neither Emily nor Luke once glanced at her. They made love to each other without ever touching, just by eating ice cream.

After coffee in the library, Marguerite excused herself with an ostentatious yawn. Emily forgave her trespasses against innocence at once.

She and Luke sat side by side on the love seat, Levin curled on Emily's lap and Kitty on Luke's. The scene was almost unbearably domestic, as if they'd been married for years—except for the undercurrent of leaping passion that ran between them. Luke put an arm around Emily and pulled her close. Before she completely lost her head, however, she remembered to ask him about his reaction to Katie.

"Oh yeah. I didn't want to say anything in front of her—or your friend—but do you realize you're harboring the enemy?

You didn't tell me your new housekeeper was Katie Parker. She's the mayor's niece."

"The mayor's niece?" So maybe Trimble had sent her after all. Emily had dismissed this possibility once she heard Katie's tale of woe.

She tried to reconcile this information with the state of the parental home in which Katie was no longer welcome. "Is there a family feud or something? Katie's parents seem awfully poor. I'd expect a mayor's relatives to be better off."

"Katie's mother married 'beneath her,' as they used to say. Trimble refused to help her, said she made her own bed and she could lie in it. To be fair, he's not so very rich himself—comfortable, sure, but not loaded."

"If that's the case, I wouldn't expect Katie to be very sympathetic toward him."

"You might think that, but the one thing he did do for them was look after Katie. Got her jobs, made sure she finished high school, that sort of thing. He's a sucker for a pretty face."

"So why didn't she go to him when her parents kicked her out?"

Luke shrugged. "That's what I'm wondering. Maybe she did, and he sent her here."

Emily lifted an indignant Levin from her lap and tiptoed to the hall door. It was fully closed, and in that sturdy old house, a closed door was as good as soundproofing. She turned back toward Luke. "I refuse to believe Katie could be spying on me. She's the sweetest girl in the world."

"She might not even know she's spying. Trimble might ask her, all innocent-like, how things are going, and she might tell him—all innocent-like—things we'd prefer he didn't know."

"Such as, for instance, how close you and I are." The words were pulled out of her.

"Yeah. Such as that." He came up to her and put his hands on her shoulders. "That being the case, I think I better go home."

She looked into his eyes, longing to pour herself into them, hating everything that stood between the two of them—the murders, the need for discretion, and not least of all, her own still-unquenchable fear.

He kissed her gently, then she walked him to the front door. "See you at the funeral tomorrow?"

"Right." He kissed her again and left.

twenty

"But what can have been his motive?—what can have induced him to behave so cruelly?"

"A thorough, determined dislike of me—a dislike which
I cannot but attribute in some measure to jealousy."
—Elizabeth Bennet and Mr. Wickham, *Pride and Prejudice*

Marguerite insisted on coming to the funeral. "I must wear my new oh-so-cunning black suit. And the hat with the little veil. And then I must see all these people you tell me about. Oh no, *chérie,* I would not miss this for all the sand on Stony Beach."

Emily resigned herself with little difficulty. After all, she really preferred not to be the center of attention at this event. She preferred to observe.

The small church was about a third full—far from the crowd that had packed it for Beatrice's funeral. Emily suspected that had Agnes's death not occurred so close to Beatrice's—which must give rise to speculation even in minds that had not sus-pected foul play before—the attendance would be limited to herself, Billy, and perhaps a handful of others. Agnes had hardly been one to spread goodwill around the town, and Billy was her only family.

Emily kept an eye on Billy throughout the service. His grief seemed neither feigned nor exaggerated. In fact, he was the only one present other than herself who seemed genuinely sorry Agnes was dead.

The eulogy was brief, Father Stephen lauding Agnes as an "upright" woman and faithful supporter of the church; with all his goodwill, he could hardly muster any warmer praise. The whole thing seemed to be over very quickly. Before Emily could summon a tear, they were standing by the grave.

Billy had purchased the plot next to Beatrice and Horace for Agnes. The dirt over Beatrice's grave was piled haphazardly, as fresh as if it had just been filled in—which in fact it had. The exhumation must have taken place the night before. Emily swallowed and focused on Agnes's coffin, now being lowered into the ground. At least Agnes would be able to rest in peace.

The blank space on Beatrice and Horace's joint headstone reminded Emily she'd not yet decided on an epitaph. She pictured Beatrice bustling about the town and was reminded of the woman described in Proverbs 31, who seemingly never slept as she both brought home the mutton and fried it up in a pan. Emily had always wondered what that woman's husband was doing while she kept so busy. She made a mental note to look up the passage when she got home and choose the perfect verse from it to sum up Beatrice's life.

Marguerite, standing beside Emily, played the scene to the hilt, dabbing a lace-edged black handkerchief at her eye as the coffin was lowered. Emily was reminded of an Edward Gorey illustration to a witty poem by Felicia Lamport about a "peachable widow with consolate eyes."

Brock came up to them when it was over. He addressed Marguerite with a leer thinly veiled by a mask of concern. "I'm so sorry for your loss," he said unctuously. "Agnes was a great old girl. Are you a relative?"

Marguerite gazed at him soulfully. Before she could manufacture some story, Emily put in, "This is my friend Marguerite Grenier from Portland. She never met Agnes. She just likes funerals."

Marguerite shot her a knife-edged glare, but Emily parried it. "Marguerite, this is Brock Runcible. I've told you about him." A pointed look at Brock added, *So don't try to get away with anything.*

Brock gave Marguerite his best show-business smile. "Then we have something in common. I find funerals fascinating. All that raw emotion. Great material for an actor to work with."

"Ah, you are an actor! Have you done any of the great French plays? Molière, Rostand, Genet?"

Brock cleared his throat. "I've concentrated on film, actually. And a little television here and there."

Emily smirked inwardly. Luke had looked up Brock's bio online. He had one film credit, a bit part; the rest was all television.

"You must tell me about it sometime." Marguerite gazed up at him from behind her veil.

"I'd love to take you to lunch and do just that." He tore his eyes from Marguerite and turned to Emily. "I'd invite you, too, Emily, but experience tells me you don't have much interest in eating with me."

A look from Marguerite warned her off, and anyway Emily had an idea Marguerite would get more out of him on her own. "As a matter of fact, I do have other plans. You two go on."

They moved off, Brock's hand on Marguerite's elbow. Definite elbow fetish, that man.

Emily turned to find Luke close behind her. "Hey, beauti-ful," he said. "Didn't want to be too obvious in front of Brock. But I would've stepped in if he got obnoxious. You think it's okay for your friend to go off with him like that?"

"Marguerite has yet to meet the man she couldn't handle. I highly doubt Brock will be that man."

"Good point. Do you really have other plans? Or can I get you to have lunch with me?"

"You are my other plans. Crab Pot? That seems like a place Brock would avoid with a woman he's trying to impress."

Luke drove her in his patrol car, leaving her car at the church. When they got to the Crab Pot, Mayor Trimble and Vicki Landau were already installed at the same table where she'd seen them before. Emily decided to try an experiment.

She walked up to the table. "Mayor Trimble, how nice to see you! I understand I have you to thank for my new housekeeper."

He blinked at her, for once apparently speechless.

"Katie Parker? She is your niece, isn't she? I assumed you sent her. And so promptly, too."

The mayor opened and shut his mouth like a codfish. Emily longed to quote Mary Poppins at him but refrained.

"Well, anyway, she's a great cook. It's a little challenging with the baby and all, but I think she's going to work out just fine."

He mopped his brow, still without a word to say. Emily turned and followed Luke to their usual table.

"That ought to disarm him," she said. "I couldn't quite tell whether he was caught out or just bewildered, but if he *was* planning to spy through Katie, at least he knows we're onto him."

Luke shook his head, grinning. "You are really something,

you know that? I couldn't've pulled off that maneuver in a million years."

Emily laughed. "Stony Beach is bringing out the femme fatale in me." She gave him a sultry look. "Or maybe it's you."

He swallowed. "I know you're bringing out all kinds of things in me. Things I thought were dead and gone years ago. Emily—well, this isn't the time nor place."

Sunny the wizened gnome shuffled up to their table and plunked down two glasses of water.

"Congratulations, Sunny, you did that just like a real waiter. Didn't even have to ask." Luke clapped the gnome on his grubby shoulder. "And I already know what I want to eat. You ready, Em?"

"Crab melt, please." Emboldened by her attack on the mayor, she added, "And could I have a salad instead of the fries?"

Sunny made an indeterminate grumbling noise that Emily decided to interpret in the affirmative.

"Fish and chips for me today. And don't forget the malt vinegar." Luke winked at Emily. "Gotta mix it up every now and then."

Emily swept a glance around the small dining room as Sunny shuffled off. "Do you ever mix it up on a higher level? Like going someplace else for lunch? Or even sitting at a different table?"

"Hey, this was your suggestion, remember? I've tried all the other places in town. This is the best. And I sit at the same table 'cause all the regulars sit at the same tables every day. If I moved, I'd be taking somebody else's spot."

"Sounds a bit boring." Emily had a sudden vision of her life back at Reed. "But I should talk. I've been eating lunch in the same cafeteria for years. Dinner, too, since Philip died. And I usually sit in the same corner by the window, eating one of half a dozen meals." She caught Luke's gaze and held it. "What happened to us, Luke? Remember how adventurous we used to be? How we wanted to travel the world, try everything there was to try? Where did that go?"

He shrugged. "I did end up seeing a bit of the world in the army—stationed in Germany, roamed around Europe on my leaves. But I didn't find anything to keep me there. I was happy to come home to Stony Beach." He played with the tines of his fork. "Or would've been, if you'd been here."

"But even if—you know . . ." She didn't want to talk about that terrible time when they were first apart. "Stony Beach was never home to me. I don't think I could have lived here all those years, even with you. Too much of a cultural backwater. At least it has a decent bookstore now, but no theater, no symphony, no ballet—I need those things, Luke. Like air." She stopped, again confronted by a vision of her recent life. She'd seen student performances and visiting artists on campus, but she hadn't ventured away from Reed for any kind of cultural event since Philip died. "At least I did then."

"You could always go to Portland for that stuff. Take a weekend now and then." He gave a little grin. "I haven't instituted a town-wide lockdown yet."

"That's true. You know, I still haven't gotten used to having money. My first thought when you said that was how expensive it would be—tickets, hotel, restaurants. But that's pocket change to me now." Her interior horizons expanded. "I could have the best of both worlds—culture in Portland, peace and quiet in Stony Beach."

"Any plan that keeps you here most of the time sounds like a good plan to me."

* * *

After lunch, Luke had to go to his office. Emily decided to walk back to her car, strolling through town along the way to visit some of her tenants she hadn't yet met. It was a gorgeous day, sunny with only a refreshing breeze instead of the near-constant bluster, and the summer crowds had begun to gather; Emily dodged strollers, dogs, and oblivious running children as she navigated the sidewalk.

She checked out a couple of gift-cum-antique shops, neither as appealing as Lacey Luxuries nor as appalling as Cash and Carry. Then she came to Sweets by the Sea, which advertised "the best ice cream and saltwater taffy in Stony Beach." That was too tempting to pass up.

She went in and browsed the side aisles, which were full of such factory-made goodies as gourmet jelly beans, fine choco- lates, and Turkish delight. Then she strolled past the bins of taffy, picking up handfuls of cinnamon, caramel, and blueberry cheesecake, a few trial singles of pomegranate, maple bacon, and orange Creamsicle, and a full pound of licorice. Taffy bags in hand, she stood in line for a two-scoop waffle cone—peanut butter and chocolate, and coffee bean—justifying to herself that she would walk it off on the way to the church. And anyway, she deserved it—she'd been a good girl, having salad instead of fries with her crab melt.

The cash register was manned by a bent little woman crouched on a padded stool. She scrabbled for Emily's coins with arthritic fingers bent into birdlike claws. Heavy makeup, no doubt intended to make her look younger than her eighty- something years, only served to accentuate her wrinkled skin and rheumy eyes.

Emily pasted on a smile. "Are you the owner here?"

"That's right. Sixty-two years ago this month I married Jim Sweet. We ran this place together for forty-seven years, till he dropped dead and left me holding the bag. Just like a man." She seemed to regard her husband's death as the last in a long line of selfish and irresponsible actions.

"If you're tired of it, why don't you retire and let your son take over?" Emily nodded toward the middle-aged man serving ice cream alongside a teenaged boy who shared his curly brown hair and receding chin.

"Him?" The old woman gave something between a cackle and a snort. "He's as bad as his father. Be bankrupt in a week if he took over."

"But he's bound to take over eventually. Wouldn't it be better to let him learn while you're still around to help him over the rough spots?" Emily was voicing thoughts she'd been longing to express to Queen Elizabeth II for years.

The old woman peered at her, her claws gripping the countertop. "What's it to you, anyway? He put you up to say that? You his lawyer or something?"

Emily realized she hadn't introduced herself. "I beg your pardon. I must have seemed terribly intrusive. I'm Emily Cavanaugh, your new landlady. I'm naturally concerned with the health of all the businesses that rent from me."

She stared in fascination as the old woman's face transfigured before her into a mask of loathing and spite. "So you're Beatrice's niece, are you? One of them Worthings." She made the name sound the opposite of worthy. "Just as high-handed, just as grubbing, just as set on having everything anyone else wants as all the rest of them, I'll wager. I don't care if you are my landlady; I don't want you in my shop. You can buy your taffy somewhere else from now on." She slammed the register drawer shut and spun her stool till she was looking at the wall.

Emily stood, gaping, unable to credit this display of venom. What could Beatrice possibly have done to deserve this woman's ferocity?

She blinked, shut her mouth, picked up her parcel, and turned to leave the shop. Just as she reached the sidewalk, she felt a presence close behind her.

"Ma'am?" said a young and cracking voice in her ear. She turned to see the boy who'd piled her cone so deliciously high.

He led her out of sight of the shop's windows. "I heard what Granny said to you. Don't mind her, please. She's a little . . ." He made a spinning motion with his finger next to his ear.

"I gathered that. But what could make her hate my family so much? What did Beatrice ever do to her?"

The boy shrugged. "No idea. All I know is it happened way before I was born. Before Dad was born, even. But see, what Granny doesn't know is, Mrs. Runcible was our best customer."

Emily gaped. "But—"

The boy grinned, crinkling cheeks on which freckles vied with pimples for dominance. "She didn't come into the shop. We delivered the stuff to her, me and Dad. The same order every month. Told Granny it was for Agnes Beech."

"An assortment? Or did she have a particular favorite flavor?"

"Some boxed stuff, but the taffy was all licorice." He pointed to her bag. "Seems to run in the family."

Emily extracted a piece of licorice from her bag, unwrapped it, and popped it into her mouth. It was delicious. "This is excellent taffy," she said when her teeth came unstuck again. "Do you make it right here in the shop?"

"Sure do. Granny does it all herself. Well, she lets me help a little now she's got so weak, but she won't let Dad touch it." A flicker of pain washed over his transparent features.

"Well, thank you." She held out her right hand. "I didn't catch your name."

"Matthew." He wiped his hand on his apron and shook.

"Matthew. Perhaps you could continue Beatrice's standing order for me. I'd hate to miss out on this wonderful taffy because your grandmother can't let go of a grudge."

"Sure thing." He gave her a wide grin and vanished back into the shop.

Emily moved down the sidewalk and addressed herself to her cone, which had come perilously close to spilling its contents during all the maneuvers of the past few minutes and was now trickling chocolate down her left hand. She had just gotten all the melted bits under control when she heard Luke's voice from the curb.

"Emily? You better come with me. One of your rentals is on fire."

twenty-one

He was declared to be in debt to every tradesman in the place, and his intrigues, all honored with the title of seduction, had been extended into every tradesman's family.

—*Pride and Prejudice*

Tell me," Emily said as Luke made a U-turn on the highway and headed back toward the south end of town.

"Sprang up out of nowhere around one o'clock. No renter in the house, thank God. Neighbor spotted smoke and called the fire department, who called me. I looked up the address, saw it was one of yours, and came looking for you. You know, you really ought to give me your cell phone number. Could've saved some time."

Emily's arm holding the ice-cream cone jerked. She caught the top scoop just as it was about to plummet onto the floor of the patrol car. "I don't have a cell phone."

He took his eyes off the road and stared at her. "No cell phone?"

"I know, I must be the last person on Earth. I just haven't felt the need for one. We don't get a lot of emergencies in Lit and Lang."

"Starting to look like you might be more prone to emergencies in Stony Beach. You better get one. If I were you, I'd do it today."

"Well, you're not me, and I don't want to." Where had that tone come from? She'd never snapped like that at Luke—had she? "I hate the things. When I'm with someone, I want to be with that person, not on call for all the rest of the world. And when I'm alone, I want to be left alone to think a coherent thought without being interrupted."

"You don't have to give your number to 'all the rest of the world.' You could just give it to me." His voice dropped till she could hardly hear it. "Unless I'm one of the people you don't want to be interrupted by."

"Don't be silly." She transferred her cone and laid her left hand on his arm as it gripped the wheel. "I always want to talk to you."

"So get a phone. For my sake. Not just so I can find you—so you can reach me if . . ." He paused as he turned off the highway onto Cedar Street. "If anything happens."

"Happens? Like what?"

"I don't know what. But I'm starting to worry about you, Em. Everything that's happening is all centered around you."

Emily blanched. So it wasn't her imagination—Luke saw it too. She'd stepped into Beatrice's place, and the storm that had gathered around Beatrice threatened to engulf her as well.

She'd seen the plume of smoke as soon as they turned south. Now she could see the flames licking the sky beyond the roofs of the intervening houses. Luke pulled up across the street, behind the fire engines, and she saw what was left of a small one-story cottage. It looked like a box full of fire, flames leaking out the windows, door, and roof. Firefighters stood around the yard, watching it burn, as others directed hoses to the surrounding trees and the roofs of the houses on either side.

"They've given up, haven't they?"

Luke nodded. "Looks like it."

He strode over to a man in a fire chief's uniform. Emily dropped her cone into a nearby garbage can and followed.

"What's it look like, Dan?"

The chief lifted his helmet, ran a hand over his hair, and settled his helmet back into place. "Whole place went up in no time flat. Looks like arson to me. We'll know more when it burns out and we can investigate."

Arson. The word settled in Emily's stomach like an overcooked dumpling. Unless it was the work of a random pyromaniac, such an act could only be directed toward her. Yet not designed to hurt her—only to cause trouble. To make her feel, perhaps, that being a landlord was more trouble than it was worth. To make her think about selling up and leaving town.

"Have you had many fires in town lately?" she asked the chief.

"First one this season."

Even a pyromaniac had to start somewhere. But Emily's gut told her this was not a random act.

"I better get to work," Luke said to her. "Question all the neighbors."

"I'll come with you."

He steered her out of the chief's earshot, wearing a look she'd seen on his face once before. No. Not this again.

"Em, I can't take you with me. In a case of arson on an insured, uninhabited structure, the first suspect is always the owner. Insurance fraud."

She stared at him. "Why would I burn down my own cottage?

It was in good shape—the accountant said they were all in good shape, with a high rate of occupancy. It would've sold in a minute if I'd wanted to unload it. It must have been worth a lot more to me alive than dead. As it were."

"I know all that. I *know* you didn't do it—heck, you must have been with me when the fire started. But it's procedure. I just can't."

She closed her eyes, willing herself not to explode at him as she had before. It wasn't his fault. He had a job to do. Still, she didn't quite manage to keep the frost out of her voice. "Is there anything I *can* do without trespassing on the province of the almighty law?"

"Tell you what. Go find Marguerite and ask her exactly what times she was with Brock, whether he left her at any point. See if we can rule him out."

"Fine." She gazed north and inland, where she could barely see the cross atop the steeple of St. Bede's winking in the sun. "It's kind of a long walk back to the church from here."

"Oh, right. I'll run you back. Few minutes won't make much difference."

They drove in silence through downtown, then up the hill to St. Bede's, where Emily's PT Cruiser sat alone in the parking lot. Luke put the patrol car in park and set the brake, then turned to her.

"Emily, if this investigation is going to come between you and me—I'd quit my job sooner than let that happen. I can't lose you again. Not when I've just found you after all this time."

Emily couldn't speak right away. Someone had put a balloon in her chest where her heart should be and then blown it up until it threatened to burst through her ribs.

She put up a hand to his cheek. "No. I can't let you do that.

We'll get through this. I've been silly, but I'll pull myself together. You just get on with your job, and I'll do whatever I can without getting in your way."

He pulled her hand to his lips and kissed it, then leaned over and kissed her lips. "I love you, Emily Worthing."

That balloon in her chest had reached her throat. She couldn't answer, though the words *I love you* were straining out her every pore. She told him with a kiss instead.

Emily drove down the hill to the highway and turned north, then on a whim parked in front of the bookstore. She noticed with a pang that the holidaymakers were avoiding the shop in droves.

A bell tinkled as she opened the door. "Be right with you," came Ben's resonant voice from the back room.

Emily browsed, not sure what she was looking for, until Ben came in. "Mrs. Cavanaugh! Nice to see you again. Looking for anything in particular?"

"I'm not sure. Actually, I have a question for you. Has anyone bought a book on fire lately? Or"—she scoured her mind for what little knowledge it contained on the subject of methods of arson—"maybe chemistry? Or electrical wiring?"

Ben gave her a quizzical look. "What's this about?"

"One of my rentals is burning to the ground as we speak. It looks like arson."

He gave a low whistle. "Nobody's bought anything like that. I did notice someone browsing in the home improvement section the other day, but I was up on the ladder and couldn't see who it was. A man, I know that much. He said he was just browsing, so I didn't bother coming down."

"Home improvement." She grimaced. "Hard to call that

suspicious in and of itself. You didn't notice anything about him? Short, tall? Old, young? Bald or hairy?"

He screwed up his eyes. "Not bald, I think. About all I did see was the top of his head. Beyond that, I couldn't say." His mouth quirked in a half smile. "I could tell you the titles of the books I was shelving, but I can't tell you what a customer looked like. Maybe that's why my store's empty most of the time."

She patted his arm. "Don't worry about it. It was just a hunch. But while we're on the subject, do you have anything about fire? How fires start, that type of thing?"

"You know, I think I just might. Over here." He led her to the back of the store to a bookcase marked MISCELLANEOUS. "Couldn't figure out where to put it, but I thought it was fascinating. It's a memoir of a fire investigator." He put a trade paperback with a lurid cover into her hands. The title *Fires I Have Known* stood out in black against a background of leaping flames.

Emily turned it over and glanced at the back cover copy. "Could that customer have looked at this book as well?"

"Possible. I didn't see him over here, but I was directly opposite, with my back turned."

"I'll take it. Maybe it'll give me some ideas."

She paid for the book and drove home, hoping Marguerite would be there before her.

As she turned up the drive, an unfamiliar car swept away from the house and passed her on its way out. Marguerite was waiting for her on the doorstep.

"*Mon Dieu!* That Brock, he has more arms than an octopus! I had to get the hotel manager to drive me back."

"You didn't go to his room? Margot, what were you thinking?"

"I was thinking, I would get more out of him in an atmosphere more *intime* than the restaurant. But he was thinking only what he could get out of me." Her shudder was more like a shimmy.

Emily opened the door. "Come in and have a sherry and tell me all about it."

When they were settled in the library, a cat on each lap, Marguerite began. "We went to Gifts from the Sea for lunch. You know it?"

Emily nodded.

"Not a bad place, for the—how you say?—boondocks. He slipped the garçon a twenty and got us a corner table with a view of the bay. We had a few cocktails—*c'est a dire*, I sipped one Kir Royale while he put back three neat whiskeys. Oh, I gave him the full treatment—the eyes, the lips, the finger on the glass."

"I get the picture, Margot. You don't have to draw it for me."

Marguerite shrugged an eyebrow as if to imply Emily was a poor audience. "I got him to talk about himself—not a great feat; it is his favorite subject. He told me all about his acting career, all the famous people he knows, all the films he has made. He must have been an extra in most of them—I see many films, and I never saw his face on-screen."

"I think you're right about that. The great highlight of his career to date was playing a murderer in an episode of *Abbott*."

"*Exactement*. With the meal, there was wine—one glass for me, the rest of the bottle for him. More flirting, but you do not wish to hear about that. *Enfin*, I contrived to help him forget I am your friend. He told me he does not plan to be an actor much longer. He plans to become *très riche* instead."

"Brock? Rich? How?"

"He was not quite intoxicated enough to spell it out for me.

But he dropped the broad hints that it will have something to do with Stony Beach."

Emily was flabbergasted. The nerve of the man! "So he still thinks he can talk me into going along with the development scheme?"

Marguerite hesitated. "He did not mention you in that context. But he did say, 'I'll be lord of the manor one day. Just you wait. These yokels are going to see some big changes in Stony Beach.'"

A shiver passed over Emily, from her scalp to her toes. "In other words, he plans to get me out of the way. One way or another."

"*Oui, ma bonne amie.* So it would appear."

Emily pulled the blanket from the back of her chair, put it around her shoulders, and hugged Levin so tight, he squirmed. Then she remembered. "I'm supposed to ask you about times. What time did you leave the hotel?"

"Two o'clock."

"Precisely?"

"*Mon Dieu,* I did not measure to the second. I was escaping from a ravening wolf! Somewhere around two o'clock, that is all I can say."

"Well, it doesn't matter. The fire was reported at one."

"Fire? What fire?"

Emily told her about the probable arson. "Was Brock with you the whole time?"

"*Oui.* Except when I went to powder my nose, but that was at the restaurant. Far from here."

"He didn't stop anywhere on the way back to the hotel?"

"*Au contraire,* he drove like one possessed. I am fortunate to be alive."

Emily desperately wanted to pin this fire on Brock. For one thing, it would mean he hoped to get rid of her by means less drastic than murder. "Did you actually see him at the funeral? Before he came up to us at the end, I mean?"

"*Oui,* I noticed him when the service commenced. I always notice a handsome man."

"And he stayed the whole time?"

"*Bien sûr.* I would have remarked it if he had left."

The funeral had started at ten thirty. Far too early for him to have set a fire that wasn't noticed till one o'clock and that then devoured the house in record time. Or at least, so she assumed. Time to read up on *Fires I Have Known.*

· twenty-two ·

Every day at Longbourn was now a day of anxiety; but the most anxious part of each was when the post was expected. . . . Through letters, whatever of good or bad was to be told, would be communicated, and every succeeding day was expected to bring some news of importance.

—*Pride and Prejudice*

Luke came by a few minutes after four o'clock. Marguerite sniffed. "Just like a man, to show up in time for food."

Luke spread his hands. "Hey, give me a break. I didn't know you had tea at four o'clock." He eyed the cake stand with its fragrant muffins and scones. "Have to admit, I could use a cup, though. Interviewing is thirsty work."

Marguerite took Emily's unspoken hint, helped herself, and retired to the parlor with a book. Emily helped Luke handsomely to tea and goodies. "So, what did you find out?"

He finished a bite of a blueberry muffin before answering. "Nobody saw anything suspicious. Pretty much what I expected. Mostly rentals around there, half unoccupied—season doesn't get going full swing till July, when the weather's a little more reliable. Transients don't pay attention to their neighbors like permanent residents would."

"Did anyone see anything at all?"

"One older woman, spends her life on the porch, apparently, says she saw people pass by that house on the way to the beach, but nobody stopped or went in the yard."

"Do the fire people know anything yet?"

"Not yet. Fire's out, but they have to wait for it to cool down before they can investigate."

Emily set her cup down with a clatter. "How can you stand this job? Wait for this, wait for that. Wait for the DNA report, wait for the fire investigation, wait for the autopsy, wait for the background check. Seems like all you do is wait." She saw the consternation on Luke's face and amended. "I don't mean that. I know you work hard. It's just—it all goes so much faster in books."

He gave a bark of laughter. "If books reported a cop's day blow by blow, nobody'd read 'em. Yeah, it's slow, but we do manage to keep busy in the meantime. Don't worry, we'll get there in the end."

He finished his muffin and reached for a currant scone. "Spy or no spy, that Katie can cook. What'd you find out about Brock?"

"His movements are accounted for, as you law enforcement types say, from ten thirty till two."

"Hmm. That's a fair alibi. Fire must've started between noon and one."

"But what if he set it up ahead of time—something that wouldn't go off till midday?" She showed Luke the book she'd been reading. "According to this, there are ways of setting up a fire hours beforehand."

"That's true. Still, if nobody saw him, we'll have a heck of a time proving it. No DNA's going to survive a fire like that."

"Did you ask about the whole morning, or just around the time it started?"

He gave her a look. "I'm not stupid, Em. Whole morning."

"Sorry. I don't think you're stupid, Luke. Honestly. Just a teacher's habit of making sure students have done their research." She stood and paced the length of the fiction bookshelves. A book by G. K. Chesterton caught her eye, and she stopped.

"I wonder . . ." She turned to Luke. "Could you go back and ask people—especially that one old woman on her porch—specifically if they saw anyone in some kind of uniform? Mailman, deliveryman, meter reader?"

He cocked his head at her. "Wouldn't they've mentioned that already?"

"Not necessarily." She pulled out a volume of Father Brown stories. "There's one story in here—*The Invisible Man*—where the murderer turns out to be a postman. Nobody noticed him because he was supposed to be there. He just kind of blended in."

Luke stood and stuffed the last of his scone into his mouth. "Why the hell didn't I think of that?" he mumbled around the crumbs. "Back in half an hour."

When Katie had cleared the tea things and retired to her room to nurse Lizzie, Marguerite decided it was time to introduce Bustopher to Levin and Kitty. "It will be best if they meet on neutral ground," she said to Emily. "The parlor, perhaps? That is not a room Bustopher favors, *n'est-ce pas*?"

Emily used treats to coax Levin and Kitty into the parlor while Marguerite went to the kitchen to fetch Bustopher. She returned, holding him nearly comatose in her arms; he'd finally "caught" his catnip mouse and bitten into it. As Marguerite explained, eating catnip had the opposite effect of smelling it. "He is as mellow as he will ever be right now. Let us see what happens if I put him down."

She laid Bustopher on the floor. Levin and Kitty, ears back, immediately sprang onto the highest surfaces they could find—a windowsill for Kitty, a tall table for Levin. Bustopher blinked and yawned, then his whiskers began to quiver. He followed his nose around the room until he spotted the intruders. Kitty he dismissed almost instantly, but he homed in on Levin. He didn't move, but crouched, muscles taut and nostrils working frantically. The tip of his tail began to twitch.

Levin adopted a similar posture on his table. But Kitty leapt down from the windowsill and crept closer to Bustopher. Intent on Levin, he didn't notice her until she was beside him. She settled on her haunches and licked him behind the ear.

Emily gaped at Marguerite. "Will you look at that?"

"It is not uncommon. She is mothering him. She sensed his pain and wants to comfort him."

Bustopher not only tolerated Kitty's ministrations but broke his stare hold on Levin and rolled onto his side, wrapping his paw around her neck as if they were old friends. Levin sat up and blinked at the two of them, clearly confused by this unexpected truce between his old friend and his new enemy. Was Kitty betraying him or paving the way for him?

At last he, too, jumped down from his perch and approached by cautious degrees to sit a few inches behind Kitty's back. Bustopher glanced at him dismissively, then returned to his blissed-out state. Eventually all three of them subsided into sleep, a cat sandwich with Kitty in the middle.

"So far so good," said Marguerite. "But do not be fooled; it is not over. When Bustopher awakes from his catnip dream and encounters Levin in the library, we may yet see some fireworks."

They went to sit in the library, keeping the parlor door open for the cats. Luke returned around five o'clock. "Bingo," he said. "The porch lady saw a meter reader go toward the backyard early this morning. Couldn't describe him, though. Like you said, man in a uniform, practically invisible."

"Is—or was—there an entrance from the back?"

"That I don't know. Easy enough to find out from the property manager, I guess."

"I'll go talk to them tomorrow." Luke opened his mouth, but Emily held up her palm. "Don't go all official on me again. It's perfectly reasonable for an owner to be looking into a fire on her own property."

"You got me there. And while you're in Tillamook, will you go to the cell phone store?"

She huffed. "All right. If you insist. But I'm getting the no-frills model, and I'm only giving the number to you and Katie and Marguerite."

"No problem." Luke turned to Marguerite. "When you were in Brock's car, did you see anything? Like a pile of clothes, or maybe a bag that could have held clothes?"

"*Mais oui,* there was a what-do-you-call-it? Athletic bag on the passenger seat. He moved it to the back so I could get in."

Luke drummed his fingers on the arm of his chair. "Wonder if it's still there."

"*Non,* he took it into his room when we went back to the hotel." At Luke's raised eyebrows, she added, "*Non,* Monsieur Luke, I do not allow myself to be seduced by suspects. I only wanted him to think I might so I could get him to talk. But he was not interested in talking. So I left."

"Hell. Now I'll have to get a search warrant, and I don't know how I'm gonna show probable cause."

"Couldn't you just go to his room to interview him and casually look in the closet?" Emily said.

"And casually open up his bag? Or casually take it away with me? I don't think that's gonna fly, Em."

"There's always the chance he'll be cooperative."

"Yeah, if he's already dumped the evidence. Still, I guess it can't hurt to try."

He got up and turned to go, then pivoted back again. "Oh, I forgot to tell you—got the results of the autopsy on Beatrice." He paused. Emily appreciated the drama but could have shaken him for keeping her waiting.

"It was arsenic."

twenty-three

"For my own part, I am excessively fond of a cottage; there
is always so much comfort, so much elegance about them. . . .
I advise everybody who is going to build, to build a cottage."
        —Robert Ferrars to Elinor Dashwood, *Sense and Sensibility*

Tuesday morning Emily drove to Tillamook. Marguerite
stayed behind, having decided with characteristic abrupt-
ness that she simply must do some work on her article on the
French Symbolists. She spread out her books and papers in the
library, dressed in an old sweater and jeans and looking every
inch the world-oblivious scholar.

The property management company had its office downtown, not far from accountant Wade Evans and attorney Jamie
MacDougal. In fact, nothing in Tillamook's downtown was
very far from anything else.

The office was abuzz with the aftermath of the fire. "Oh,
Mrs. Cavanaugh, I'm so glad you came in!" said the manager
after Emily had introduced herself. "I just tried to call you. We
need you to sign the claim forms for the fire insurance."

Emily sat across the desk from the manager, a pleasant-
looking woman of about forty who, Emily guessed, was usually

neater in appearance than she was right now—dark blond hair escaping from a loose bun, light blue shirt collar half in, half out of her navy jacket. "Where do I sign?"

"There"—she flipped pages and pointed with her pen—"and there. Thank you so much."

"I wonder if I could ask you a few questions about the cottage that burned."

"Certainly. I assure you, all your cottages are very well maintained. No electrical faults or anything like that. And we checked it after the last tenant left. We always have the places cleaned between tenants, and the cleaner is instructed to make sure appliances are unplugged, heaters off, and all that."

"Excellent. My questions were along different lines. Did the cottage have a back door?"

"Um . . . Let me see . . . I'm not personally familiar with every single property, you understand. I might have a plan somewhere." She stood and flipped through a drawer in the file cabinet behind her desk. "Oh yes, here it is. One Fifty Cedar." She laid a set of drawings in front of Emily.

Emily checked the rear elevation. It showed a door leading into the half basement at the back of the sloping lot. "Do you know how secure this door was?"

"Well, as I say, I'm not personally familiar . . . But Mrs. Runcible insisted on dead bolts for all the outside doors."

Emily frowned over the drawing. Surely even a dead-bolted door could be forced if one didn't care about leaving evidence. If one knew all the evidence would shortly be burned to a cinder.

Emily asked for a copy of the plans just in case they might come in helpful. With the scaled-down photocopies in a folder under her arm, she thanked the manager and turned to leave.

An assistant passed her in the office doorway and whispered something to the manager.

"Mrs. Cavanaugh?" the manager called after her. "I've just been informed—one of your business tenants has given notice."

"Oh, really?" Emily had thought all the downtown businesses were in good health. "Which one?"

"Sweets by the Sea. It seems . . . Well, they're not going out of business." The manager gave a sheepish cough. "It seems they want to move into Mr. Runcible's empty spot. Apparently, Ms. Landau arranged it."

"I see. Well, thank you for telling me. I'm sure we'll find a new tenant soon."

Emily set off for the cell phone shop, which was down the highway back in the direction of Stony Beach. So Brock was a sheep stealer on top of everything else. No big surprise there. Nor was it surprising Mrs. Sweet would jump at a chance to cut off a connection with "one of them Worthings." But it was enlightening that her animosity did not extend to the Runcible bloodline.

Emily felt an itch to get to the bottom of this decades-old mystery. Maybe Luke could help.

She found the cell phone shop but hesitated outside the door, as nervous as if she were going for her first job interview. Why hadn't she asked Luke to come with her? She knew nothing about models, features, prices. Her ignorance just begged a salesman to take unfair advantage.

If only she could call him and ask him to meet her here. But she'd have to buy a cell phone before she could do that. She squared her shoulders and pushed open the door.

She strolled around the shop, keeping close to the walls, examining the displays and trying to look like someone who had a clue. She read the cards describing the features of the different phones, but the words—well, hardly words, more like alphabet soup—meant nothing to her. *3G? 4G? GPS? Android? QWERTY?* Wait a minute, didn't QWERTY apply to typewriters? She thought the tech world had moved beyond that.

"Can I help you?" said a voice from behind the counter. She turned to answer and froze, a pounding like an old manual typewriter filling her chest. The voice belonged to a boy who could almost have been the double of Luke at eighteen.

Emily blinked, swallowed, then managed, "Please. I've never had a cell phone. I don't have a clue what I'm looking at."

He grinned, his mouth quirking up on the opposite side from Luke's. When he came up to her, she saw his eyes were blue, not gray, and his hair was lighter and curlier than Luke's had been. She breathed a little more freely. At least she wasn't hallucinating.

"This is the newest and best model right here," he said, reaching for a sleek black rectangle that looked like what most of her friends kept in their pockets—but not like anything she would call a phone.

"I was thinking of something totally basic. It's for emergency calls only. I don't need all the frills and furbelows."

"Well, we do have last year's model for about half the price." He reached for one that looked nearly identical to the first.

Even his hands were like Luke's, strong with long, square-tipped fingers. Before she could stop herself, she blurted, "Are you related to Luke Richards?"

"Sure. He's my uncle. You know him?"

"We're . . . good friends. I first met him when he was about your age. You look a lot like him."

"Yeah, they all say that. The family, I mean." He looked her up and down out of the corner of his eye, and his expression took on a wary respect. "Did Uncle Luke send you here?"

"He did. But he didn't mention he had a nephew working here."

"Oh, I just started a couple weeks ago. He probably didn't know."

Emily gave him her sweetest smile. "I'm sure he'll be very happy to hear you have a good job and take good care of your customers. What was your name again?"

"Brian." He grinned and threw up his hands. "All right, you win." He led her to the counter and pulled out a tray from the back of the display. It contained an object that reminded Emily of a Star Trek communicator. "This is our most basic, no-frills phone. Just a phone. It's got a kinda lame camera and you can text with it, but that's about all. They don't make 'em any simpler."

"How much?"

"Contract or no-contract?"

Once he had explained what that meant, Emily opted for no-contract and waited while he did mysterious things with the phone. She got him to explain how to make a call and how to answer one. Anything more could wait till she got home and read the manual.

As soon as she was outside the store, she called Luke. "This is your local Luddite, speaking to you under duress from her brand-new cell phone."

"Hey, you got one! Good girl. That didn't hurt too much, did it?"

"I'm sure it would have been more painful except that the clerk turned out to be your nephew. You should've warned me you had a young double walking around the county. Gave me quite a turn."

"Brian's working at the cell phone store? Good for him. Yeah, sorry 'bout that. Never occurred to me you'd run into him. Did he take good care of you?"

"Once he found out I knew you, he did. Before that he was trying to sell me way more than I needed."

Luke chuckled. "Just doing his job. But it's good to know I have a little intimidation power. At least in my own family."

"So, aren't you going to ask for my new number?"

"Don't need to. The phone'll remember it. I'll make a contact for you as soon as we hang up."

That was so much gobbledegook, but presumably he knew what he was talking about. "All right. I'd better head home. Oh, I got the plans for the cottage that burned if you want to see them."

"Absolutely. Stop by the office on your way back, would ya?"

Emily stopped at the large chain grocery store on her way out of town, filling her cart with items from Katie's list and dreaming of all the wonderful things Katie would make with them. When she got to Stony Beach, she remembered she'd forgotten to buy stitch markers, so she pulled up in front of Sheep to Knits. Brock was just coming out of the shop as she approached. Instead of the suit she'd seen him in before, he wore white slacks, a navy double-breasted blazer, and a red ascot in the open neck of his white shirt. Today's role: the gentleman sailor.

"Brock, I didn't know you were a knitter."

"Very funny." He gave her a slightly acid smile. "Just talking to my tenant, like a good landlord."

"I see." Emily recalled with a pang that she'd never followed up on her promise to Beanie to reason with Brock about the rent. The way things were going, he was hardly likely to listen to her, but she had to try. "I hope you're not raising the rent on Beanie. I doubt she can afford it, and this shop needs to continue. It adds some class to the neighborhood."

"Beatrice's rents were ridiculous. Nowhere near what the market will bear. She may have been rich enough to run her business like a charity, but I can't afford to."

"Not even with your new tenant coming in? I find it hard to imagine you'll be charging Mrs. Sweet 'market' rent. She may have hated Beatrice and, consequently, me, but I hardly see her jumping at the chance to—what, double her rent?"

Brock blinked and put up a hand to adjust his ascot. "Mrs. Sweet and I have come to a special arrangement she can well afford." He put on a veneer of compassionate concern, but Emily could see a flicker of prurient interest underneath. "I am sorry, though, to deprive you of a tenant just when you're having other troubles. So sorry to hear about your fire."

"News travels fast in this town."

"I could see the smoke from my hotel. Desk clerk knew all about it. Such a tragedy."

"Hardly that. More of a nuisance. The cottage was insured, and no one was hurt. Good thing it wasn't a windy day, though, or the neighboring houses might have caught—that could have been a tragedy." She put all her professorial sternness into the last phrase, just in case.

Brock, however, was oblivious. "So, I hear it went up pretty quickly?"

"Uncontrollable by the time the fire department got there."

She could have sworn she saw his mouth twitch toward a smile, but he swiftly pulled it back. "Any idea what caused it? Electrical fault, probably, huh?"

"The property manager assures me the wiring was sound

and nothing was left plugged in. I believe the investigators are pursuing possible arson."

Was that a spark of fear in his eyes? If so, he was a good enough actor to quell it. "Arson! Good heavens! Right here in peaceful little Stony Beach?" He furrowed his brow in apparent concern. "Are you sure this place is safe for you? It'd be so easy to just sell out and go back to Portland. Back to your friends, your job, your life. After all, what kind of life can you have in Stony Beach?" His voice was smooth, caressing, almost hypnotizing, like the voice of the Green Lady in *The Silver Chair*.

She dug her nails into her palm to ground herself. "In my experience, the easy road is very seldom the right one. After the fire, I'm more convinced than ever that this town needs me, or at least a person of integrity in my position. Since I don't see anyone like that standing in line to take over, I plan to stay put."

As the words left her lips, she wondered if she had just pronounced her own death sentence.

Brock's face reflected an unsuccessful struggle to decide how to play the rest of this scene. In the end he inclined his head in her direction and strode off.

More shaken than she cared to admit, Emily pushed open the shop door. She could hear a voice cursing vigorously from the back room.

"Beanie?" she called. "It's Emily."

Beanie pushed aside the sixties-style bead curtain that separated her back room from the shop, wiping mascara from her cheeks. "Oh, hi, Emily. He did it. That . . . not-cousin of yours raised my rent. More like shoved it in a rocket and sent it to the moon." She hiccupped on a sob. "I can't do it. I'm going to have to sell up and go back to Portland."

Emily laid a hand on her tattooed arm. "No, you won't. I've

got a place going empty at the end of the month. You can move in there for the same rent you paid Beatrice. I think it's even a little bigger than this one. Where Sweets by the Sea is now."

Beanie gaped at her. "No way. That's prime real estate. You mean it?"

"Absolutely. What would Stony Beach be without a yarn store?"

A wide smile split Beanie's face, and she threw her arms around Emily. "You are *so* my new BFF! How can I ever thank you?"

"No need to thank me. Just let Ben Johnson help you move."

"Ben?" Her pert little nose scrunched. "Bookstore Ben? Why would he want to help me? I've said hello to him, and that's about it."

"Let's just say I think it's time you got better acquainted. You're going to be closer neighbors now, after all."

Beanie shrugged. "Whatever. I mean, he's a hunk and all, but you know he's got to despise what I write. His shop's full of all that highbrow stuff."

"I think you might be surprised at just how eclectic his taste can be."

To cheer Beanie further, Emily bought fifteen balls of the most expensive yarn in the shop—a hand-spun, hand-dyed alpaca-silk blend in a marvelous combination of jewel tones that she thought would look lovely on Katie. Then she threw in enough of the cashmere, in a soft peach, to make a blanket for Lizzie. She locked the yarn in her car—big-city habits die hard—and walked the few blocks to Luke's office.

He met her at the door. "I'm starved. Want to talk over lunch?"

"Fine, but do you want to look at these plans first?"

"Oh, sure." He shoved stacks of papers to the sides of his desk. "Roll 'em out."

She raised an eyebrow at him. "They're plans, not cattle." She spread the photocopies across the desk. "See, here's a back door into the basement. That porch lady wouldn't have been able to see back there, would she?"

Luke shook his head.

"So that supposed meter reader could've broken in there. It was dead-bolted, but if you were going to burn the place, you wouldn't care how much mess you made getting in."

"No, but you'd care how much noise you made. He'd need to either break the jamb or saw around the lock—noisy proposition either way."

"True." Emily chewed her lip. "You said that porch woman was old—was she hard of hearing by any chance?"

"Yeah, kinda. Kept saying, 'Speak up, young man, and don't mumble!' " He chuckled. "Kind of fun being called 'young man.' Don't get that very often anymore. But she could hear me when I did speak up, so I bet she'd hear somebody breaking in. Didn't ask about that, though. Better go back and talk to her again."

"We could stop by there on the way to lunch."

He shot her a sidelong glance as he gathered the photocopies into a stack. "You're a sly one, Emily Worthing. You're just bound and determined to get your toe into this investigation, aren't you?"

She faced him and put her hands up to his chest. "Who, me? I just want to be near you, that's all." She aimed a kiss at his chin.

He dipped his head and caught the kiss on his lips. "Yeah, right. Well, I guess you can come along. But you have to promise not to breathe a word without my say-so."

She stepped back and saluted. "Yes, sir. Lips zipped, sir."

twenty-four

"When a woman has five grown-up daughters, she ought to give over thinking of her own beauty."

"In such cases, a woman has not often much beauty to think of."

—Mrs. and Mr. Bennet, *Pride and Prejudice*

From Luke's office it was only a few blocks to the fire site, but they took the patrol car "'cause it looks more official," as Luke said. Sure enough, the porch lady was on her porch, watching the fire investigator sift through the rubble across the street.

The woman was not as elderly as Emily had expected from Luke's description—probably not more than ten years older than Luke and herself. But she was effectively glued to the porch swing by her enormous bulk—Emily guessed it at around four hundred pounds. Every time the woman pushed off with her toe, the chains holding the swing groaned as if begging to be relieved of their burden. A walker stood to one side of the swing, but Emily feared it would take a hoist to lift her.

"Here you are again, you handsome young hunk," the woman said with a grotesque attempt at coquettishness. "You just sit yourself down. Have a glass of lemonade and some

M&M's." She used her foot to push a small plastic table toward Luke.

Then she caught sight of Emily, hovering on the porch steps. "Oh, I see you brought your lady friend today. Guess that means there's no chance for me." She giggled, causing all her fat rolls and the entire swing to jiggle ominously. "Sorry, sweetie, only got the one extra chair. But you can perch yourself on the porch railing, a little thing like you."

Emily couldn't remember the last time she'd been called "little." It didn't quite measure up to Luke's "handsome young hunk," but she'd take it. She obligingly hopped up onto the broad wooden rail, praying to avoid splinters. This house wasn't as well maintained as the ones she owned.

Luke helped them both to lemonade, forgoing the M&M's. The combination didn't sound appealing to Emily, either, but she thought the lemonade would be welcome on this warm day. Then she tasted it. This was adult lemonade. She set the glass down on the rail beside her.

"I've got just a couple more questions for you, Miss Barnes." Luke pitched his voice just south of a yell.

"Ask away, dear boy. I've got all the time in the world." She made a toasting motion with her glass and drank deeply.

"We talked about what you saw yesterday. But I never asked you what you heard."

"Well, now, that's an interesting question. What did I hear?" She cocked her head this way and that as if reliving the sounds of the previous day. "I heard the ocean."

"Yes, ma'am, I'd expect that." Luke shot a twinkle toward Emily.

"I believe I heard a bird or two, though the birds don't seem to sing near as much as they used to. All they do now is squawk."

Emily nodded along with Luke. The more pleasant varieties of birdsong would be lost to failing ears.

"Heard some kids yelling across the way. Dog barking. Somebody left their dog behind when they went to the beach, can you believe it? Dang thing barked its head off for an hour."

"Anything out of the ordinary?" Emily admired Luke's patience, but he would have to work Miss Barnes around to the point eventually.

"I believe there was a crew working on a house a block over. Lots of banging, sawing, that kind of thing. On and off all morning. They quit and came over to gawk when the fire got going."

Luke shot a significant look at Emily. Now they were getting somewhere.

"Any of that building noise sound like it might be closer than the rest?"

The porch lady made a moue with her fleshy lips. "Now, there I'm afraid I just can't help you. I can tell you *what* I'm hearing good as anybody, but just exactly where it's coming from—that's beyond my gift."

"Well, thank you, Miss Barnes. You've been very helpful." Luke stood and took a long swig of his lemonade before Emily could think of how to stop him. His eyes bulged and he coughed, but he set down the glass with aplomb. "And thank you for the lemonade. Very refreshing."

"Thank you, Miss Barnes." Emily supposed the ban on speech did not extend to the basic pleasantries.

Once they were safely in the patrol car, they both burst out laughing. "Oh my word!" Luke said. "I'm not sure now I oughta believe a word she says. She might be hallucinating if she drinks that stuff all day long."

"It was pretty early in the morning when she saw the meter reader. She couldn't have been too drunk yet."

"True. And she didn't seem drunk just now. Guess she can take a lot of liquor with a size like that."

"And she probably wouldn't hallucinate builders. Unless she just wanted to drool over a bunch of 'handsome young hunks' like you." She gave him a playful poke.

"You should talk, you sweet 'little thing.'" He poked her back. "But no, I saw those guys myself, I just didn't connect the dots. Anybody who wanted to break into your house would've had plenty of cover, noise-wise."

"Should we see what the investigator's come up with?"

"Sure thing." Luke nosed the SUV down the street twenty yards solely to justify having gotten into it in the first place.

"How's it look, Bob?" he called to the top of a man's head. The man must have been standing on the floor of the half basement the back door had led into.

"That you, Luke?" The head moved back till Bob could look up and see them. "Come on down here. Got something to show you."

Emily followed Luke down the steep slope of the side yard, then picked her way over the charred remains of the back wall, wishing she'd worn pants and sensible shoes.

Luke introduced her as the landlady, and Bob gave her a nod.

"See here?" Bob pointed to a rough-edged ring in the middle of the cement floor that was blacker than everything around it. "I'd bet my badge it started right here. Classic pile of oily rags, more'n likely. Traces of accelerant just here, not in the rest of the house."

"That'd go up quick, would it?"

"Pretty quick. This back part being lower, it'd take a little while before anyone'd see smoke from the street—by then the fire'd be going pretty good."

Luke scratched his jaw, poking rubble with the toe of his boot. "Oily rags. Any way that could be set up ahead of time? To start when the arsonist was long gone?"

Emily bounced on her toes, longing to shoot up her hand like Hermione Granger. She'd read about just such a scenario in *Fires I Have Known.* But she assumed she was still bound to silence.

"Sure thing. Classic method. Stick a tall candle to the floor with some wax, pile the rags around it, light the candle. Candle burns down to the rags and boom. You got the prettiest little fire you'd ever want to see. Big enough candle, you could be across the state line when it hits."

He knelt down and with his gloved hand picked at something shiny amid the charcoal. A nail. He tossed it aside and stood. "That is, assuming you're not the kind of arsonist who does it for fun. That case, you'd want to hang around and watch."

"We're not thinking pyromaniac on this one. More like an attempt to cause trouble for Emily."

"I guess he succeeded there. Sorry for your loss, ma'am."

Emily waved a hand. "It's not like I was attached to the place—I'd never even seen it. I can always rebuild, or even sell the property. I'm just glad no one was hurt."

Bob cut narrowed eyes from her to Luke, and Emily wondered if she'd sounded too cavalier—too much like an owner-arsonist. But it didn't matter what Bob thought. It might be his job to determine how the fire started, but it was Luke's job to figure out who lit the match.

* * *

When Luke and Emily walked into the Crab Pot, Mayor Trimble and Vicki Landau were at their usual table, but not exhibiting their usual demeanor—boisterously friendly on his side, icy-smooth on hers. Instead they leaned over the table, heads close, whispering at each other with all the force of a steam boiler about to blow.

"Trouble in River City?" Emily murmured to Luke as they took their seats.

"Lovers' quarrel or conspirators', I wonder? Keep your eyes peeled and see if you can catch anything."

Emily made a show of perusing her menu while straining her ears toward the other table. She thought she caught the word *Brock* a time or two but couldn't be sure. He was on her mind anyway, so she couldn't trust herself not to be making it up.

Just when further menu perusal seemed impossible to justify, the mayor and Vicki left the restaurant. Vicki strode ahead of Trimble, her blond mass of hair vibrating with fury, and he followed, dragging his feet.

"Whew! I didn't know how much longer I could keep that up," Emily said. "Did you catch anything?"

"Nothing I could swear to in a court of law."

"Me neither. But I'd wager it's business, not personal. I mean, she was by far the angrier, and of the pair of them, who's likelier to betray whom? But I have to pity him, being on the receiving end of her tongue. How can anybody get that riled up over money?"

Luke shook his head. Sunny shuffled up, took their order as if it were his death sentence, then shuffled off again. The

thought of *death sentence* reminded Emily of her recent conversation with Brock. She related its highlights to Luke.

"Sounds like he was pretty interested in the fire."

"More than a sympathetic interest, I'd say. And he tried
hard to convince me it was time to throw in the landlord towel
and vamoose."

Luke slammed his water glass onto the table. "I know in my
bones he started that fire. He's an actor—he'd know how to look
like a meter reader, how to make himself up in case anyone got
a good look at him. And with his background, he could easily
know how to break into a house and start a delayed fire. But
I can't prove it."

"What about the bag of clothes? Have you given up on that?"

"Oh, forgot to tell you. I went by his hotel last night after
dinner. The bag was sitting in the open closet, all innocent-like,
so I asked him, all innocent-like, if I could take a look. He said
go ahead."

"And?"

"It was empty. We gave him too much time. He dumped the
evidence."

"Well, he must have dumped it somewhere, right? Is there
a fireplace in his room?"

Luke gave a bark of laughter. "We're not talking about the
Ritz here, Em. No fireplace."

"Does the hotel have an incinerator? Or a Dumpster?"

"No incinerator. Got a couple of my guys to go through the
Dumpster. Nothing."

She drummed her fingers on the tabletop. "What about
the laundry?"

"He wouldn't be that stupid. If he sent stuff to the hotel
laundry, we could trace it right back to him."

"If, as you say, it's not the Ritz, they probably don't collect guests' laundry—just have machines on-site somewhere for people to use. He could shove the stuff into a machine when no one was looking and just walk away. How could you trace that?"

"If he was careful not to leave fingerprints—and if he turned on the washer—any DNA would be gone." Luke gazed at Emily with a new kind of admiration. "You're not so shabby at this, you know?"

She felt herself blush like the schoolgirl he had long ago called beautiful. This praise was even more welcome.

Then reality hit. "But if that's what he did, we're back where we started from. No evidence."

"Unless somebody saw him. Or he wasn't quite as careful as he should've been."

Sunny shuffled up and tipped two laden plates onto their table. Luke looked longingly at his burger and then picked it up in a paper napkin. "Time's of the essence on this one, Em. I'm gonna have to eat and run. See you back at the ranch?"

"All right." Her car was a short walk away.

Emily ate her sandwich and then headed back to Windy Corner. She'd used her new cell phone to let Katie know she wouldn't be home for lunch, so Marguerite was finishing a lei-surely if lonely repast when Emily came in. "Such a wonderful hostess you are, *chérie*, to leave your guest alone for luncheon. Is there such superb food in Stony Beach that you can forgo Katie's cooking without a pang?"

"It wasn't the food. It was the case. Luke actually let me go with him on an interview." She told Marguerite about the porch lady and her lemonade.

Marguerite laughed until she had to wipe her eyes. "Ah,

I should have liked to be there. She sounds like quite a character. And did you find out anything useful?"

"Only that Brock could easily have set the fire, but we have no evidence to prove it."

"Evidence. Pah!" Marguerite snapped her fingers. "The man is guilty, *évidemment*. What more do you need?"

"Luke needs some evidence even to arrest him, and a whole lot more to get him convicted. This is America, Margot. Still at least nominally a free country."

"You need evidence? So create some. There is no doubt a hair of his on my so-lovely black suit, after he pawed me in the hotel. Take it and plant it wherever you like."

"Margot!" Emily was genuinely shocked. "Luke would never do that! He plays by the rules, and even if he would stoop to such a thing, it could cost him his job."

"So you do it. And do not, how you say, spill the beans."

"No. No way. Honestly, Marguerite—what if we did that and he turned out to be innocent? Would you send an innocent man to prison?"

Marguerite sipped her coffee as if the murder and mayhem were a million miles away. "Whatever that man is, innocent he is not. He may not have committed a crime according to the law, but he deserves whatever he gets."

Emily threw up her hands, literally and figuratively. "You are impossible. Thank God you're not directly involved."

She poured herself a cup of coffee from the pot on the sideboard. "How was your morning? Did you make any progress on your article?"

"*Mais oui,* it is finished, except for a few things I will have to look up when I get back to Reed. That library of yours, it has some magic in it. *Très bien* for focusing the thoughts. When I was finished, I played with *les chats*. You will see they are getting to be quite good friends now, even with Bustopher out of his catnip stupor."

"He'll even let them in the library with him?"

"*Oui,* as long as they stay out of his particular chair."

"That's a relief. I was afraid I'd have to choose between my own cats and my library for the length of Bustopher's life." That would have taken much of the joy out of living at Windy Corner.

Marguerite gave her a shrewd look. "So, you will stay at Windy Corner indefinitely? You will leave me alone to handle all those men in Lit and Lang on my own?"

"You know you love it. All the more attention for you," Emily teased, but then grew serious. Had her heart in fact made that decision without giving her head a chance to intervene?

twenty-five

"Mr. Elliot is a man without heart or conscience; a design-
ing, wary, cold-blooded being, who thinks only of himself;
who for his own interest or ease, would be guilty of any
cruelty, or any treachery, that could be perpetrated without
risk of his general character. . . . Oh! he is black at heart,
hollow and black!"

—Mrs. Smith to Anne Elliot, *Persuasion*

After lunch the sun was so warm and the breeze so mild,
Marguerite decided to lie on the beach. As a good Portlander, she held to the motto *carpe sole*—seize the sun. Emily's
fair complexion had never been conducive to sunbathing, and
she wanted to be available when Luke returned from his fishing expedition. She took *Persuasion* onto the shaded terrace,
along with a bowl of taffy.

Soon the tribulations and adventures of Anne Elliot blocked
out all the engrossing dilemmas of Emily's real world. Captain
Wentworth's attitude gradually shifted from disdainful to
concerned to vaguely jealous of Mr. Elliot's attentions at Lyme,
then to admiration and reliance on Anne's cool head and com-
petence when Louisa took her fall. Then, abruptly, Wentworth
was out of the picture, and Mr. Elliot loomed in his place.

Mr. Elliot, the handsome, suave, and plausible, the oh-so-
complimentary, and all the time scheming to get his hands on

his inheritance a little faster and to ensure it would not be snatched from his grasp. Soon Emily found her imagination had endowed the young Mr. Elliot with a more mature face and a rather less plausible manner: in short, the face and manner of Brock Runcible.

It was obvious Brock was trying to get his hands on the whole of Beatrice's property. That explained his advances to Emily when they first met, and when those failed, his suggestions of partnership in their business affairs. Veronica Lacey's implication that he'd expected to inherit more from Beatrice than in fact he had done. Brock's hints to Marguerite that he predicted wealth in his own future. It all fit together.

If he wanted the property that badly—and had expected to come by it automatically through her will—what was to stop him from hastening the day by getting rid of Beatrice?

Mr. William Elliot was not a murderer (at least not known to be; who knew what had really happened to his wife?). But then he didn't need to be. He had money already and wanted only a title. If Sir Walter Elliot, the incumbent baronet, had announced his engagement to Mrs. Clay, thus making a new heir possible, Emily felt certain the baronet's life would not have been worth a day's purchase. Some poison absorbed through the skin would have been added to the creams with which he attempted to preserve his youthful complexion, and Sir William would have replaced Sir Walter, with or without an Elliot wife at his side.

But *how* could Brock have done it? She still needed proof. She could hardly convince a jury of Brock's guilt by merely drawing parallels between him and a fictional villain.

She was musing on this when Luke walked around the corner of the house. "Katie told me you were out here."

"Luke, listen. I think I've figured it out." She told him her deductions based on *Persuasion*.

Luke sat beside her, listening attentively but with a growing expression of skepticism. "Emily, you can't accuse a man based on a book. So what if he reminds you of this Elliot guy? That doesn't make him guilty."

"No, of course not, but don't you see? It all fits. It all points to Brock." She laid the book down with a sigh. "Did you find anything in the laundry?"

"Nope. No uniform, no complaints about an abandoned load in a washer, nothing turned in to the lost and found."

Emily's spirits sank, but whether because of the dead end itself or because her hunch had not been borne out, she couldn't say. "I guess I'm not such a brilliant detective as you thought."

"Hey, ninety percent of leads we follow don't pan out." He squeezed her shoulder. "Don't kick yourself. It was still a good idea."

"Maybe it was a real meter reader after all. Maybe we're imagining this whole thing."

"Nah. I checked with the power company. They didn't send anybody out yesterday. He's our man, all right. We just have to nail him."

Emily passed him the bowl of taffy. "Have a piece. It'll help us think." She recalled her visit to Sweets by the Sea and the news of their impending move into Brock's property. "Say, I meant to ask you. Do you have any idea why old Mrs. Sweet hates Beatrice so much?"

"Mrs. Sweet . . . let me think. . . . That goes back way before my time, but I think my grandmother said something about it once. She's a great one for local gossip, my granny." He unwrapped a piece of peanut-butter-and-chocolate and chewed it thoughtfully. "Can't remember what it was. I just know it happened before I was born, back when they were both young."

Emily stared. "Over fifty—sixty years ago? And she still hates her?"

"You wouldn't believe how long some people can nurse a grudge. 'Specially if it dates back to adolescence. Anything happens then gets kind of seared into you, y'know? Hard to let it go."

Emily gazed at his profile, her mind's eye stripping away the roughened, slightly sagging skin to reveal his youthful ruddy complexion. She said softly, "I know."

He turned to her, his gray eyes dark with emotion. She could see words springing to his lips that she longed to hear—but not quite yet.

Just then Marguerite's head appeared as she climbed up the hill from the beach. *"Bonjour, Monsieur* Luke."

"Good afternoon." Emily watched Luke through narrowed eyes as he took in Marguerite's appearance. She'd thrown a loose cover-up over her swimsuit but was still showing quite a few inches of very shapely leg. After one quick look, Luke kept his focus on Marguerite's face.

"So, how goes the sleuthing?" Marguerite asked, helping herself to a swig from Emily's iced tea. "Have you found your precious evidence?"

"Not yet, I'm afraid. No sign of that uniform," Luke replied. "How was the beach?"

"Very pleasant. Lying in the sand, watching the little sailboats so far away—most relaxing."

A light went on in Emily's brain. "Sailboat! That's it!"

Luke raised an eyebrow at her. "What is this, a word game? Sailboat?"

"When I saw Brock this morning, he was dressed for sailing. What if he went out yesterday, too? What if he dumped the uniform into the ocean?"

"Then you would be one brilliant lady. And we'd be just as stuck as we were before. Unless somebody saw him, which is about as likely as my chief's budget getting approved."

"He would've had to rent a boat somewhere. Whoever rented him the boat might have at least seen him take the stuff on board."

"Worth a try, I guess." He hauled himself to his feet. "Who'd have my job?"

Emily sang a snatch from *The Pirates of Penzance*: "*When constabulary duty's to be done, to be done, a policeman's lot is not a happy one.*"

He laughed. "That's catchy. You just make that up?"

"Me? That's Gilbert and Sullivan. Haven't you ever seen *The Pirates of Penzance*?"

"Can't say I have. Is it on Netflix?"

"It's an operetta. Well, there is a movie of it, so I guess it could be on Netflix. We'll have to look for it sometime. You'll love it. Though I see you more as the pirate king than the head constable."

"I'm not sure if that's a compliment or an insult."

"Oh, a compliment. You'll see. He's not one of your more bloodthirsty pirates. And the constable is a total wuss."

Luke grinned. "Well, I'm glad you don't see me as a wuss, anyway." He bent to kiss her.

"Do not mind me. I am not here at all, oh no." Marguerite's voice cut between them.

"Sorry." He straightened, then aimed a continental bow toward Marguerite. "Good day to you, Mademoiselle Grenier."

Luke turned to leave but then hesitated and pivoted back to face Emily. "Come with me?"

She sprang to her feet. "You don't mind, do you, Margot?"

"*Moi? Mais non,* I shall amuse myself *avec les chats* and your so-marvelous library. But do come back for dinner, will you? I do not care to dine alone."

"Of course." Emily felt a pang at being such a poor hostess, but then Marguerite had essentially invited herself at what she knew was not a relaxing time for Emily. And anyway, Marguerite had encouraged her to pursue a relationship with Luke—how could she do that without spending time with him?

The harbor was on the far south end of town, where the beach ended and Tillamook Bay began. Rough-shingled houses of fishermen clustered on the east side of the highway, which ran close to the marina. At this midafternoon hour, boat traffic was light; the fishing boats had gone out in the early morning and returned before noon, while most of the pleasure boats had gone out some hours before and would not return till near sunset.

Luke parked the patrol car, and they strolled along the dock. Emily breathed in the marine atmosphere, the rank but exhilarating compound of salt water, paint, and fish; the incessant cries of the gulls and the slow slap of waves against boat hulls. The fishing boats and motorboats did not much interest her, but she loved the sleek lines of the sailboats, their elegance and grace, their promise of freedom. She hadn't been out on one since her last summer in Stony Beach—with Luke. She stole a glance at him—the smile playing about his mouth told her he was remembering too. She slipped her hand into his and squeezed.

They stopped in front of a large, crudely lettered sign that read, JOES BOAT'S. RENT BY THE OUR OR DAY. Emily longed to grab the errant apostrophe and place it in *Joe's* where it belonged; but the missing *h* was nowhere to be found.

Lounging next to the sign on a rickety wooden chair was a man for whom the term *old salt* might have been invented. Emily wondered whether he cultivated the image: navy peacoat, leathery skin, a few wisps of white hair under a filthy cap, pipe clenched in his blackened teeth.

"Hey there, Joe," said Luke. "How's business?"

Joe extracted the pipe from between his teeth and stared at it as if the pipe had spoken rather than Luke. Then he replaced it in his mouth and spoke around it. "Can't complain, can't complain. Tourists get stupider every year, but I can't complain."

"What've they done now?" Luke winked at Emily as he leaned back against the railing opposite Joe.

"Couple yesterday took out my best sloop, the *Marianne*, and didn't get back till almost dark. Coulda wrecked her. Came back today, but I said no way—go rent from Sammy." He jerked his head toward a younger man washing the deck of a small boat fifty yards away. "He don't care what kind of idiots take his boats, long as he gets their money. Told 'em that to their face." He gave a wheezy chuckle. "If looks could kill."

Luke shot Emily a sidelong glance. "What'd this couple look like? Did they give a name?"

Joe snorted. "Mr. and Mrs. Smith. If they were married, I'll eat my hat." He chewed on his pipe, eyes on the horizon. "Fella was tall, dark, movie-star type. Even had on one of them whaddy-acallits 'round his neck."

"An ascot?" Emily put in.

"That's the bugger. Gal was a looker, though." He sketched

an hourglass shape with his hands. "Blonde. Little scrap of a skirt over a bikini." He whistled. "Some legs."

"What time did they go out?"

"Latish. 'Round about this time, I guess."

"Have any gear with them?"

Joe lifted his cap to scratch at his bald scalp. "Lemme see now. . . . Gal had a basket, like one o' them fancy picnic baskets, all fitted out. Couple bottles of champagne sticking out the sides. Guess that's what kept them so late." He wheezed again.

"Was the man carrying anything?"

"Some bag. Towels and such, I reckon."

"Athletic bag? Blue with a white swoosh on the side?"

Joe squinted into the lowering sun. "Now that you mention it, believe it was. Matched his jacket and pants." He wheezed so hard, Emily was tempted to thump his back. "Said to myself, 'Now, there's a fella knows more about lookin' like a sailor than bein' one.'"

"Why'd you rent to him if you didn't think he could handle the boat?"

Joe shrugged. "Said he had experience. Anyway, I need the money. Savin' up to retire. He wrecks the boat, I get the insurance. Can't lose either way."

Emily wondered what that retirement would look like. For many men, playing around with boats was the dream retirement they saved up for as they slaved in an office for forty years.

Luke clapped the old man on the shoulder. "Thanks a bunch, Joe. Have one on me." He slipped a five-dollar bill into the pocket of Joe's ancient shirt.

"Don't mind if I do." He hauled himself to his feet and shuffled off in the direction of a decrepit tavern at the far end of the marina.

Luke turned to Emily. "Looks like you were right. I'd take that description of Brock to a lineup any day of the week."

She nodded. "I wonder who the woman was? I haven't seen Brock with anyone other than Marguerite."

"Who knows? Good-looking blonde doesn't narrow it down very far. Anyway, it's Brock we're after. If he wants to mix business with pleasure, that's his affair."

"I wonder. I keep getting the feeling there's a brain behind all this that's better than Brock's."

"Could be, but a good-looking blonde?"

"Brains are approximately evenly distributed among genders and hair colors, Mr. Clever Policeman. Marilyn Monroe and Jayne Mansfield were both well-endowed with brains as well as their more obvious assets."

"Point taken." He put his hands on her waist and smiled. "I guess I thought redheads had a monopoly on the brains-and-beauty combo."

She gave him the kiss he was clearly asking for. "I guess you're forgiven."

He returned the kiss with interest and then said low in her ear, "Can I tempt you into my lair this evening? We could look on Netflix for that pirate movie."

Emily's body longed to say yes, but her conscience shook a stern finger at her. "I can't, Luke. I promised Marguerite I'd be home for dinner, and I really should stick around after that. I've been neglecting her all day."

He sighed, pulled her tight against him and then let her go. "Rain check?"

"Rain check." She hadn't made any promises about when he might cash that rain check in.

twenty-six

"What glorious weather for the Admiral and my sister!
They meant to take a long drive this morning . . . I wonder
whereabouts they will upset to-day. Oh! it does happen very
often, I assure you—but my sister makes nothing of it; she
would as lieve be tossed out as not."

Captain Wentworth to Louisa Musgrove,
Persuasion

The next morning, Marguerite demanded to go sightseeing.
"I have seen your so-lovely house and your beach, but
nothing else have I seen. I look on the Internet and see there is
much cheese made in this Tillamook, yes? It is *sans doute* infe-
rior to *le fromage français,* but I will taste it nevertheless. You
will take me to the Blue Heron and the Tillamook Cheese Fac-
tory, and then we will drive to the lighthouse at, where is it,
Cape Meares, yes? I wish to see this lighthouse and this so-
peculiar octopus tree. Then I will consider you have done your
hostess duty. I have done my duty as cat whisperer, so then
I shall think about going home."

Emily didn't greatly mind. There seemed to be nothing
more she could do to help Luke at this point, and she was quite
fond of cheese and lighthouses herself.

The cheese factories left Emily satisfied, with plenty of
delicacies to take home, and Marguerite smug in the confirma-

tion of the superiority of French cheese. The drive to Cape Meares was lovely, first following the outer edge of Tillamook Bay and then turning inland through rolling forested land, tending gradually uphill to the fingerlike promontory that held the lighthouse. They parked at the base of the finger and walked downhill along the trail to the tip, stopping to admire the views of ocean and spruce forest along the way. Marguerite was disappointed not to see any whales, but the oddity of the Octopus Tree, a gigantic spruce with multiple trunks that spread out at the base before soaring skyward, seemed adequate compensation.

Emily steered the PT Cruiser out of the parking area and back along the access road to the main highway. Marguerite, replete with cheese and fresh air, dozed beside her. Soon the road took a sharp dip off the height of the promontory. Emily put her foot on the brake as the car began to accelerate. Nothing happened.

She pumped the brakes. Still nothing. She shifted into second gear; the engine whined but continued to accelerate. The sour taste of panic rose in her throat as she gripped the wheel. She'd had the car checked over just a few weeks ago, before she left Portland. What could be wrong?

The road curved gently, with little oncoming traffic. Her knuckles went white as she concentrated on keeping the car on the pavement. There was no shoulder to speak of; if she swerved from the asphalt, she would shortly find herself up close and personal with a towering spruce.

She'd been going about forty miles per hour when she started the descent. From the corner of her eye she watched the speedometer climb to fifty, sixty, seventy. The road bore more sharply to the right—a curve she would, for choice, have taken at forty. Her pulse whooshed in her ears as she careened around the bend. But up ahead—oh, blessed relief, the road took a final dip and then headed uphill again. If she could just make it through that dip without bouncing off the road, she'd have gravity on her side. She'd have a chance.

The wheels stayed on the road as she jounced across the dip at seventy-five, then zoomed up the other side. *Let this hill be long enough to slow us completely.* The slope was much less steep on this side, but longer. Down to sixty, fifty, forty. At the top of the hill a turnout led into a grassy area that sloped up from right to left. Her mouth dry with relief, Emily steered into the turnout, shoved the gearshift into first, then made a sharp left turn, ran the car up onto the grass, and yanked on the emergency brake, praying the car would stop before it hit the trees.

When she thought the steering wheel would crack from the pressure of her grip, the Cruiser finally skidded to a halt with the front bumper kissing up to a giant spruce trunk. The bumper might be dented, but at least Emily and Marguerite were not.

Marguerite awoke, sputtering. *"Qu'est-ce qui se passe?* Where are we?"

"The brakes failed. We could easily have been killed. You just slept through the most brilliant bit of driving you were ever likely to see."

"Mon Dieu!" Marguerite put her hand to her chest, rolling her eyes. "I came here to relax. If I had wanted this kind of adventure, I would have gone to the Alps!"

Emily rooted in her purse till she found her cell phone. Luke's insistence on the hated device now seemed providential. With shaking fingers, she punched in his number.

"Holy crap!" he said when she'd told him what happened. "Where are you?"

She gave him her location as best she could.

"I'll be there as quick as I can. You're not hurt?"

"No. Just shaken up."

"No ambulance then, just me and a tow truck. Take about half an hour, though—you okay for that long? I could send someone from Tillamook a lot faster."

"No, I'd rather have you. We'll be okay."

"Better get out of the car, just in case."

"Right." She hung up and opened the door, then leaned there until her legs stopped shaking enough to walk. She and Marguerite found a fallen tree to sit on a few yards away from the car. But Emily couldn't stop her teeth from chattering, though the day was warm.

Marguerite cast a shrewd glance at her, then went back to the car and opened the back doors and the trunk. She came back with a ragged wool blanket and wrapped it around Emily's shoulders.

After a few minutes the shaking subsided, and Emily felt limp and exhausted. She sagged against Marguerite's shoulder. Would Luke never come?

Then suddenly he was there, raising her to her feet and holding her tight, murmuring unintelligibly into her ear. She must have fallen asleep. She'd been in hell, reliving the terrifying descent in her dreams with a series of endings, each bloodier than the last. In Luke's arms she was at peace.

Luke directed the tow truck to his favorite garage in Tillamook and drove Emily and Marguerite home. Emily dozed again through the drive. Luke got her settled in the library with a blanket and a cat, then asked Katie to bring in some cocoa. After a few sips, Emily had revived enough to talk.

"When's the last time you had your brakes checked?" Luke asked.

"Couple of weeks ago. They were fine."

"So we're looking at deliberate sabotage."

"Looks like it to me."

Luke stood and paced the length of the room. "You could've been killed today. Somebody is out to get rid of you. The fire wasn't enough to scare you off, so the next step is murder." He stopped in front of her and frowned down into her face. "Emily, I want you to go back to Portland. Stay with Marguerite for a while—you shouldn't be alone."

"What good would that do? If they're that set on getting rid of me, they could do it just as easily in Portland. Maybe easier."

"Well, you might be right about that. But I've got to do something to keep you safe." He scrubbed his hands over his stubble of hair. "Come stay at my place."

Emily raised an eyebrow at him.

"I'm not suggesting . . . I mean, I've got a spare room if you want it. I'm just thinking, they wouldn't dare try anything if you were with me."

"But I can't be with you twenty-four-seven. You've got a job to do."

"You can come to the office. Ride around with me. Hell, I could even deputize you now—nobody could call you a suspect when you're obviously a victim. You'd have to be crazy to fix your own brakes."

Marguerite put in, "No one has asked my opinion, but may

I point out that you will be stranded here, a mile from town, your car laid up in the garage. I agree with Luke."

Emily frowned at her. Marguerite had a valid point, but Emily couldn't help thinking she was really motivated by a desire to see Luke and Emily sleeping in the same house. Preferably in the same bed.

"See there?" said Luke. "Now you have to come. I won't have you stuck out here by yourself."

Emily ticked off on her fingers. "A: I won't be alone; Marguerite's here, Katie's always here, and Billy's here three days a week. Including now. B: I still have feet. A mile isn't all that far to walk."

"It is if something happens in the middle of the night. You can't make a quick getaway on foot."

"I can use Marguerite's car."

"You forget, *chérie*, I return to Portland tomorrow. I am sorry to abandon you, but I have a summer class to prepare for. I do not fear for you when you have so strong a protector as your good sheriff here." She batted her eyes at Luke.

Some friend! Emily was stumped but refused to give in. She didn't trust herself alone in a house with Luke, and she still felt far from ready to end up in his bed. Besides, to accept Luke's offer would be like admitting to the killer that he had beaten her. She would never be ready to do that.

"Let's table this discussion for now. Shouldn't you be concentrating on finding out who tampered with my car?"

Luke glowered but didn't push it further. "Fair point. You didn't see or hear anything out of the ordinary last night?"

Emily and Marguerite both shook their heads.

Luke called Katie in and repeated the question to her. "Not

a thing," she said. "Lizzie slept through the night last night, and I conked out. It would've taken a train wreck to wake me."

"Is Billy around?"

"Sure, I'll get him." Katie went out the French doors and came back with Billy so quickly, Emily wondered if he'd been listening outside the window while weeding the flower beds, like Samwise Gamgee. He did bear a certain resemblance to a hobbit, now that she thought about it.

Billy stood straight, his hands clasped in front of his spherical belly like Tweedledum about to recite a poem. But where was Tweedledee?

"You weren't around yesterday or last night, Billy, is that right?"

"That is correct, Lieutenant. I was sleeping the sleep of the just in my own modest cottage on the south end of town, all in innocence of any mischievous shenanigans taking place on the mistress's property."

"What time did you get here this morning?"

"Punctually on the dot of eight, sir, as is my wont."

"Notice anything out of order? Any signs of a strange car? Anything funny around Mrs. Cavanaugh's car?"

"Now that you mention it, sir, I did remark some tire tracks on the side of the road outside the gates. There was a bit of a shower last night, as I am sure you are aware, and the ground was wet."

"Excellent. I'll go check that out in a minute. Anything else?"

"Not that I can remember, sir."

"How about you come outside with me and take a look at where Mrs. Cavanaugh parks."

"Certainly, sir."

Emily followed them out to the end of the driveway in

front of the garage, which she had not yet gotten around to exploring.

Luke squatted in the gravel next to the indentations left by the Cruiser's wheels, behind Marguerite's red Peugeot. "See that damp patch?" He pointed to a darker spot in the gravel that Emily never would have noticed. "Was that there before?"

"I cannot say with certainty, sir, but I doubt it."

Luke took a plastic bag from his pocket and used it to pick up a piece of gravel from the dark patch. "I'd bet my badge this is brake fluid." He turned to Emily. "You ever park in the garage?"

"Not yet. I assume Aunt Beatrice's car is still in there."

"Indeed it is, madam," Billy said. "Unfortunately, the Mercedes is no longer functional; Mrs. Runcible kept it for sentimental reasons. The Vespa runs perfectly, however."

"The what?" Emily said as Luke shot Billy a look Emily suspected would usually be accompanied by handcuffs.

"The Vespa, madam. A species of motor scooter. Mrs. Runcible used it exclusively since the Mercedes passed on to its eternal rest."

Emily smiled smugly at Luke. "There, you see? I won't be stranded."

Luke gritted his teeth, and his nostrils flared. "You ever ride a scooter before?"

"No, but how hard can it be? I know how to ride a bicycle."

"It's not the same thing."

"If Aunt Beatrice could do it, I can do it. Billy, would you please open the garage?"

Billy took out a ring of keys worthy of a Victorian butler, selected one, and opened the padlock that held the two swinging doors of the garage together. He swung open the left-hand one, went in, and turned on the light.

There before Emily stood the sweetest little scooter imaginable, its light green surface a little dusty but otherwise immaculate. Instead of a standard motorcycle frame with pedals, it had a broad footrest with a shield in front of it so a lady could ride in a skirt quite modestly and safely. Emily loved it on sight.

Billy pulled a chamois out of his back pocket and whisked away the dust. "Allow me to roll her out onto the drive for you, madam." He grabbed a key ring and a helmet off the wall, rolled the Vespa across the gravel, and parked it on the asphalt of the main drive.

Emily boarded the scooter, leaving the kickstand engaged, and settled the matching light green helmet over her bun. If she hadn't put herself in the position of needing to assert her vehicular independence, she'd never have dreamed of riding something like this. But at least with the kickstand in place, the scooter felt quite stable and manageable beneath her. She reminded herself of her own claim: If Aunt Beatrice could do it, she could do it.

"How do you make it go?"

Billy reached in front of her, inserted the key into the ignition, which was tucked away on the shaft below the dashboard, and turned it. "The transmission is automatic, madam. Speed is controlled by turning the right hand grip, so, and these levers are for the brakes." He pointed out the various switches on the dashboard. "Here we have the lights and the turn signals. And this switch locks the speed, rather like the cruise control on an automobile."

Emily turned her right hand and revved the engine slightly. "I feel just like Audrey Hepburn in *Roman Holiday*."

"I hope you drive better than her," said Luke, "or we won't

have to worry about anybody murdering you—you'll get yourself killed all on your own."

"Don't worry. I'll take it slow to begin with. Want to hop on and help me?"

He shook his head, neither his frown nor his arms-folded posture relaxing at the suggestion. "One of us better stay alive to catch this killer."

"'My courage always rises with every attempt to intimidate me,'" she quoted. She released the kickstand, gave the right handle a tiny twist, and the Vespa puttered down the drive. *No sweat,* she thought, and gave it a bit more speed. Coming to the bend where the drive circled in front of the house, she braked a little, then leaned into the turn. Picking up speed as she gained confidence, she drove all the way to the highway and back. She was a natural at this, like Harry Potter the first time he rode a broom. The breeze on her face through the open visor, the vibration of the scooter underneath her, the feeling of power over a machine that outweighed her were exhilarating; she felt like a teenager again.

"Nothing to it," she said, removing her helmet.

"Well, I have to admit you did better than Audrey Hepburn," Luke said. "Just one little problem. You need a motorcycle license, or at least a learner's permit, to drive this thing on a public road."

She sidled up to him. "And who's going to give me a ticket if I drive without one?"

He looked down at her, his jaw working. She gave him her most coquettish smile.

At last he broke into a grin and threw an arm around her shoulders. "All right, you win. But only for emergencies. Anything else, you call me and I'll give you a ride."

She took off her helmet, reached up, and kissed him on the cheek. "I'll get a permit as soon as I can."

Luke looked around at their audience—Marguerite, Katie, and Billy were all watching with indulgent smiles. "All right, folks, show's over. See you inside."

They took their dismissal—Billy and Katie submissively, Marguerite with a charming little pout. When they were all out of earshot, Luke said low to Emily, "Look, Em, you do realize we can't rule out either Katie or Billy on this brake job? You could be sleeping with the enemy here. So to speak."

"But what about the tire tracks? They suggest an outsider, don't they?"

"Yeah, but who's to say they weren't put there deliberately just for that purpose? Billy was awful quick to mention them. Most people wouldn't even notice a thing like that unless they were looking for it."

"But you can trace them to a specific vehicle, can't you?"

"Should be able to, yeah. Fact, I better go take a look right now."

Emily walked with him down to the end of the drive. There were the tire tracks, just as Billy had said, on the dirt by the side of the road just beyond the head of the drive. Luke pulled out his phone and measuring tape, and squatted beside them. He took several pictures from various angles and distances, then measured the width of each track and the dimensions of the tread pattern.

"See that?" Luke pointed to a flat spot near the top of the right-hand track. "That's where the tire's been repaired. Narrows these tracks down to one particular car. We find this car, we've got our man. Let's go compare these to Billy's truck."

Billy's tires were a quarter-inch wider than the tracks; the tread pattern was different and much more worn. "See?" said Emily. "It wasn't Billy. And Katie doesn't even have a car."

Luke straightened and put his tape measure away. "Point taken. But do one thing for me?" He put his hands on her shoulders and held her gaze. "Make a will. Today. I don't care who you leave your money to as long as you don't leave a penny to Brock. And make sure he knows it."

Emily folded her arms. "Oh, so you do take my Mr. Elliot theory seriously after all?"

"Never said I didn't. Just said it wouldn't prove anything." He slid one arm across her shoulders and walked her toward the house. "Better get your lawyer to come here. Or I could drive you into town. I think you've had enough driving for one day, don't you?"

"Definitely. It's about closing time anyway. I'll see if Jamie can come here."

• twenty-seven •

The old gentleman died; his will was read, and like almost
every other will, gave as much disappointment as pleasure.
—*Sense and Sensibility*

Lured by the promise of a home-cooked dinner, Jamie read-
ily agreed to come to Windy Corner to help Emily with her
will. "I should've insisted you do this right away," he said when
she'd told him about her afternoon's adventure. "I hold myself
responsible for what happened to you today."

"Don't be silly. I'm a grown woman; I should have taken the
initiative myself. It's just that this inheritance is so new to
me, I've hardly had a chance to think about what I want to do
with it myself, let alone how I want to pass it on."

But she had thought about that while waiting for Jamie to
arrive, and she was ready to make her dispositions: Windy
Corner plus a hundred thousand dollars to Katie, so that she
would have a home for herself and Lizzie and enough money to
get the place off the ground as a B&B if she so desired. Another
hundred thousand to Marguerite, so she could take her trip
around the world and even buy a suitable wardrobe for it. The

extra fifty thousand Dr. Griffiths had requested for the clinic trust. A nice fat cash bequest to Reed, earmarked for scholarships, and the rest of the money plus all the Stony Beach real estate to Luke. Jamie drew up a draft then and there on his laptop and e-mailed a copy to his office for safekeeping. Beatrice had no printer, so Emily agreed to come into Jamie's office the next day to sign the printout.

"Will it be valid before I sign it?" she asked, concerned about the delay.

"I'm afraid not. It has to be signed in the presence of two witnesses, preferably people who don't inherit. In fact, in your case, I'd say that's essential, since there's someone standing by who'd be all too eager to dispute the will. We don't want to give him any ground to stand on."

"Or any time to stand on it." Then she remembered. "I think Katie has a printer. And Billy can be one witness. But we still need another one."

Emily went to the kitchen and asked Katie if she could spare a minute from making dinner.

"Sure, it's all in the oven." Emily ushered Jamie into Katie's room.

Jamie took one look at Katie and turned so red, Emily feared his face would explode.

"Do you two know each other?" Emily asked, wondering if Jamie could even be Lizzie's father—what else could account for such embarrassment? And it would explain Lizzie's red hair.

But Jamie shook his head. Katie said with a friendly smile, "I don't believe we've met."

Emily made the introductions, observing Jamie's face. His eyes told her the truth. It wasn't embarrassment that crimsoned the poor boy's cheeks; it was instant, overpowering love.

Katie turned a little pink but kept her head. She was such a lovely girl, this couldn't be the first time a young man had fallen for her on sight. She unplugged the printer cord from her own laptop and handed it to Jamie.

He fumbled at the connection, his fingers shaking, so Katie gently took the plug back and inserted it herself. In the process, their hands touched, and Jamie jumped as if hit by an electric shock. Katie took over and printed the will.

The noise of the printer woke Lizzie in her cradle, invisible on the far side of the bed. Jamie jumped again at her cry, and a look of utter consternation swept over his features.

Katie picked the baby up to soothe her and then shot a worried look at Emily. "Oh dear, I was hoping to get your dinner on the table before she woke."

"It's my fault. I'll take her, unless she needs to eat right away. Would you ask Billy to come in, please? And we'll need dinner put off a bit to give us time to sign the will."

Lizzie snuggled into Emily's neck, and she carried her into the library. One-handed, she punched in Luke's number. "I've got a will made, but I need another witness. Can't be you or Katie or Marguerite. Do you know anyone you can draft in a hurry?"

"Sure, I'll rustle up a deputy and be there in fifteen minutes."

Emily sat down to proofread the will, but Lizzie turned squirmy. "I can take her," Jamie said. His color had drained completely, and his freckles stood out dark against his white skin. With expert hands, he took Lizzie from Emily's arms and bounced her gently.

"You seem pretty comfortable with babies," Emily said. "That's unusual in a young man."

"I'm the oldest of five. Plus I have lots of little cousins."

Emily felt her way carefully. "I thought perhaps you had an aversion to babies, from the way you reacted when she first woke up."

Jamie reddened again. "Oh no, I love babies. It's just—I guess this means Katie's married, huh? Or taken, anyway."

"Not married. Not taken. Just a mom."

Jamie's face took on a glow as if he were a new father himself. He didn't speak, but began to hum "Annie Laurie" softly under his breath as he jiggled Lizzie around the room.

Emily found no typos in the will. By the time she'd finished reading it, Billy was standing by and Luke had arrived with two deputies. "I brought Pete to witness and Heather to notarize. Assuming you need a notary."

Jamie thanked him and looked around for someone to hand Lizzie off to who wasn't needed for the signing ceremony. Marguerite backed off as if the baby's skin were coated with poison, but Luke held out his arms. "Come here, you. I'm a sucker for a pretty girl." He carried Lizzie over to the windows and babbled nonsense to her as if he'd been holding babies all his life. Emily teared up, watching him. If only . . .

Jamie called her attention back to the matter at hand. As she took his blue-ink fountain pen in her fingers, she had the feeling she was signing her life away—but in fact she was probably saving it. Peculiar and wrong that so much should hinge on a bit of ink on a piece of paper. Billy and Pete signed after her with similarly solemn faces, as if Death had entered the room along with them.

Heather applied her seal, and the ceremony was complete. Emily offered sherry all around. They all sipped in somber silence for a moment, then gradually thawed out. Marguerite flirted with Pete, a handsome young blond, while Heather, cute and petite with hair as red as Jamie's, darted barbed looks their way and attempted to flirt with Jamie. He, however, was already far beyond her reach.

Katie shimmered in, Jeeves-like, as they were all finishing their sherry, and whispered to Emily, "Is everyone staying for dinner? Because it's ready, but I'm not sure there's enough to go around."

"No, just us and Jamie. I'll give Luke a hint, and he'll get the others away."

Emily sidled over to Luke and took Lizzie from his arms. "I'd invite you for dinner, but your deputies would be stranded, and I'm afraid we don't have enough to feed them."

"No problem. I've got work to do anyhow." He glanced around to make sure no one was looking, then gave her a quick kiss. "See you tomorrow."

Lizzie was beginning to fuss and bump her open mouth against Emily's shirt, so Emily was relieved when Katie finished setting out the food and took the baby back from her. Marguerite and Emily kept the conversation going through dinner; Jamie never said a word beyond please and thank you in response to offers of food and drink. When Katie left the room, his gaze retreated to some distant cloud. When she returned with dessert, his eyes fastened onto her until her face was nearly as red as his own. She stayed in the dining room while they ate their blueberry cobbler, fussing about the table and doing who-knew-what at the sideboard.

When they'd finished, Emily said to Marguerite, "Shall we be very English and leave Jamie alone with a glass of port?"

Marguerite nodded with a conspiratorial smile. But Jamie jumped to his feet and said, "No, no, I'm afraid I have to go.

Have to drive back to Tillamook, you know. No port for me." He gathered his things and bustled out without a backward glance.

Alone in the library, Emily and Marguerite burst into laughter. *"Le pauvre petit!* Never did I see a case so bad. But he must not despair—I think his lady love is not completely indifferent, *n'est-ce pas?"*

"I'd say not. He'll find his tongue eventually, and then I imagine they'll get along just fine."

A drizzle had begun while they were eating; after Jamie left, it escalated into a full-fledged storm. Katie built a fire in the library. Emily cozied up to it with her knitting, and Marguerite played with the three cats on the hearthrug: Kitty jumped for the toy mouse Marguerite dangled, while Bustopher and Levin wrestled like kittens over a squeaky toy. The scene was outwardly as cozy as a Dickens Christmas, but underneath Emily felt far from calm; it was all she could do to keep her hands steady on the needles. When a flash of lightning cast a white glare across the room, followed by a deafening crash of thunder and then the doorbell, she jumped and dropped two stitches. She nearly fainted with relief when Luke walked into the room.

Marguerite excused herself with a staged yawn. "Now that you have someone to keep you company, *chérie,* I will go enjoy that so-lovely clawfoot tub of yours." Emily gave her a grateful smile.

"Got a call from the mechanic just now," Luke said as he flopped into Bustopher's unoccupied chair. "Your brakes were definitely tampered with. Fluid line cut down by the back wheel."

Emily shivered. She hadn't doubted it before, but having

actual proof that someone had tried to kill her threatened to send her back into a state of shock. "I think I need a sherry," she croaked.

Luke poured a sherry for each of them. "Talked to Brock earlier. Dropped a hint about your new will. Shook him up, but he rallied. I guess that acting training is good for something even if it doesn't get him decent roles."

"Did you question him about my car?"

"Sure did. He claims he was with 'a lady friend' all night, but he wouldn't give me her name to back him up. I got a look at his tires, though. Don't need a search warrant for that." He gave her a sidelong glance.

"And?" Emily was figuratively on the edge of her seat, and he chose this moment to tease her.

"They match. Flat spot and all."

"So what'd he have to say about that?"

"Oh, he had a story, of course. Said he and his lady went for a drive early in the evening and just happened to pull over at that spot. He implied she couldn't wait till they got to the hotel to get her hands on him." Luke snorted. "Then I pointed out he must've been there after the rain, which came later—sometime between midnight and dawn."

"Aha! You got him. He couldn't squirm out of that, could he?"

"Nope. Just gave me a look and said, 'Country sheriffs really shouldn't try to play Sherlock Holmes. The tracks were made in the dry dirt, and the rain set them. Elementary, my dear Watson.' He can do a fair British accent, I'll give him that much. But he knows as well as I do rain would've wiped out dry tracks. He was sweating, literally. Tough thing about real life—no makeup people to powder you up so the sweat doesn't show."

"So did you push him for the name of his lady friend?"

"I did, but he wouldn't budge. Now I know for sure I've got a charge of attempted murder, I'll go to town first thing in the morning and get a warrant for his arrest. That ought to loosen his tongue."

"Of course, even if he does give her name, she might back him up."

"Might. But I don't see Brock inspiring any strong personal loyalty, do you? And the fact he doesn't want to identify her suggests there may be something we can hold over her to make her tell the truth. Might be married, for instance."

"Good point. And she's probably the same good-looking blonde who went out with him on the boat. She could be a gold mine."

"Exactly." Luke stretched, yawning. "By the way, did you hide that will?"

"Not to say hide. It's locked in the desk." Emily pointed with her chin at the immense rolltop across the room.

"If I were you, I'd hide it. Brock's gonna be pretty anxious to find out who cut him out."

"Good point." Emily put down her knitting, walked over to the desk, and unlocked the shallow drawer. "I know just the place. But you'd better come with me—so somebody can find it if . . ." She couldn't finish that sentence.

He followed her upstairs and into Beatrice's room. "Beatrice showed me her hiding place." She went to the ornately carved mantelpiece and twisted a medallion in the center below the mantel shelf. The panel dropped open to reveal a small steel door with a combination lock. "In fact, I wouldn't be surprised if she'd left something there—I doubt anyone else would know this was here."

"You know the combination?"

"She wasn't terribly sneaky about that—I think she relied more on nobody knowing the safe existed. She just used her initials." Emily spun the dial to clear it, then carefully turned it to *B–W–R*. The door clicked and swung open.

Inside was a fat envelope, which proved to contain an exact copy of Beatrice's will, the same version that now resided in Jamie's office. Underneath that was a velvet box. Emily opened it to see a Victorian-style choker consisting of six rows of tiny, perfectly matched pearls with a large cameo in the middle.

Luke whistled. "I never saw her wear that—did you?"

"No. She showed it to me once, though. I'd forgotten all about it till now. In fact, I think that's why she opened the safe—she showed me this and told me it would be mine one day. It belonged to her grandmother." Emily traced the profile of the cameo with her finger. This piece would not have been Beatrice's style—her clothes were always severely practical, though custom-tailored of the best materials. But the choker would complement Emily's Edwardian-inspired wardrobe perfectly.

"I think I'll keep this out." She closed the box, placed both folded wills inside the safe, and restored the safe to its former invisibility, making sure she left no telltale cracks around the secret panel.

As they left the room, Luke checked his watch. "Getting late. I hate to leave you unprotected like this. Sure you won't reconsider coming to my place? Just for tonight—after tomorrow he'll be in jail."

"Brock's not likely to try anything now that he knows you're onto him. I'll be fine." Brave words, but she didn't feel as confident as she sounded.

"You wouldn't let me sleep on your couch?"

"My couch! If it comes to that, I have about half a dozen empty bedrooms." She bit her lip, weighing safety against independence. "All right, you win. I would feel better with you under the same roof tonight. I'll give you your choice of rooms."

"Just a sec." Luke ran down the stairs and came back a minute later, soaking wet and carrying a small overnight bag. "I packed a toothbrush just in case you said yes. One good thing, fella'd have to be nuts to get up to mischief on a night like this." A thunderclap punctuated his pronouncement.

Luke chose the front room next to Marguerite's because its bay would give him a view of both the drive and the approach to the front door. "I'd perch on the roof where I could see three sixty if it weren't for this rain."

He placed an easy chair where he could see out either the windows or the open door to the hall. "Any chance Katie could come up with a pot of coffee?"

"You're not planning to sit up all night?"

"That is exactly what I'm planning to do. Not to say I might not doze in the chair a bit, but I'm not gonna get too comfortable. Not when your life is on the line."

She walked into his embrace. "I'm glad you're here."

He kissed her lightly. "No distracting an officer on duty, ma'am."

"I'll go see about that coffee."

twenty-eight

As they approached Barton, indeed, and entered on scenes of
which every field and every tree brought some peculiar, some
painful recollection, [Marianne] grew silent and thoughtful.
—*Sense and Sensibility*

Emily fell into bed, exhausted, but slept fitfully, dreaming of
riding in an out-of-control car driven alternately by Brock,
Luke, and her long-dead father. At one point she startled awake,
some unknown noise having penetrated her dream. She strained
her ears but heard nothing more, and soon she slept again.

When she came down in the morning, Luke was just leaving the bathroom, freshly shaved but with deep shadows under
his eyes. She wanted to run back upstairs and hide her dishev-
eled hair and puffy raccoon eyes, but it was too late—he'd seen
her. He smiled as if she were dressed for a ball.

"Good morning, beautiful," he said as he wrapped his arms
around her ratty old bathrobe.

"Lack of sleep seems to have affected your eyesight," she
said, turning her lips away from his attempted kiss. "I haven't
brushed my teeth yet. And I know I look like something my
cats would be too finicky to drag in."

He took her chin and turned her face back. "You're alive and unharmed. That makes you a beautiful sight—and eminently kissable." He suited the action to the word.

He tasted minty fresh and smelled like lavender soap. "I could get used to this," she murmured.

"So could I."

"Did you see anything last night? I thought I heard something, but I couldn't be sure."

"Yeah, I spotted somebody prowling around about two this morning. Heard a noise over by the garage, shone my high-powered flashlight over there and caught sight of somebody in black. He lit off when I put the spotlight on him. Or she. Couldn't be sure if it was a man or a woman."

"But you're sure he left?"

"Pretty sure. I followed him with the light as far down the drive as it would go. Then I went out and had a look around. All clear."

Emily leaned against him, trying to still her beating heart. "I have a really bad feeling about this, Luke."

"Heck yeah. Having your life in danger's not exactly a day at the beach."

"I don't mean just that. I mean, now that I've cut Brock out of my will and he knows it, I'm not an obstacle to a fortune anymore. If he—or someone—is still out to get me—well, it has to be personal. Doesn't it? Somebody actually hates me enough to kill me." She tightened her arms around him. "Who would hate me that much? And why?"

"I don't know, baby. To me you're the most lovable creature on Earth." He stroked her back. "I don't think it's really about you. I have this gut feeling it's still about Beatrice. I just don't know how."

"I'm not sure if that's better or worse. How can I make amends for something I didn't do?"

He kissed her forehead. "Too early in the morning for such deep questions. Let me at least get some coffee in my belly before we get into that."

"Of course. Go on down and ask Katie to get breakfast on. I'll be there in a minute."

Luke put away an impressive quantity of bacon and eggs. "Lack of sleep sure gives you an appetite," he said in response to Emily's bemused look.

She picked at a boiled egg and nibbled a piece of toast. Lack of security just as surely took hers away.

Marguerite drank café au lait and ate a brioche in perfect equanimity. Then she sent Katie to bring down her packed bag, and took her leave. *"Merci, chérie,* for a most interesting visit." She pecked the air beside Emily's cheeks.

"Thanks for coming, Margot. And thanks for working your magic on the cats."

"Ce n'est rien. I have my reward in my finished article. I hope you will permit me to return next time I need to do some writing. I am persuaded your library has some magic in it for those who work with words."

"You're welcome anytime." Emily waved her off down the drive and then turned to Luke. "I suppose you're leaving me too?"

He checked his watch. "Want to be at the courthouse on the dot to get that warrant. You could come along if you want."

Emily hesitated, weighing the benefits of staying close to Luke against the unpleasantness of the errand. "No, I don't think so. I certainly don't want to be there when you arrest

Brock. I'd prefer never to set eyes on him again, though I suppose I'll have to at his trial."

"Right. I'll come back when it's all over." He kissed her and got in the patrol car. She stood on the porch and watched the car go down the drive.

The rain had given place to a light fog, and Emily decided she needed a walk on the beach to clear her head. Remembering Agnes's fate, she descended the wooden stairs carefully, holding on tight to the banisters and testing each step before trusting it with her weight. At the bottom she looked up and down, debating which way to walk. Toward town she saw several walkers; to the north the beach was empty. She headed north.

With the surf pounding in her ears, the gulls crying overhead, the fresh breeze in her face, and the sand soft beneath her feet, some measure of her anxiety soon dissipated. She didn't exactly forget her worries, but they hung back for a time, like a heavy backpack she had laid aside but would soon have to sling over her shoulders again. She drifted, half-conscious, surrendering herself to the ocean as if floating on its waves, and soon she found herself at the entrance to the cove.

Her legs suddenly felt like jelly. She ducked inside the cove to sit on a driftwood log and rest. Absently, she kicked aside an empty beer can. Blasted teenagers, littering up her cove.

She looked deeper into the dark hollow. As her eyes adjusted to the gloom, she saw signs of more than casual habitation. On a natural ledge in the rock lay a folded blanket and a pillow; a flat spot in the sand showed where they had been spread out. Next to them stood a half-empty bottle of amber liquor and a couple of glasses, along with a half-dozen unlit candles in various stages of burning, all stuck down to the rock with wax. She moved closer to investigate. The blanket felt like a fine, soft wool, and the liquor was Glenlivet. Beside the blanket lay a plastic bottle of something. Massage oil.

Someone was using *their* cove—hers and Luke's—as a love nest. Someone with adult tastes and means.

Up to now she'd been worried, scared, shocked, and deeply disturbed by the violence around her. Now she was furious. This spot was sacred to her memories. How dare these people violate it with their tawdry affair?

She grabbed the Glenlivet bottle by its neck and flung it above her head to smash it against the rock. Then she stopped, hand in midair. Two well-heeled adults, presumably in possession of homes and beds of their own, who would go to such trouble and inconvenience to have sex must have something to hide. All of this could be evidence.

She lowered the bottle and replaced it on the shelf, chiding herself for having messed up the one item most likely to carry good fingerprints. But at least she had grabbed the neck of the bottle; someone pouring the scotch into a glass would be more likely to hold it around the middle. She might not have flunked Detecting 101 after all.

Maybe she could discover something else to redeem herself. What other clues might this cove hold?

She stood in place and pivoted, examining every surface. A second blanket had been nailed into the rock to one side of the cave entrance, with another nail to hitch it to on the other side. Nothing else to be seen. But as she turned to face the ledge again, she caught a whiff of something. Cologne. A man's scent, and a rather potent one at that. A musky smell. Where had she smelled that before?

Of course. Brock.

This was where Brock had his rendezvous with his anonymous

blonde. In fact, he could have parked at the top of Emily's drive in order to come down here, and not to tamper with her brakes at all. It would be the most convenient parking spot to the cove.

She had to tell Luke right away. His probable cause had just become less probable.

She pulled out her cell and punched in his number but got only silence. What was she doing wrong? She stared at the phone's tiny screen. What did those grayed-out bars at the top mean again? Oh, right—no reception. Hardly surprising inside a cave.

She went outside and tried again. This time she heard a ring, and soon after that a faint echo of Luke's voice. The wind and the surf between them carried his words away. She covered her right ear with her hand and hit the volume switch several times. "Luke?"

"Emily? Are you okay?"

She enunciated each word. "I'm okay. I found something, but I'm on the beach and I can't hear you very well. I'll call back from the house." Then she hung up.

She half walked, half ran back to the house and stopped on the porch to catch her breath. Sitting on the porch swing, she tried again. This time they could hear each other.

"Did you get the warrant yet?"

"Just got it. 'Bout to head back to Stony Beach now."

"I think there might be a flaw in our theory." She told him about her discovery.

"That sneaking bastard. I've got half a mind to arrest him just for violating our cove."

"I know. I felt the same way. But of course you can't, can you? I don't think it's technically private property."

"No, guess not. Could get him for vandalism, maybe, but

he'd get off with a slap on the hand." He was silent for a minute; she could hear him sucking his teeth. "Just the one blanket, you say?"

"One on the shelf and one hung up to cover the entrance."

"So one to lie on but none to cover up with. No sign of a fire?"

"No."

"Be pretty cold in that cove at night, wouldn't you think?"

She shivered just thinking about it. "Yeah, I guess it would."

"And for him to leave those tire tracks, he would've had to arrive after the rain got going. That was well after midnight, coldest part of the night. Not a great time to lie in a freezing cove, even with a blonde to warm you up."

Emily's spirits began to perk up. "So you think your probable cause still holds?"

"Still looks pretty probable to me. I'm going to go get him now."

Two hours later Emily was reading in the library in front of a fire, wrapped in her finished shawl and sipping hot coffee, still cold to her core from the feeling of hatred surrounding her. Even *Sense and Sensibility*, which she'd moved on to after *Persuasion*, couldn't keep the cold entirely at bay. Outside, the fog had turned to drizzle. As a Portlander, she didn't expect June to be a true summer month, but here on the coast the weather was even drearier than in town. She began to contemplate abandoning this sinking ship.

But no. She had to see it through. As a good academic, she'd never been able to resist a puzzle, and there was still a puzzle here to be solved. Besides, not even in Portland could she sleep soundly knowing there could be someone walking the world who wanted her dead.

She jumped at the sound of the doorbell and relaxed only when Luke walked into the room. He collapsed into the chair opposite hers.

"It's done. He's behind bars. We can breathe a little now."

The news did not bring her the relief it should have. "I don't know, Luke. I don't feel any safer than I did before. Even if we're pretty sure he fixed my brakes, we can't be certain he's responsible for the deaths as well. We still have no idea how Beatrice was poisoned, and we can't pin Brock to the scene for Agnes either. It feels to me like we still have a lot of work to do."

Luke sighed and sat up. "Can a fella get a cup of coffee before you push him back out into the rain?"

"Of course." She poured him a cup from the tray that stood on a table between their chairs. "I didn't mean to rush you."

He swallowed the lukewarm coffee in three gulps. "Better get down to the cove. You wanna come?"

Stay by a warm, dry fire with one of her favorite books or traipse through the chill rain to the cove with Luke. No contest. "I'll get my coat."

Luke grabbed a professional-looking camera from his car and slung it around his neck, and they headed to the beach. They walked along the sand in silence, hand in hand, memories washing over them. Years and troubles fell away until Emily felt like a teenager again, trembling with anticipation and a queer, delicious fear. She slipped her arm around Luke's waist, and he tightened his on her shoulders.

When they stepped into the cove, he drew her aside from the entrance and kissed her deeply. "Emily," he said into her ear. "I may be a grown man with a job to do, but I don't know how much longer I can wait. I want us to be together, Em. For real.

For always." He pulled back and held her face in his hands. "Don't you want that too?"

In that moment, she wanted it more than anything else on Earth. But there was still a barrier between them—a barrier of her own making, but one she was not yet ready to tear down. "We have to get through this, Luke. I can't—relax until I know for sure Beatrice and Agnes's killer is behind bars."

He sighed and dropped his hands. "Yeah. Better get to work."

They turned to face into the cove, their eyes adjusting to the darkness.

The ledge was empty.

Emily waded to it through the loose sand and ran her fingers across the ledge as if the objects might still be there, but invisible. "I don't understand. It was all here just a little while ago. What could have happened?"

"Somebody got the wind up. Must've been Brock's blonde—I got to him too soon after you called for it to've been him. But she's had two hours to hear about his arrest and get out here to clear up the evidence."

Emily turned to Luke, ready to cry with frustration. "What are we going to do?"

"You didn't get any pictures?"

"Pictures? I didn't bring a camera."

"Your phone. You must have a camera in your phone—they don't make 'em without anymore."

Emily pulled her phone out of her pocket and stared at it. "Camera? Where?"

He pointed to a tiny circle of glass in the cover. "There's your lens."

"Oh." She opened the phone and stared at it. None of the buttons looked like a shutter. "Never occurred to me. I don't have a clue how to use it."

Luke laughed. "You are really something, Emily Worthing, you know that? Straight out of the Dark Ages. Here, let me show you." He took the phone from her and pushed buttons until a picture of a camera appeared on the screen; then the screen shifted to show the empty ledge in front of them. He pushed another button, and the phone emitted a click and a whir.

Luke peered at the result. "Have to admit, it wouldn't have done a lot of good if you had remembered. Not enough light in here to get a decent shot." He closed the phone and handed it back to her. "Might still be able to get some fingerprints off the ledge. You didn't touch it just now, did you?"

"No." Even in her distress, her subconscious had somehow reminded her to keep her fingers above the surface.

Except for clear spots where the various objects had stood, the ledge was dusted with a fine layer of sand. Luke took close-up flash photos of each section. "Not much here, but the boys might be able to get something." He took more photos of the sand around the flat spot where the blanket had lain, where neither he nor Emily had walked. "Might get a footprint or two if we're lucky."

Emily sniffed the air, where Brock's scent still lingered. "If only we could bottle up this smell. That puts him here as clearly as any fingerprint."

"To you, yeah, but not to a jury. Cologne you can buy over the counter—could be anybody's. Could be the kids' who left the beer cans." He pointed to a pile of them, half buried in sand next to the driftwood log where Emily had sat before.

Emily grabbed the hair at her temples. "Are we never going to find anything definite? I feel like I'm swimming around in a fog, with nothing to hold on to except wraiths in the mist that dissolve as soon as I touch them."

He slung an arm around her shoulders. "Think about it, Em. Was there anything in here that would tie Brock or anyone else to murder?"

"Well—now that you mention it, no. Not in itself."

"Exactly. So why are we interested? Two consenting adults want to carry on in an out-of-the-way place, what's it to us? Legally speaking, I mean."

She was momentarily stumped. The whole scene had affected her so deeply, there had to be a good reason it was incriminating to somebody.

"One or both of them needed to hide the affair, or they wouldn't have gone to all this trouble."

"Right."

"And the woman obviously doesn't want to be associated with Brock, since she got out here so fast to remove the evidence."

"Right again."

"So that means—they're in it together? Or she at least knows about it. Might be an accessory. And she's afraid he'll give her away."

"Bingo. If you look at it that way, the fact that all the stuff is gone helps us more than the stuff itself. Assuming we can get some proof of identity." He scratched his head. "I am sorry the blanket's gone—that would've been a DNA gold mine."

"If we got floodlights in here, I bet we'd find something. A blond hair in the sand or *something*."

"Now you're talking." He pulled out his phone and called his office. "They'll be out here in fifteen minutes."

Emily turned and buried her head against his chest. "Oh, Luke. Our cove—a crime scene. We'll never be able to come here again."

He wrapped his arms around her. "Would you really want to? We have the memories whether we still have the place or not. And at my age, I prefer a bed. I personally can live without sand in my butt."

That made her giggle. "Me too."

He led her over to the driftwood log and they sat—companionably at first, her head on his shoulder, their hands intertwined. He stroked her palm in little circles with his thumb. Who knew the palm could be so sensitive? Then he kissed her, and before long she wouldn't have cared if she had sand in every crevice of her body.

The sound of an engine roused them, and they sprang apart. Emily hurriedly tucked stray locks of hair into her bun and tugged her shirt straight. They heard heavy objects being dragged through loose sand, then Luke's two deputies, Pete and Heather, stuck their heads through the cave entrance.

"Chief?" called Pete, squinting into the dark.

"Right here." Luke's voice cracked a bit before it took on professional authority.

Emily hung back while the three of them put on white bunny suits and got to work with floodlights, tweezers, swabs, and plastic bags. Time slowed to match the pace of their painstaking work. Between weariness, cold, hunger, and frustrated arousal, Emily's nerves overloaded, and she drifted into a state of suspended animation where she felt none of those things, nor any sense of time passing. As if hypnotized, she watched the white figures dissolving in the bright light.

At last Heather cried, "Aha!" She straightened and held up a long blond hair caught in her tweezers.

Luke thumped her on the back. "Good work, Heather."

After a few more minutes Pete, who had moved away from the blanket area to examine the sand close to the rock wall, raised his arm in triumph. "Jackpot. This was almost buried." Gripped in his tweezers was a used condom.

Emily's stomach turned, but Luke whistled. "Can't ask for a better sample than that." He stood up and arched his back, vertebrae popping. "Let's pack up and go home."

twenty-nine

"And how you will explain away any part of your guilt in that dreadful business, I confess is beyond my comprehension." . . .

"I do not mean to justify myself, but at the same time cannot leave you to suppose that I have nothing to urge."
—Elinor Dashwood and Willoughby, *Sense and Sensibility*

Luke sent his deputies off in their Jeep to deliver the samples to the lab, then walked Emily back to Windy Corner. He opened the door of his patrol car and leaned his arm on the top of it. "Course it's gonna take weeks to get results, but at least we've got Brock put away. He can stew in there till we're ready, and then we'll reel in his lady friend. That's assuming we don't get him to talk before that." His jaw tightened. "I have a feeling he'll talk."

Emily didn't like the steely glint in Luke's eyes. "You wouldn't—hurt him?"

"Nah. I won't say that never happens in this country, 'cause I've heard stories that'd make you think you were in the Middle East. But it doesn't happen on my watch. Jail's just not a real nice place to be, 'specially for a softie like Brock. Few days of it, and an offer of bail in return for information could start to look pretty good."

"I don't much like the idea of having him out on bail."

Luke snorted. "Judge wouldn't either. Didn't say he'd get bail—just said we'd offer it."

"You'd lie to him?"

"Not lie—just make a promise we can't keep." He took his arm off the door and cupped her chin. "Emily, if we're right, this man has killed two women and attempted your life. He may have an accomplice who's willing to carry on the work in his absence. Do you think I'd stop at a tiny white lie to keep you safe?"

She swallowed. When he put it that way . . .

"I'm going to the jail to have a go at him now. You stay safe, hear?"

She nodded. "You too."

He kissed her lightly, then got into the car and drove off. She felt like a shipwrecked sailor from whom the last life ring had just been whisked away.

Emily went back to the library and *Sense and Sensibility*. Katie brought her some hot chicken soup, which she sipped gratefully in front of the fire, wondering if she would ever feel warm again.

Soon she lost herself in the adventures of Elinor and Marianne, the two sisters of opposite temperaments who took their disappointments in love so very differently—Elinor bearing up in brave silence against the onslaughts of the vindictive Lucy Steele, who insisted on confiding her fears regarding her secret engagement to Elinor's beloved Edward, while Marianne dissolved in hysterical weeping merely because Willoughby was called unexpectedly to London. But Marianne's true heartbreak was not far off, while Elinor's long-suffering would eventually be rewarded.

Late in the afternoon, while Emily was enjoying another of Katie's delicious teas, the doorbell rang and Katie brought a package into the library. "It's from Sweets by the Sea," she said. "Did you order some candy?"

Emily set down her cup and took the package, a box about a foot square and four inches deep wrapped in brown paper. "Not exactly. I did tell them to continue Beatrice's standing order for me, but I didn't expect it to come so soon. I'm still working on the taffy I bought the other day."

She unwrapped the box and opened it. A pound of licorice taffy, a bag of assorted gourmet jelly beans, and a box of Turkish delight.

Emily wrinkled her nose. "I should have asked exactly what was in that order. I can't stand Turkish delight. It always makes me think of Edmund and the White Witch."

Katie bit her bottom lip. "Mind if I have it then? I adore the stuff. The Witch would've had me hooked forever, I'm ashamed to admit."

"Help yourself." Emily handed her the box. "Just don't eat it all at once, okay? I don't want to have to nurse you and take care of Lizzie at the same time."

"I'll be good. I'll have one piece, and then you can hide the box for me till after dinner."

Katie took her time choosing from what looked to Emily like two dozen identical pieces. She took her treasure to the kitchen while Emily hid the box inside the window seat. "Just like Mr. Spenalzo," she said to Bustopher, who was lounging on the top of the seat back.

Emily read on till dinnertime. When her stomach called her back out of nineteenth-century London, she realized she hadn't been hearing any dinner-preparation noises from the kitchen or dining room. Instead she heard Lizzie's snuffling waking-up cry and a deep groan from Katie's bedroom.

She knocked softly on the bedroom door. "Katie? Are you all right?"

"No," came the hoarse reply. Emily opened the door to see Katie curled on her bed in the fetal position. With another groan, she rolled to her feet and stumbled into the adjacent bathroom, whence issued sounds of the most unpleasant bodily functions.

Lizzie was working herself up into a full wail now, so Emily picked her up and soothed her. "Katie? Do you need a doctor?"

"No. Yes. Maybe." More distressing noises. "I've never gotten sick from one piece of Turkish delight before."

"Flu, maybe?"

"Haven't heard of any stomach flu going around. Haven't been around anyone to catch it."

"I'm going to call Doctor Griffiths." In light of all the evidence converging on Brock, Emily's suspicions of Sam Griffiths had pretty much fallen by the wayside. In any case, she couldn't mean any harm to Katie.

With Lizzie in her arms, Emily awkwardly dialed the clinic and caught Sam on her way out. "Be right there," Sam said.

Sam was indeed there in five minutes. She examined Katie and asked about what she'd eaten that day. "The only thing out of the ordinary was the Turkish delight," Emily told her.

"Let me see it," Sam said.

Emily retrieved the box from Mr. Spenalzo's resting place. Sam took a piece and held it to her nose, then touched a fingertip to the powdery coating and brought it to her tongue. "This isn't just sugar," she pronounced. "Can't be sure without a test, but I have a gut feeling . . ." She glanced at Katie on the bed. "Pardon the pun—but I bet it's mixed with arsenic."

Emily felt the blood leave her face. "Arsenic? But that's what killed Beatrice."

Sam shot her a sharp look. "What makes you think that?"

"The autopsy. They exhumed her and did a postmortem. She was full of it."

Sam went white in her turn. Her hands shook, and she nearly dropped the box of candy. Emily took it from her and laid it on the dresser.

Sam took out a handkerchief and wiped her face. She took a deep, shuddering breath and turned to Katie. "You only ate the one piece?"

Katie nodded.

"Feel like the worst of it's over?"

"I think so. I'm just weak."

"I'll give you a little something for the pain. Just rest for to-night, and you'll be fine by morning." She fumbled in her bag and brought out a hypodermic and a tiny vial.

Katie looked at Emily with the baby in her arms. "What about Lizzie? And your dinner?"

"You have some breast milk in the freezer, don't you? We'll be fine."

Sam gave Katie the injection, and then Emily took the box of candy and ushered Sam back into the library. "Now it's time for some honest explanations. You knew it was arsenic with Beatrice, didn't you? Or at least you suspected."

Sam sank into a chair and covered her face with her hands. "I suspected. A tiny suspicion—easily could've been natural causes. Too late when I got there—nothing I could've done for her, truly—you have to believe that."

Emily hesitated, then nodded. Sam was a professional, a physician through and through; she'd never be able to stop her-self from saving a patient if she could.

"But I knew any question about her death, question of—

murder—would hang up the will being proved. Needed my money for the clinic. Had a kid die on me few months ago, acute appendicitis. Could've saved him if I'd had the clinic. Beatrice was an old woman, would've died soon anyway. Meanwhile, I could be saving so many other lives." She looked up at Emily. "I was wrong. I see that now. Suppose you'll turn me in."

Emily gazed at her, then turned and walked Lizzie around the room. Sam was a dedicated doctor who cared deeply for the community she served. Should one error in judgment—of which she'd clearly repented—cut her off from that service forever?

But that one error of judgment had led to Agnes's death—as well as what were now two attempts on Emily's own life. That Turkish delight had been meant for her.

Sam's voice dwindled to a whisper. "Could cost me my license."

"I know. You realize if you'd spoken up, Agnes might still be alive?"

"I've barely slept since she died."

"But on the other hand, you found the arsenic this time, which could be just what we need to nail the killer."

Sam looked up, a spark of hope in her eyes.

Emily made her decision. "Let's say you're on probation. But you put one toe out of line, and . . ." She made a slashing motion across her throat with her free hand.

"Thank you." Sam got to her feet and gripped Emily's hand in both of hers. "I won't let you down."

Lizzie's intermittent fussing escalated into a full-scale hungry wail. "I'd better get this baby a bottle. Can you see yourself out?"

Emily watched Sam out the front door, then went into the

kitchen and took a plastic envelope of breast milk out of the freezer. "Now what?" she muttered to herself. The envelope looked as if it might fit into a bottle, but where to find a bottle? She opened cabinet after cabinet and finally found a plastic column with a rubber nipple sitting beside it. She took everything to the table and sat, angry Lizzie over her shoulder. Pinning the baby with her forearm, she fumbled the milk envelope into the bottle with its top hanging over the sides, then wrestled the rubber nipple in place over all. It was trickier than the hardest cable pattern she'd ever knitted.

But Lizzie couldn't drink frozen formula. Jiggling Lizzie, who by now was screaming in frustration, Emily scoured the cupboards again for a pan and filled it with the hottest water the tap would produce, then stood the bottle upright in the water. She didn't dare heat it on the stove for fear the plastic would melt.

Willing the milk to thaw at improbable speed, Emily did a slow bouncing walk around the kitchen, singing, "Hush, little baby," over Lizzie's desperate wails and hoping Katie's medicated sleep was deep enough for her not to hear. After a few rounds, she stopped to check on the milk. It wasn't warm, but at least it was thawed. She'd give it a shot.

She took the bottle and sat at the table, shifting Lizzie to lie prone in the crook of her left arm. She put the bottle to the baby's lips, but she turned her mouth away, wailing louder. "It's good milk, Lizzie. Mommy's milk, just like you're used to. Come on, try it." She nudged the nipple against Lizzie's open mouth, but she only turned her head again.

Emily shook a drop of milk onto her finger and touched it to Lizzie's tiny pink tongue. The baby's eyes opened wide, and she stopped in mid-wail. Emily repeated the process with a larger drop, then gave Lizzie a third drop while inserting the nipple into her mouth at the same time. This time Lizzie clamped her mouth on the nipple and sucked greedily.

Emily sighed with relief, feeling as if she'd just scaled Everest. She sat back in the chair and crooned to the baby as she drank. This was what it would have been like if she'd had one of her own—except she wouldn't have had all the bother about the bottle. The sweet warmth of Lizzie's head against her arm, her tiny fingers curled around Emily's pinkie as she held the bottle. It was well worth the screaming.

At last, replete and exhausted from her tantrum, Lizzie drifted off, and the nipple slipped from her lips. Emily put her feet up on the opposite chair, shifted the baby in her arms, and napped as well.

Luke's voice roused her through a desperate dream in which Lizzie was her own child and someone had poisoned her. She watched, helpless, as the baby struggled for her fragile life, wishing desperately that she could be the one to die instead— she couldn't go on living without her child.

The dream was so vivid that when she opened her eyes to see Luke standing before her, she couldn't immediately distinguish reality from the dream. She glanced down at the baby motionless in her arms and gasped. "My God, she's dead! Luke, our baby's dead!"

Just then Lizzie's mouth made a little sucking motion in her sleep. Luke squatted before them. "She's fine, see? She's moving." He tucked Lizzie's blanket more closely around her, then put his hand to Emily's cheek. "Em, wake up. It's me. Lizzie's fine. You're fine. You must've been dreaming."

Emily blinked, gasping for air as the dream receded. "Oh,

Luke. I dreamed somebody poisoned her. She was ours, and they poisoned her."

He put his hand behind her head and kissed her. "Now why would you go and dream a thing like that?"

"Because of Katie." She realized with a start she'd been so busy with Lizzie, she'd never called Luke to tell him about Katie. "She ate some Turkish delight and got terribly sick. Sam fixed her up. She's sleeping now. But Sam thinks it was arsenic. And, Luke—that candy was meant for me."

He sprang to his feet, his face like a thundercloud. "Where is it?"

"In the library." She led him in there and showed him the Turkish delight and the larger box it had come in. "I asked the boy at Sweets by the Sea to continue Beatrice's standing order for me. I didn't realize it included Turkish delight. I hate the stuff, so I let Katie have it. She only ate one piece, thank God. If she'd had more, this baby might have become mine for real." Emily hugged the baby closer. "Not that *that* would be so very bad."

Luke flipped the lid off the box with his fingernail. "What made Sam think it was arsenic?"

"She tasted a tiny bit of the sugar. Arsenic has a bitter taste, doesn't it?"

"Yeah." Luke touched his finger to a piece, tasted it, and grimaced. "I think she's right. I'll get this to the lab first thing tomorrow—too late tonight." He pulled a plastic bag out of his pocket and slipped it over the box. "Now, tell me exactly what happened with Sweets by the Sea."

"I already told you about Mrs. Sweet being so hostile, right?" He nodded. She related her conversation with Matthew as closely as she could remember it. "He only mentioned licorice taffy, so I thought that was it."

Luke stood and paced the room, one hand on his hip, the other scratching his head. "No reason to think Matthew had anything to do with this. He said he and his dad did these orders without the grandma's knowledge?"

"That's what he said. But maybe she found out."

"I think she must have. I can't see George Sweet being involved any more than Matthew." He stopped and pounded one fist into the opposite palm. "Damn, I wish I could remember what my granny told me about her and Beatrice. Hard to believe any grudge could stay fresh for sixty-odd years, but this sure as hell looks like it could've been what happened to Beatrice, too."

Suddenly a number of facts converged in Emily's mind. *"Strong Poison!"*

"Yeah, arsenic's pretty strong."

"No, I mean the book. The mystery by Dorothy L. Sayers."

"Sorry, no clue." He grimaced. "No pun intended."

"I found a copy upstairs in the room Brock used to use, hidden inside the headboard. It's all about arsenic. The killer doses himself with arsenic over time so he can share a meal full of it with his victim and not get sick. Then Lord Peter Wimsey traps him by feeding him Turkish delight and pretending he's covered it with arsenic powder. Just like somebody did for real here."

Luke stared at her. "You found the book in Brock's room?"

"And remember the rat poison in the attic? And the piece of brown paper in Beatrice's fireplace? This box came wrapped in brown paper. It all adds up. Plus, Agnes told me she was sneezing all day the day Beatrice died—and she was allergic to roses. It's rosewater Turkish delight."

"So either Brock really is involved, or someone's trying awful hard to make us think he is. Be pretty tough for somebody to plant the book and the poison, though. Have to be somebody who had regular access to the house." He shot her a sharp look. "And since Agnes is dead, and Katie wasn't here yet, that pretty much means Billy."

"I refuse to suspect Billy. Even if he did bear a grudge against Beatrice and Agnes, can you see him plotting something this elaborate? And what would he have against *me*?"

"I know. I want to pin it on Brock too. But what does all our evidence against him amount to, when all's said and done? It's all circumstantial." Luke counted off on his fingers. "A book and a can of rat poison don't prove murder, especially since I can't imagine how he'd get into a sealed package at the candy store to plant the stuff. He had the opportunity with Agnes, but we can't prove anything without the DNA. We can put him at the scene for your brake job, but we can't prove he did it. We know he was having an illicit affair, but so what? People who screw around don't necessarily commit murder." He ticked off the fourth finger and threw up his hands.

"Which means it could be Mrs. Sweet after all." Emily's stomach went cold. "So . . . you think her grudge—whatever it was—could extend to wanting *me* dead? That's a powerful lot of hatred. Hard to believe she'd have waited all these years to act."

"True. But that's all we've got to go on right now. Tell you what—my granny's still alive in a nursing home in Seaside. We'll go up there tomorrow and see what she can tell us. She's got all that ancient history down pat, even if she can't remember what she had for breakfast."

"I'd love to meet your granny, history or no history. But isn't there anything we can do tonight?"

"I don't think so. I could go question the Sweets, but I'd like to hear what Granny has to say first—give me more leverage to make them talk."

"In that case, we may as well have some dinner. I'm starved. Could you sneak quietly into Katie's room and bring the cradle in here so I can put Lizzie down?"

Luke brought in the cradle with catlike tread, and Emily laid the baby down as gently as if she were a priceless and fragile objet d'art. Lizzie did wake, but lay quiet in the cradle, staring up at Emily. Emily smiled at her, and for the first time she'd seen, Lizzie smiled back. Emily couldn't tear herself away.

"You two stay right there. I'll rustle up some grub." Luke opened the fridge, rummaged through the cupboards, and stuck a frying pan on the stove while Emily and Lizzie carried on an inarticulate but highly satisfying conversation.

By the time Lizzie's eyes began to drift shut again, Luke was putting plates on the kitchen table and scooping something onto them from the frying pan.

"What's this?"

"Joe's Special. Hamburger, mushrooms, onions, spinach, and eggs."

"Smells wonderful." It tasted good too. "Goodness, a man who can cook as well as fight the bad guys. What more could a woman ask for?"

"You forgot the red-hot lover part." He winked.

"Oh no, I didn't." She leaned over and kissed him. "But I've known about that for a long time. This is the first time I've tasted your cooking."

The edge off her hunger, she could think clearly again. "Speaking of red-hot lovers—did you find out anything about Brock's blonde?"

Luke shook his head. "Not a word. He was getting pretty frayed around the edges after just a few hours in jail—I didn't think it'd take much to loosen his tongue. It rattled him bad when I asked him about her, but he wouldn't give her name. He wasn't afraid of anything the law could do to him—he was afraid of *her*. What *she'd* do to him if he talked."

"Even supposing her to be such a virago, what could she do to him in jail?"

"Not much, you wouldn't think. Security's not so tight as a federal prison, but it's tight enough. All he'd need to do is refuse her visits. But he seemed to think she had some kind of supernatural power. 'She'll get me,' he said. 'I don't know how or when or where, but she'll get me in the end.'"

Emily was always reluctant to believe the worst about any of her own sex, despite plenty of evidence from literature and life that the female of the species could be deadlier than the male. She glanced over at Lizzie, stirring and making little noises in her cradle, her reddish fuzz of hair damp with sweat. "You could never grow up to be like that, could you?" she crooned to her. "Thank God, at least you're not a blonde."

At that Lizzie let out a wail, as if insulted by the mere suggestion. Luke picked her up and soothed her while Emily prepared another bottle. She turned with the bottle ready to see Luke jiggling the baby on his shoulder like an old hand.

"Here, give that to me," he said. He took the bottle from her, shifted Lizzie into the crook of his arm, and guided the nipple into her waiting mouth.

"You're a natural," Emily said in wonder.

"You forget, I've had one of my own. Long time ago, but some things you never lose."

She almost told him then. But something still held her back. *Let's just get through this case. When my life isn't in danger, then I'll tell him. Then we can start over, right from the beginning.*

thirty

"Aye, it is but too true. He is to be married very soon—a
good-for-nothing fellow! I have no patience with him. . . .
He has used a young lady of my acquaintance abominably
ill, and I wish with all my soul his wife may plague his heart
out."

Mrs. Jennings to Elinor Dashwood, *Sense and Sensibility*

Luke slept in the guest room again, while Emily took the
baby to bed with her. She left another bottle of milk thawing
in the fridge, expecting to be roused in the middle of the night,
but Lizzie miraculously slept until six. By that time Katie was
awake and feeling nearly herself again.

"I forgot to ask the doctor whether the arsenic would get
into my milk," she said as she welcomed Lizzie into her arms. "I
think I'd better throw out whatever I've got now just in case."

"No problem. There's a bottle waiting in the fridge." Emily
retrieved the bottle, warmed it, and fed Lizzie while Katie ex-
pressed her possibly poisoned milk. Then Emily handed the
baby back to her mother. "You take your time. I'll get my own
breakfast."

She went back to the kitchen to find Luke already making
coffee. She got out some eggs and cheese. "One thing I can cook
is scrambled eggs."

Luke fried bacon and made toast. Emily took Katie some toast and juice.

"I'll have to run that candy over to the lab before we head up to Seaside," Luke said as he washed down the last of his bacon. "Then I better do some paperwork. Visiting hours don't start till ten, anyway. Pick you up at nine thirty?"

"All right." Emily had been mulling something over, and this seemed like a good opportunity to pursue it. "Pick me up at Saint Bede's."

"You gonna walk to Saint Bede's?"

"Well . . . Actually, I was thinking of taking the Vespa."

"Emily, remember what we agreed? Only for emergencies."

"This is an emergency. A spiritual emergency. I haven't been inside a church except for a funeral in weeks. I really need this, Luke." She tried to combine an arch look with one of spiritual intensity—an effort so absurd, it made her laugh at herself.

Luke laughed with her. "All right, you win. But just this once. I'm going to pick you up a motorcycle manual while I'm in Tillamook, and tomorrow we'll go get you that learner's permit."

When Luke had gone, she showered and dressed in her brown tweed suit, putting her hair in a flat braided bun instead of her usual poufy style. Then she went to the garage and wheeled the Vespa out onto the drive. She mounted the brown leather seat, settled the helmet over her hair, and patted the perky green dashboard. "Here we go, girl. Time for our maiden voyage."

She was a little wobbly at first and wished she'd ridden some the day before, just to keep in practice. But by the time she hit the highway, she was riding as if she'd been using this form of transportation all her life.

She rode the mile into town, then turned left on Third

Street and up the hill to St. Bede's. The church was dark, but Father Stephen emerged from the parsonage next door as she parked the Vespa.

"Mrs. Cavanaugh! My, but you startled me. I heard that engine and expected to see Beatrice outside my door."

"Sorry, Father. I had a bit of an accident in my car, so I'm using this for the time being. Would it be all right for me to go into the church for a little while? Just to be alone."

"Certainly. I'll get the keys." He unlocked a side door for her. "If you should need me for anything, I'll be right next door."

"Thanks. Oh, by the way, I've decided on an epitaph for Beatrice. Could you take care of that for me?"

"Certainly." She handed him a slip of paper, and he read it aloud. "'Strength and honor are her clothing; / She shall rejoice in time to come.' Proverbs 31, isn't it? Very appropriate. I'll call the engravers today."

Emily entered the cool, dim space and took a grateful breath of flower-scented air. She truly longed for her own church, the tiny Russian Orthodox church of St. Sergius of Radonezh, not far from Reed and home. Her other home, that is. Windy Corner felt at least as much like home now as did the house she'd shared with Philip for more than twenty years. But Windy Corner had not yet come to feel to her like a place of prayer.

At St. Sergius, the air would be scented with incense instead of flowers. The nave would be dimmer and cooler, the only sun coming through panes at the base of the dome high above and glinting off the gold-leaf halos on the icons that covered every wall. Here, what light there was on this cloudy day entered the nave through stained-glass windows along both sides and behind the apse. Instead of an iconostasis, across the front of the altar area stood a carved wooden rood screen. Aunt Beatrice had seen to it that this church stayed as "high" and traditionally Anglican as possible.

The atmosphere of sanctity was fainter here, but it would have to do. Emily knelt on the cushioned altar rail and attempted to compose her mind and heart to prayer. She was out of practice, she was ashamed to admit. The past few weeks had been some of the most turbulent of her recent life, and prayer should have been her first recourse; but she had been leaning on Luke's strength, plus an unexpected reserve of her own, instead of God's. Luke's strength, as well as her own, could go only so far. She suspected their end was coming soon.

One by one she lifted all her fears and concerns to the cross behind the altar until she felt peace flow through her. The sense that her greatest trial lay ahead deepened, but she found a verse from the Prophets—one she didn't know she knew— washing over her mind and heart: "But let justice run down like water, and righteousness like a mighty stream." Justice would be done, and she would come safely through the storm.

When she heard Luke's car pull up outside, she was ready.

Seaside lay about fifty minutes to the north along Highway 101, which at times passed inland through dense forest, at times skirted various little bays and estuaries, and for a few breathtaking miles ran along the side of a cliff that sheered straight down to the breakers hundreds of feet below. Emily enjoyed the scenery and the companionable silence she and Luke shared. That was one good test, surely, of a viable relationship—the ability to be silent together without awkwardness.

They left the highway at the south end of town and headed inland to the small neighborhood surrounding the hospital.

Sensible place to put a nursing home, Emily thought, hoping this would be one of the nicer homes where the stench of urine and dead dreams would not be too overpowering.

It looked nice from the outside, at least—typical coastal architecture of weathered cedar shingles and steep gables; it might have been a set of condominiums rather than a nursing home. Inside, a cheerful nurse greeted Luke like an old friend and told him to go on up. "Mrs. Richards will be very happy to see you."

They took the elevator to the third floor and walked down a bright yellow corridor lit by skylights. Luke paused outside an open door. "Granny?" he called. "It's me, Luke."

"Come in, dear," came a high, quavery voice. They entered a spacious room that looked—and smelled—more like a studio apartment than a hospital room. In one corner stood a bed neatly spread with a brightly colored quilt; a tiny kitchenette occupied the opposite corner. Family photographs covered the walls. One large portrait of a serious young Luke in army uniform nearly stopped Emily's heart.

In the center of the room, a frail, impossibly wrinkled woman sat in a recliner in front of a soundless television, crocheting. Her hands were shrunken, darkly veined, and so knobby from arthritis, Emily wondered how she could hold the hook; but her eyes when she looked up at them were bright with intelligence.

Luke leaned over to kiss his grandmother's cheek, but her eyes were fixed on Emily.

"Brought somebody to meet you, Granny." He pulled Emily forward. "This is Emily, the love of my life."

Emily felt herself redden at this introduction. Mrs. Richards reached for her hand to pull her closer. "Emily? You mean *the*

Emily? The one who didn't answer your letters?" Her eyes narrowed and her clawlike hand tightened painfully on Emily's wrist.

"We worked all that out, Granny. She never got my letters 'cause she moved, and I never got her letters 'cause Mom didn't send them on. It wasn't Emily's fault."

The claw's grip relaxed slightly. "So is my Lukey the love of your life too, young lady?" the old woman asked, her tone implying the answer had better be yes.

"Yes, ma'am," Emily said, slipping her free arm around Luke's waist. "Absolutely."

Mrs. Richards released her wrist and gave it a friendly pat. "That's all right, then. Sit yourselves down and tell me all about it. But maybe you'd like a cup of coffee first?"

"I'll get it." Luke reached the kitchenette in two strides and pulled open a cupboard; a half-full pot of coffee stood ready on the warmer.

"So how did you come back into my Lukey's life, dear?" Mrs. Richards resumed her crocheting without looking at it. The pink yarn and simple shell-stitch pattern suggested a baby blanket.

"My aunt Beatrice died, and I came to Stony Beach to settle her estate. I saw Luke at the funeral, and since then . . . ." She glanced at Luke to see how much she ought to reveal. He nodded vigorously. "We've been trying to find out who killed her."

"Killed her! My, my! I heard about poor Beatrice dying, of course. Such a sad thing, and her still with so much life ahead of her. But I never dreamed she'd been killed." A note of salacious interest belied the sorrow in the old woman's words.

Luke brought over three cups of coffee, handed them around, and sat on the other side of his grandmother. "Took us a while to figure it out." He recounted the events of the last weeks in a few sentences. "As a matter of fact, there's something we hope you can help us out with."

Mrs. Richards sat forward in her chair, her fists closing around her hook and yarn. "Anything I can do, dear. You know I'm only too happy to help."

"I remember you told me years ago there was some kind of quarrel between Beatrice and old Mrs. Sweet."

"Oh my, yes. Beulah Landau she was then. Prettiest girl in Stony Beach, if you can believe it—hair just the color of yours, dear." Mrs. Richards fingered a tendril that had escaped from Emily's bun. "Sassy little thing, too. Bold as brass. And she had her heart—or at least her ambition—set on Horace Runcible. He wasn't bad-looking himself back then, and already starting to build up a fortune. Couldn't go to war, being flat-footed, but he made a bundle out of it here at home. Shrewd man, was Horace. Knew a thing or two about most everything. Including women." She chuckled.

"So Beatrice took Horace away from her?" Emily put in. Luke shook his head almost imperceptibly.

Mrs. Richards frowned, her wrinkled cheeks nearly meeting her overhanging brows so her still-bright eyes only just peered through. "Just you let me tell my story in my own way and my own time, young lady. Beulah thought she had Horace right where she wanted him. They went around together for months, driving up to Seaside for a party, over to Portland to the opera—she was a showy piece, and he showed her off good. She was picking out her trousseau, just waiting for him to pop the question, when Beatrice came to town."

The old woman smiled into the distance as if watching a movie play in her head. "Beatrice was visiting a college friend,

I think, somebody long gone now. At any rate, she got invited to all the same parties Horace and Beulah did. She was a handsome woman, not showy like Beulah, but tall and dignified, with a skin like pure porcelain. And a tongue on her that would slice you in half. She didn't run after Horace—he got introduced to her at a dance, had one fox-trot with her, and he was down for the count."

She rubbed her crabbed hands together. "It was her wit that got him, I think. Beulah may've been a looker, but she didn't have two thoughts to wave at each other in her whole pretty head that didn't have to do with money. Plus she had no sense of decency. Way I figure it, Horace was moving up in the world, and he knew he was going to need a wife that would do him proud. Beatrice was pure class."

Emily smiled to herself at this glimpse of her aunt as a young woman. She could just see Beatrice flattening poor Beulah with a single epigram.

Mrs. Richards had fallen silent, so Emily ventured a remark. "So Beatrice married Horace, and Beulah settled for Mr. Sweet?"

The old woman went on as if Emily hadn't spoken. "Beulah came to the wedding. Grandest affair Stony Beach ever saw. Eight bridesmaids, every one in yards of lilac silk and tulle— this was right after rationing was finally over. Beatrice's train stretched clear down the aisle of Saint Bede's, and her veil was imported lace. Beulah sat right at the back, fuming through the whole ceremony, and when they walked out as husband and wife, she spat on that train—a good old hack, like a man's. Beatrice didn't notice, but I did. I sneaked up during the reception and cleaned it off. Didn't want them to have bad luck right from the start."

"Where did Mr. Sweet come in?"

"Oh, he was a local boy, always had a crush on Beulah, just like half the boys in town. But he had his business going, doing pretty well, so she chose him over a couple of others who didn't have a nickel. Poor man, I reckon he regretted it before the honeymoon was over. She gave him hell right up to the day he died." Mrs. Richards shook her head. "She did make that candy shop pay, though. Rumor has it, she's got quite a packet squirreled away, though what use she'll ever have for it I surely couldn't say."

Mrs. Richards fell silent again, and this time she returned to her crocheting. Luke spoke up for the first time since she began her story. "Did you say Beulah's maiden name was Landau?"

"That's right. Her father was old Henry Landau, who built the Driftwood Inn. The Landaus were a force to reckon with back then—had half the town in their back pocket. But when Henry Junior inherited, he let it all go to seed. Beulah like to had an apoplexy when he sold the Driftwood to Beatrice."

"So what relation is Vicki Landau? The real estate agent?"

"Why, she's Henry Junior's granddaughter. Beulah's great-niece. Pretty girl, as I recall. Too bad she didn't get Beulah's red hair. But her mother died when she was just a little thing. Her father, Henry the third, he just went to pot after that. Beulah pretty much brought Vicki up. I'm afraid the child may have picked up a bit of Beulah's sour temper."

"And I have a sneaking suspicion she inherited Beulah's grudge." Luke shot a look at Emily. "I think we've found our blonde."

Emily sat up with a jolt. "But—Vicki and Brock? I thought she was having an affair with the mayor."

"Playing both sides for the main chance, is my guess. I think it's time I had a word with Ms. Landau, don't you?"

They took their leave, promising to return soon for a good long chat.

"Anything you want to know about Stony Beach, you just come and ask me, hear?" Mrs. Richards gave Emily's hand a parting pat. "I've lived in these parts for ninety-five years. Not much goes on I don't hear about, even up here."

Emily was tempted to come back on her own—she was sure Luke's grandmother must have quite a trove of stories about Luke, about all the years of his life Emily'd had no part in. She wanted to hear every one.

She and Luke drove back to town, speculating on the possibility of Vicki's involvement. "I know she's in cahoots with the mayor," Emily said. "Remember that model of the planned development? And that argument we witnessed at the Crab Pot—they could've been fighting over Brock. Maybe she wanted to pull him in, and the mayor said no."

"Or maybe he was already in, business-wise, and Trimble suspected Vicki was getting too personal. My gut feeling is all three of them are guilty as hell—though maybe not of actual murder."

"But how are we going to get any evidence?"

"I'm putting my bets on the candy store. I might be able to lay my hands on something there, if I can get to it before they know we suspect anything."

Luke dropped her at the church to collect the Vespa, and Emily rode back down to Windy Corner. When she rounded the bend of the drive that brought the house into view, she was so startled, she nearly fell off the scooter. A red Porsche stood in the circle before the front door. Brock's red Porsche.

Emily stopped the Vespa on the pavement to avoid the noise of wheeling it over gravel. She took off her helmet and pulled out her cell phone. Luke's message came on. "Luke, it's me. I just got home, and Brock's car is in front of my house. I don't know what's going on, but I don't like it. I think you'd better get over here right away."

She crept crouched on tiptoe through the grass and up to the ground-floor windows, flattening herself against the house to peek into each room in turn. She couldn't see into the hall without climbing onto the porch, and the stairwell window was above her head. But she could get a good view of the dining room through the bay; it was empty. She heard a noise to her right, from the direction of the kitchen.

Holding her breath, she inched along the wall to the kitchen window. She had to move out a bit to see inside, but she crouched down until her eyes barely cleared the sill. At first she could see nothing through the sheer white curtains. Then a glint of light off metal caught her eye, and the scene came into focus.

Katie sat in a chair by the table, her back to Emily. Her hands were roughly tied behind her with twine. More twine bound her ankles to the legs of the chair. Strapped into a bouncy seat on the table, little Lizzie fussed, working herself up to a proper indignant cry because Katie did not come to her rescue.

And standing in front of the two of them was Vicki Landau, impeccably turned out in a red suit and pearls, pointing a pistol at Katie's head.

thirty-one

[To Edward Ferrars] "Engaged! But what was that, when such friends were to be met?"

"Perhaps, Miss Marianne," cried Lucy, eager to take some revenge on her, "you think young men never stand upon engagements, if they have no mind to keep them, little as well as great."

—Marianne Dashwood and Lucy Steele,
Sense and Sensibility

The window was open a couple of inches. Emily maneuvered herself where she could see and hear without being seen.

"I'm disappointed in you, Katie," Vicki was saying in a calm, friendly voice. "You're not acting like a loyal Trimble at all. Don't you want your favorite uncle to get rich? I'm sure he'll set you up quite nicely if you'll only do your part." She moved the barrel of the pistol toward Lizzie. "Just tell me where the will is hidden, and you and your precious baby will be fine."

Emily's heart constricted. She'd been kind to Katie, but what did a week's worth of kindness count for against a lifetime of family loyalty? She couldn't even remember now whether she'd told Katie about her own legacy under the will. Would it be better or worse if Katie knew?

But Katie didn't know where the will was hidden. Emily was sure of that.

"I tell you I don't know!" Katie's voice bordered on hysterical.

"She's hidden it somewhere. I don't know all the hiding places in this house—there must be hundreds. You think I wouldn't tell you if I knew? With my baby's life on the line?"

Emily thought fast. She could sneak in through the front door, retrieve the will, hand it to Vicki, and stop this nightmare. Or would the nightmare then only begin? What could Vicki want with the will, anyway? She must know she and her coconspirators would not profit by it.

She could only want one thing: to get all the legatees out of the way before killing Emily herself. Then the estate would default to Brock, if he were proved innocent, or to the State of Oregon, which would be only too happy to sell that prime stretch of beach real estate to Trimble and company.

So Katie and Lizzie were in equal danger either way. And once Vicki had the will, Marguerite and Luke would be added to the hit list as well.

Emily peered down the drive, straining her ears. No sound of an approaching patrol car. What was keeping Luke? She dialed his number again. Still no answer.

She couldn't stand by and watch Katie and Lizzie get hurt. Especially Lizzie. Her heart threatened to jump out of her body at the thought of that precious, innocent life being sacrificed to a hatred and greed that had nothing to do with her.

Emily would have to play the hero herself.

Unfortunately, her literary background didn't help her much in this situation. As a professor, the greatest danger she'd faced in real life was that of being stabbed in the eye by a mortarboard on commencement day. And her reading had always focused on the classics, with a few forays into genteel detective stories in which the sleuth's work was entirely intellectual. She knew nothing about handling a crisis situation like this.

But she did know how to analyze characters. Now which character did Vicki remind her of? Yes, of course—Lucy Steele from *Sense and Sensibility*. A mask of friendliness covering bitter jealousy. A shrewd eye on the main chance, with loyalty that lasted only as long as her intended's prospects were good. Vicki had forsaken Mayor Trimble for Brock when Brock looked likely to come into the property. Now that Brock was disinherited and in jail, she was hitching up to the mayor's wagon again.

Emily didn't need to overpower Vicki or persuade her out of her evil intentions; all she had to do was stall her until Luke arrived. And all that would require was a pretense of acceding to her demands. Surely the promise of turning over the beachfront property would be enough to pacify Vicki's spite as well as her greed—at least for now.

Emily took a deep breath, drawing on the strength of which she'd felt the promise back at St. Bede's. The hour of her greatest trial had come.

She slipped around the corner of the house to the kitchen door and tried it silently. It was unlocked. She backed down the steps, then mounted them with deliberate disregard for noise. She pushed open the back door, calling, "Katie?"

When Vicki swiveled to point the gun at her, Emily did not need to feign shock. Although she'd been expecting it, she could never have been prepared for the feeling of having an undoubtedly loaded pistol, held in a sure and firm grip, aimed with precision at her heart. She felt the blood drain toward her feet and just managed to catch herself against the counter.

"Vicki! What—what's going on?" She willed herself into control. "You'd better put that thing down—you could hurt someone."

"That's the general idea," Vicki said sweetly. "Probably more than one someone. But if you're very cooperative, I might not make you watch the others die."

"You're talking nonsense, Vicki. What can you possibly hope to accomplish by more murder?"

"If at first you don't succeed, try, try again. My aunt raised me with that motto. I'm going to get my hands on that beach-front property one way or another, Emily Worthing. Worthings out—Landaus back in. Right on top, where we belong."

Emily raised her eyebrows. "Well, if the property is all you want, you can have it. What's a piece of land weighed against the lives of my friends?"

Vicki's eyes narrowed. "You'd deed me the property? For nothing?"

"Of course, if that's what it takes to stop this bloodbath."

The muzzle of the pistol wavered. "My aunt also taught me never to trust a Worthing."

"You can dictate a statement of intent right now and watch me sign it. Katie can witness—after you untie her hands, of course."

"One hand, that's all she'll need." Vicki sidled over to the table, keeping the gun leveled at Emily. With her left hand she undid the straps that held Lizzie in her bouncy chair and scooped the loudly protesting baby up under her arm. "And I'm using all the insurance I can get."

Oh God, not Lizzie. Don't let her hurt Lizzie. Again Emily willed herself calm. She mustn't make one false move.

Vicki jerked her head toward the hallway. "Into the library. I know you've got paper and pen in that desk of yours."

Around that desk of hers was more like it. The floor within a three-foot radius of the desk was littered with papers, pens, stamps, and all the other paraphernalia the drawers had contained. Clearly Vicki had already satisfied herself the will was not in the desk.

Moving slowly and deliberately, knowing Lizzie's life depended on her not arousing Vicki's suspicion, Emily retrieved a blank sheet of paper and a pen from the pile and sat down at the desk. "What do you want me to write?"

"I, Emily Worthing Cavanaugh, do hereby—"

"Just a minute, I can't write that fast. You do want this to be legible, don't you?"

Vicki waited, tapping her foot. She shifted the wailing baby into a more comfortable position—for her—the baby's bottom resting on her hip, her head hanging out over her arm. Emily's desire to take Lizzie in her arms and comfort her was almost as strong as her fear that Vicki would shoot the baby the moment she tried.

"All right, go on."

"Do hereby promise to deed to Victoria Beulah Landau—"

"How do you spell Beulah?" Emily asked, although she knew perfectly well.

Vicki spelled it, then went on dictating. Emily drew out the process as much as she could without infuriating Vicki beyond endurance.

At last the document was finished, and it was time for Emily to sign.

"Back to the kitchen," Vicki said. "Katie has to see you sign it."

Emily picked up the pen and paper and walked ahead of Vicki into the kitchen. What on Earth was keeping Luke? He should have been here ages ago. Emily didn't think her strength could hold out much longer. Her nerves were at breaking point as it was.

She set the pen and paper on the table and pulled out a chair across from Katie.

Vicki waved the gun toward Katie. "Untie her right hand *only*. Unless you want me to shoot them both off."

Katie's hands were tied separately to the slats of the chair back, then looped together. Emily untied the right while attempting surreptitiously to loosen the pressure on the left.

Vicki waved Emily back to her chair with the gun. "Now sign."

Emily wrote in her best Parker-perfect handwriting—which bore no resemblance to her real legal signature—"Emily Ann Worthing Cavanaugh." Her middle name was actually Alice.

"Now write, 'Witnessed this day,' and a blank line, then 'by' and another blank line."

Emily complied.

"Hand the pen to Katie."

Katie took the pen as if it were made of dynamite. She shot Emily a pleading look. Emily gave her a tiny nod.

Emily held the paper steady as Katie wrote the date, signed, and printed her name underneath. Emily noticed she'd spelled her name "Kathryn," although she'd seen *Katherine Parker* written in one of her books. Good girl.

Vicki transferred the pistol to her left hand as she picked up the paper, folded it, and stuck it in the inside breast pocket of her suit jacket. "Now that we've got that out of the way, it's time to settle some old scores."

Emily had barely a moment to panic at that pronouncement when she heard a faint scraping noise. She glanced over Vicki's shoulder and saw a head through the panes of the back door. Luke put a finger to his lips as he silently turned the knob.

Stall her. Get her to monologue. "Scores? What score could you have to settle with me, now that you have that property?"

Vicki sneered. "You think I'd settle for one little strip of land when your aunt stole all of Stony Beach from us? The Landaus were headed for glory before she came along. Then it all started to go downhill. But you Worthings haven't won yet. This town's going to be Landau Beach before I'm done. You and your legatees are all going down—just as soon as I find out who they are."

Maybe Emily's character analysis had been wrong. Maybe Vicki wasn't an Austen character at all, but a Dickens one— Estella to Beulah Sweet's Miss Havisham. If that was the case, she didn't just have a vindictive heart—she had no heart at all. How could such a person be touched?

Vicki aimed the gun at Emily's head and pulled back the safety. Emily kept her eyes on Vicki's so as not to betray what she saw happening behind her.

Luke stepped quietly into the room, his own pistol gripped in two hands and pointed at the back of Vicki's head. "Put down the gun, Vicki, and nobody gets hurt."

Vicki whipped around, and Emily saw Luke's face go white as he realized what she was holding in her left arm. Emily silently rose from her chair and stepped away from the table.

"Come on now, Vicki. It's over and you know it. I found arsenic in the kitchen at Sweets, and your aunt told me all about it. How the two of you poisoned Beatrice and then tried to do the same to Emily. Funny how a lifetime of hatred can loosen your tongue."

"It's not over till that usurper is dead!" Vicki screamed. "I'm going to own this town. You're on her side, not the law's. You'll go down with her."

"You've got no quarrel with Katie or the baby. Trimble won't thank you for hurting them. Just put the baby down, nice and easy, and let the adults work this thing out."

"Put the baby down?" An evil smile crept across Vicki's face. "All right, I'll put the baby down." She opened her arm. Lizzie's tiny hands grasped at her coat sleeve but couldn't hold. She plummeted toward the floor.

The scene unfolded before Emily in slow motion. As Vicki's arm opened outward, she rounded the corner of the table. She heard Katie scream as if from a mile away, but Emily herself felt perfectly calm. As Lizzie fell, Emily dived. She hit the floor just in time to cushion the baby's fall.

Her slide knocked Vicki sideways, and she fell. A gunshot exploded in Emily's ears, deafening and disorienting her. Then she saw Luke's boot come down on Vicki's outstretched wrists. The boot was dotted with red. Why would Luke wear polka-dot boots? More red bloomed on the brown leather. She looked up to see Luke gripping his right shoulder with his left hand.

"Get her gun, Emily. Quick."

Getting a good purchase on Lizzie and holding her carefully out of the way, Emily slithered across the floor and pulled the gun out of Vicki's helpless hands. Holding it with her fingertips by the end of the stock, she set it carefully on the far counter, muzzle pointing toward the wall.

"Give the baby to Katie and help me."

Emily laid Lizzie gently into the sobbing Katie's outstretched arm, then untied her other hand.

"What can I do?" The gunshot had blasted coherent thought clear out of her head.

Luke spoke through gritted teeth. "Get a towel or something to stop the blood."

Of course. She grabbed a clean towel from a drawer, ran it under Luke's armpit, and tied it tightly above his shoulder. He dropped his left hand and transferred the pistol to it.

"Don't think I can't shoot left-handed," he said to the woman writhing and snarling under his boot. "Game over."

Deputies Pete and Heather stormed through the back door, each holding a gun in two outstretched hands.

"All right, you two, fun's over. Get this woman up and cuffed." As Pete grabbed Vicki's hands, Luke lifted his boot and sank into a chair. "Better call me an ambulance, Em."

"I called them to stand by when you called us," Heather said as she helped Pete cuff Vicki's hands behind her back and raise her from the floor. "Should be here any second." The sound of wheels on gravel confirmed her prediction.

Leaving Pete to hold the secured Vicki, Heather went out to tell the paramedics it was safe to come in. As the medics got to work on Luke, Emily tore her eyes from him to glance at Vicki.

In that moment, Emily believed she knew the origin of the legend of the werewolf. Vicki was unrecognizable as the chic, attractive businesswoman Emily had met less than two weeks before. Hanks of brassy yellow hair hung over her lowered face. She glared at her captors through reddened eyes, her breath coming in loud rasps. Her lips, from which the red lipstick had smeared onto her cheeks, curled back over her teeth, and a growl issued from her throat.

She had allowed her malice, envy, and avarice to eat into her soul until scarcely anything human was left in her. She was lower than a beast. And yet somewhere inside her, Emily knew, the image of God still flickered, obscured but unable to be eradicated. Emily's heart stirred with a divine pity.

The medics finished bandaging Luke's shoulder and got him

onto a gurney, over his protests that he could walk just fine. "Coming?" he said to Emily.

She looked at Katie, who had put Lizzie to her breast regardless of the crowd around her and was cooing to her as if they were the only two people in the world. "Will you be all right?" Emily asked.

"We're fine," Katie said, and tore her eyes from Lizzie to look Emily in the eye. "Thanks to you. You saved my baby. I don't know how to thank you."

"If it hadn't been for me, the two of you would never have been in danger in the first place. Don't thank me. Thank God."

"Somebody better untie her ankles before we go," Luke said from his gurney. "In case she needs to pee or something before you get back."

Emily clapped her hand to her mouth and bent to do as he suggested. She rubbed Katie's ankles to get the blood flowing in them again, then stood. She felt this image of the mother and child would be imprinted on her heart for the rest of her life.

"I hope I'll always be around to protect the two of you. You mean more to me than you can possibly imagine." She bent to kiss the top of Katie's head and caressed Lizzie's downy red hair. To think she had almost lost them.

It was time Luke knew the truth.

thirty-two

She went to Mrs. Goddard's accordingly the very next day,
to undergo the necessary penance of communication; and a
severe one it was.

—Emma

Vicki's bullet had entered Luke's right shoulder below the collarbone and exited above the shoulder blade, miraculously avoiding shattering any bones. At the hospital in Tillamook they cleaned and dressed the wound, put his arm in a sling, and kept him overnight to be sure there was no infection.

Emily stayed by his side as long as they would let her, but he was too woozy from pain medication for a serious talk. She returned the next morning, after serving Katie breakfast in bed.

"I'm perfectly fine, Mrs. Cavanaugh," Katie had protested.

"I know. Just let me do this for you for my own sake. Please."

She'd held Lizzie while Katie ate, then kissed the two of them good-bye. Now she sat by Luke's bedside again, sipping acidic hospital coffee no amount of cream could palliate and helping him eat his breakfast.

"You never think about how much you need your dominant

hand till you lose the use of it," he said, chasing bits of scrambled egg around his plate with the fork in his left hand.

Emily stood a piece of toast against the plate as a barrier for him to push the eggs against. "Just think what a romantic figure you'll cut in court, with your right arm in a sling. 'Valiant officer wounded while saving innocent women and children.'"

"Seemed to me like you did most of the saving," he said with a heightened note of admiration in his voice that made Emily thrill. "The way you dove for that baby and knocked Vicki over in one fell swoop—I've never seen anything like it. I'd've expected that from Katie, maybe—it's amazing what a mother can be capable of when her child's in danger—but I have to admit it surprised me coming from you."

Emily set down the toast and folded her hands in her lap. "In a way I almost feel as if Lizzie is my child. And Katie too. Odd as that might sound."

She looked up at him. "Luke—there's something I've never told you. About—what happened after you went away."

He put down his fork and searched her face. "What is it, beautiful?"

"There was a particular reason I badly wanted to get in touch with you. I mean, I wanted to stay in touch anyway—I wanted us to be forever. But—I couldn't wait till the next summer to see you again. Literally *couldn't* wait."

She closed her eyes and took a deep breath. It had all been over so very long ago—yet in another way it would never be over.

"The thing is—I was pregnant."

"*Pregnant?*" His voice was a shocked whisper. "And I never knew? What happened? Did you give it up for adoption?" He took in her stricken expression and echoed it with his own. "You didn't—get rid of it? Not our baby?"

"No. No. I could never have done that. But I was desperate."
She took another shuddering breath, willing the tears back. "I
was four months along, my jeans were getting tight, and I knew
it wouldn't be long before people started to notice. You'd
dropped off the face of the Earth, and I didn't dare tell my dad;
he would've spontaneously combusted. I told Geoff, or he figured it out—I don't remember. Anyway, he said to go to Aunt
Beatrice. She was a bit of a tyrant, but she was kind underneath.
I think she would've helped me. I wrote to her."

The tears refused to be held back any longer. She struggled
for air to speak. "I wrote to her. But before I could mail the
letter"—Luke reached out to her with his good hand, and she
grabbed it like a lifeline—"I lost the baby."

"Come here, you." Luke pulled her up onto the bed beside
him and folded her tight in his good arm. He rubbed her back and
planted kisses on her hair as she sobbed out a lifetime of grief.

When she had calmed a little, he asked her, "Does that have
anything to do with your never having children?"

She sat up and reached for a tissue. "When I miscarried, I
didn't dare go to a doctor—didn't have a doctor I could trust,
because we moved around so much. I just got through it somehow
on my own. I bled for weeks—thought I'd never stop bleeding.
But years later, when I'd tried so hard to carry a baby and
couldn't, I got checked out. They told me there was something
wrong from the first miscarriage—scar tissue or something—
so an egg couldn't implant properly. I'd never be able to have a
child." She blew her nose vigorously and looked back at Luke.
"I didn't just lose our child—I lost all my children. Forever."

He ran his fingers down her cheek. "My poor baby."

"So you see, when Katie and Lizzie came into my life—I felt
like I'd been given another chance. Katie was like what our

daughter might have been grown up—I always thought our baby was a girl, and Katie has your coloring—and Lizzie was like my own baby. I couldn't lose them. Not even if saving them meant losing my own life."

Luke's face took on a faraway expression. "Katie's parents threw her out, right? And Lizzie's daddy's out of the picture? I wonder if there's some way we could legally adopt the two of them. After you marry me, that is."

Emily stared, certain she'd heard him wrong. "After I *what*?"

"Marry me." He saw her gaping and grinned. "No, it's not the pain meds talking. I'd planned to ask you a little more formally. First I thought the cove, but after that got desecrated, I figured maybe another dinner at Gifts from the Sea. And I planned to have a ring to offer you too. But after what we've been through, it seems kind of silly to stand on ceremony. Will you?" He threw off the bedclothes, hoisted himself out of bed, and knelt in his hospital gown at her feet. "Will you do me the great honor of becoming my wife?"

Why she should be so stunned, Emily didn't know. After all, she'd known for some time that Luke still loved her; he'd hinted he wanted their relationship to move onto firmer ground. But marriage? After all these years?

"I—I don't know, Luke." She saw his face fall and put her hand to his cheek. "I do love you—you know that—but . . . I can't explain it. I just feel like we need to take more time."

"Thirty-five years isn't enough for you?"

She gave a pale smile. "But we've only been back together for a couple of weeks. And it's all been so crazy. I've hardly had time to breathe, let alone sort out what I feel or what I want to do with the rest of my life."

Half-formed thoughts from recent days began to take shape

in her mind. "And we have to think about—well, whether we're really compatible. I mean, obviously the passion is still there, and we've been getting along pretty well, but—we haven't had any time together that was just normal life. We're really very different people, Luke. Where would we even live? I can't see myself in your house with your gigantic TV, and I'm not sure you'd be comfortable at Windy Corner, tripping over antiques every time you turn around."

Luke shrugged his good shoulder. "That's all details. We can work all that out." He gripped her hand. "I wasn't kidding when I told Granny you were the love of my life. Were you?"

She softened. "No. I wasn't kidding either."

"Then it'll work itself out. It's got to."

"And I believe it will, Luke. I really do. I just don't want to rush into anything. Don't forget that as of now, I still have a job in Portland nine months of the year. I don't want a marriage where we only see each other on weekends."

He sighed and climbed back into bed. "All right, you win. We'll take some time to work things out. But will you promise me one thing?"

"What is it?"

"Don't disappear from my life again. Ever. I don't think I could survive that a second time."

She leaned over the bed and kissed him. "I won't disappear. I promise."

Luke was discharged later on Saturday morning and sent home with instructions to rest for the remainder of the weekend. For once he seemed inclined to cooperate, so Emily tucked him in and went home. She needed some time alone to think about her future.

Levin and Kitty greeted her with reproachful yowls over her long neglect. She took a few minutes to fuss over them. Bustopher had apparently deduced that Katie was the new source of good things to eat and had taken to following her everywhere like a puppy. But Levin and Kitty, though they liked their dinner as well as the next cat, held a loyalty to Emily that could not be so easily swayed.

Katie served Emily's lunch in the dining room—a delicious hot quiche lorraine, with fresh strawberries and spinach salad. Emily took a bite and sighed in contentment. "You know, Katie, you're really too good a cook to be cooking for just me. Not that I want you to stop."

Katie finished filling Emily's water glass. "I've been thinking about that, actually." She moved around the table and pulled out a chair. "Can we talk?"

Emily's heart sank. Surely Katie wasn't going to say she wanted to leave and find a professional cooking job in Portland or somewhere. After all they'd been through.

She forced a smile. "Sure. What's on your mind?"

Katie sat and leaned toward her, elbows on the table. "You remember when we fixed up that room for Ms. Grenier? And I said the house would make a great B and B? I'm sure you haven't had time to think about it, with everything happening, but I've been thinking about it. And if you did want to do it, I would absolutely love to be the manager."

"You think you could handle that? With Lizzie? It'd be a lot of work."

"I know, but I think we could do it. You'd probably want to make some changes to the house first—like adding bathrooms, for a start. That would take a while, so by the time we got going, Lizzie'd be a little older, wouldn't be nursing every five minutes. Women keep house with babies all the time—this would just be on a little bigger scale. And maybe—if you agree—I could get in a little help when things got really busy. Somebody to change beds and stuff."

"Goodness, now it's beginning to sound like a hotel. I don't know, Katie. That would be a big step for me. If I'm going to be living here full-time, I'm not sure I want to share my house with a lot of strangers."

"Oh." Katie slumped back in her chair. "I guess I thought you'd be going back to Portland in the fall. Then the house would be empty most of the time. I was mainly trying to think of a way to keep myself busy while you were gone."

"The truth is, I haven't made a final decision about that yet. I certainly don't need to work anymore, and I've been getting kind of tired of teaching the last few years. I might see if I can get a sabbatical for next year and see how I like living here full-time."

"Well, I guess we can just go on as we have been, in that case. Certainly less work for me, just having you to take care of." Katie didn't sound as enthusiastic about that prospect as Emily would have been in her place. Ah, the energy of youth.

Marguerite's parting words came back to Emily: *Your library has some magic in it.* "You know, there is another alternative. Maybe a little less scary—to me—than a B and B."

Katie looked up, the light back in her eyes.

"Marguerite said something about what a great place this was for her to write. I expect there are a lot of people who need a quiet place to write. People who might not be able to afford regular B and B or hotel prices. Maybe we could make this house into a writers' retreat. Open only by invitation or referral from someone I know."

Katie leaned forward again, hands clasped on the table.

"Oh, that would be fabulous! I'd get to meet some real writers. And the house would love it, I know it would. This is totally a literary house."

She jumped up and began to move about the room, nearly dancing. "And we could theme each room around a different writer. We could have an Austen room, all light and eighteenth-century. Keep that Victorian room just like it is, red and spooky, and call it the Brontë room. Maybe pick somebody exotic and do a foreign room, Indian or something."

"Beatrice's old room would simply have to be Forster. *A Room with a View*."

Katie clapped her hands. "I love it! But don't you want that room for yourself?"

"I'm happy with my tower room. In fact, I might think about fixing up more of the attic space for a bathroom and a private sitting room. That way I could get away from the guests if I wanted to."

Katie froze. "Oh yeah. I'd be right in the middle of everybody down here. And Lizzie, too. That could be a problem."

Emily thought fast. "I'm pretty sure there's an apartment over the garage where Beatrice's chauffeur used to live. We could fix that up for you, and then we'd have a ground-floor room for people who can't handle the stairs. We could call it the Dickens room—for all those crippled villains of his."

Katie's mouth quirked. "How about the cupboard under the stairs as the J. K. Rowling room?"

Emily laughed. "A bit cramped, don't you think? But we could put a Rowling sign on the door and still use it as a broom cupboard." She stood and hugged Katie. "You know, I think this is going to be a lot of fun."

· thirty-three ·

"But I will not stay to rob myself of all your compassionate goodwill, by shewing that where I have most injured I can least forgive."

Willoughby to Elinor Dashwood, *Sense and Sensibility*

On Monday, Luke went to work, in his sling, then came to Windy Corner for dinner. Katie outdid herself with boeuf bourguignon—so tender Luke could eat it one-handed—and flaming crêpes suzette for dessert.

"Katie, this is a meal fit for a king," Luke said as he dug into his dessert.

"You two are my heroes," Katie replied with a catch in her voice. "You saved me and Lizzie. I could never do enough to repay you."

"I'll have to make a habit of saving good cooks, then. I could get used to this." He winked at Emily.

As they sipped their coffee in the library, Luke filled Emily in on the events of his day. "Brock sang like Sinatra soon as he knew we'd arrested Vicki. Told us the whole story."

"Even his own part in it?"

Luke nodded. "He wasn't responsible for the actual murders,

though he knew about 'em. Vicki had a whole clutch of co-conspirators, apparently. She and her aunt sent Beatrice the poisoned Turkish delight. Vicki had her claws into Brock by then, and he'd convinced her he was set to inherit the lot. Then, when it went to you, it was Vicki's plan for Brock to marry you and get the money that way. Only his heart wasn't in it 'cause he was so far under Vicki's spell." He shot her a sidelong glance. "Lucky for me, I guess."

Emily reached over to squeeze his hand. "You should know me better than to think I'd fall for anyone like Brock, even if he'd been as sincere as a hundred Romeos. Especially with you right there in the picture."

He returned her pressure with a smile. "Agnes was like we thought: a cover-up—Brock overheard something that made him think she knew about the Turkish delight. Vicki got the mayor to fix that one up. He's been under her spell for some time—hadn't even guessed she was two-timing him with Brock."

"So what excuse did Vicki give Trimble for doing Agnes in?"

"Claimed they weren't trying to kill her, just get her injured and out of the way. But he knew about Beatrice's murder, all right, just not about Vicki's plan to marry Brock. He thought the deal was Brock would sell out to them and push their develop-ment plan ahead. He figured he'd go down as a coconspirator if Vicki got caught." Luke made a wry face. "In which he was not mistaken."

"You're not going to tell me Brock is completely innocent in all this?"

"No way. He was complicit in the two murders, and it was him that set fire to your rental house."

"I knew it! I was certain we had him there if anywhere. And

I was basically right about him being Mr. Elliot, wasn't I? Even though that wasn't the whole story?"

"Yeah, I'd say that was pretty well on target. It was him who fixed your brakes, too."

Once again Emily went cold. "So he really does hate me."

"I have to admit, it did seem kinda personal. He rambled on about stuff that happened when you were kids. I didn't know you knew him that far back."

"I didn't remember him myself at first, but when I found his stuff in the headboard, it all came back to me. I guess Geoff and I weren't very nice to him. Did he mention anything specific?"

"Something about you locking him in a secret passageway?"

Emily clapped her hand to her mouth. "Oh my gosh, I'd forgotten all about that! It was Geoff's idea—I didn't want to, but Geoff wouldn't listen. I did sneak back later and let Brock out. But I guess I could've stopped Geoff if I'd tried hard enough."

"So where is this secret passageway? Just out of curiosity. Unless you think you're going to need to hide from me someday."

"Don't be silly, I'd never want to hide from you. It's right over here." She got up and walked over to the corner where the fiction shelves bowed out into the room. "If I can remember where the catch is . . . Ah, yes." She pulled down the top spine of a volume at the end of a shelf titled *One Thousand and One Arabian Nights*. The bookcase creaked open just a crack.

"Open Sesame." She tugged at the edge of the bookcase. "This probably hasn't been opened since we played in it. Come give me a hand."

Luke lent the strength of his good shoulder, and the bookcase opened out to reveal a spiral staircase.

"Got a flashlight?" she asked.

"Natch." He turned his back so she could grab it out of the back of his belt. She turned it on the staircase, and her face fell.

"Dust and spiders. I was afraid of that."

"We don't have to go up. Where's it lead to?"

"Beatrice's room. Disguised as a closet. The door locks at that end."

Luke examined the edges of the bookcase opening. "I don't see a keyhole here."

"No. This end locks automatically. There's a release—Geoff and I knew about it, but Brock didn't. He was too short to reach it anyway." She showed him a knothole in the paneling of the stair enclosure. "You just push this and it opens."

"So he was in here in the dark? With the spiders? How old?"

She shrugged. "Six? Seven? It was cruel, but he kind of brought it on himself. You wouldn't believe what a little pill he could be back then. We called him Eustace—you know, like the kid in Narnia who almost deserved it."

"He sure doesn't think he deserved it. He's got quite a grudge against your whole side of the family—which at this point, I guess, comes down to you. He feels like you all stole his inheritance—Horace's whole estate should've come to him."

"You know, I think Beatrice would have split it more evenly if she'd thought he'd make good use of it. But she saw through him. Besides, she built the estate up quite a bit on her own after Horace died. I'd say the portion Brock got was just about fair."

"Which will now revert to you, I assume. If he goes down for arson and attempted murder."

"I suppose it will. I don't care for my own sake—I've got plenty—but I am glad those tenants won't have Brock for a landlord. Him or whatever developer he would've decided to sell out to." Emily sneezed. "This dust is getting to me." She made to leave the enclosure.

Luke pulled her back. "Just a minute. We can't let this nice dark secret space go completely to waste." He pulled the door nearly shut, then wrapped his good arm around her and kissed her deeply. "Ever do anything like that in here before?"

"You know I haven't. If I had, it would only have been with you."

"I have a new goal. I'm gonna kiss you in every hidden corner of this amazing old house."

"Sounds good to me." She glanced up at a huge web right over Luke's head. "As soon as Katie gets rid of the dust and spiders."

That night Emily dreamed of her sixteenth birthday. On the real day so long ago, Beatrice had thrown a party for her—quite a small one, as Emily knew hardly anyone in town. She and Luke had barely met then, though he'd already turned his teasing smile on her in a way that made her glow from head to foot.

But in the dream, Luke was there as her established boyfriend. Philip was there too, though in life she wouldn't meet him for several years; but he and Luke chatted like old friends. Geoff and Beatrice attended, of course, and Ethel, Agnes's predecessor, officiated, assisted by Agnes herself. In life, Emily's father's absence had been the elephant in the room, the gaping space no one else could fill. But in this dream, he sat on the love seat with her mother, hands entwined—her mother, a gentle soul who had died, worn down and brokenhearted, when Emily was eight. Horace, who had also been dead some years by the time of the real party, nodded at Emily across the table, and at his side was the sulky young boy she still thought of as Eustace—Brock.

Emily, in mysterious dream fashion, was both her teenaged self and her present self, and those around her seemed to be all ages at once. The cake and ice cream were as delicious as only Ethel could make them, and the presents rained down in an endless stream. But the greatest gift of all for Emily was to have all these loved ones gathered around her, all those she had lost from her childhood on. She thought her heart would burst with joy.

When the festivities were winding down, she sat at her mother's feet, resting her head on her lap as her mother stroked her hair. Eustace came and stood before her, face red, toe scraping the carpet.

Emily's joy faded as her stomach began to roil. "Forgive, darling," her mother said softly. "Forgive. He didn't know what he was doing."

Aunt Beatrice, sitting opposite, added her voice. "Forgive them all, Emily. They have suffered more than we. And they will go on suffering until they learn how to love." At Beatrice's side, Agnes gave her crisp nod.

"Teach them, my darling," her mother crooned. "Teach them by loving them first."

Emily awoke with tears streaming down her face. She knew what she must do.

She asked Luke to drive her to the jail. "Are you sure you want to do this?" he asked her as they parked outside. "Those people won't be exactly happy to see you, y'know."

"I know." Half of her wanted to run the opposite direction, but the dream still upheld her. "This is what I have to do."

She went to the women's side first. The guard brought in Vicki and Mrs. Sweet together. The wild look was gone from Vicki's eyes, but the hatred remained.

"Come to gloat over us, have you? Just like a Worthing," Mrs. Sweet spat. Her eyes were a laser beam of pure malice, but Emily was protected by the shield of her family's love.

"No. I've come to apologize for anything I or my family have done to hurt you. And to ask if there is anything I can do for you."

"You? Do for us?" Vicki's once-elegant voice came out in a growl. "Like send us a poisoned cake, for example?"

"Like pay for a top-notch lawyer. I'm quite serious."

"We don't want your money," Mrs. Sweet said. "Got enough of our own. Trust ourselves to some lawyer you've got in your pocket? Not a chance."

Emily took a deep breath, remembering Beatrice's words as the dream faded: *All you can do is offer. You can't make them accept.*

"I'm sorry you feel that way. If you should change your minds, the offer stands."

She signaled to the guard, who let her out. Luke escorted her to the men's side, where Brock and Trimble were already waiting. Brock sat, his head in his hands, while the mayor's eyes darted around the room as he fidgeted with the neck of his jumpsuit.

Emily looked at the man who had tried to kill her—the man who mere days ago had filled her with horror—and felt only pity. "Brock, I've come to tell you I'm sorry for anything my

312 KATHERINE BOLGER HYDE

family did to hurt you. I'm sorry we locked you in the secret passage, and I'm sorry you didn't come out better under Beatrice's will. Is there anything I can do to help you now? Get you a good lawyer, for example?"

He dropped his hands and stared at her through bloodshot eyes. "You'd do that for me? After I let that harpy talk me into . . . what I did?"

"I would. I forgive you, Brock. It gives me no pleasure to see you suffer." She turned to Trimble. "The offer extends to you as well. I don't think I have anything to apologize to you about, do I?"

A shadow of Trimble's old bluster returned to him. He waved his hands. "All forgotten, all forgotten. A lawyer, now—that'd be swell. No harm meant, get it, no harm meant. Put it all behind us." He gave her a nervous smile, then subsided like a leaky balloon.

Outside, Emily filled her lungs with cool, slightly cow-scented air. On the exhale, she let go all the fear, anger, anxiety, and pain of the last two weeks. She felt empty, but clean.

She turned to Luke, who regarded her with a line between his brows. She put up her thumb and smoothed the line away. "It's over," she said. "Now we can begin."